D0497800

MOTHER
OF THE BRIDE
MURDER

Books by Leslie Meier

MISTLETOE MURDER
TIPPY TOE MURDER
TRICK OR TREAT MURDER
BACK TO SCHOOL MURDER
VALENTINE MURDER
CHRISTMAS COOKIE MURDER
TURKEY DAY MURDER
WEDDING DAY MURDER
BIRTHDAY PARTY MURDER
FATHER'S DAY MURDER
STAR SPANGLED MURDER
NEW YEAR'S EVE MURDER
BAKE SALE MURDER
CANDY CANE MURDER
ST. PATRICK'S DAY MURDER
MOTHER'S DAY MURDER
WICKED WITCH MURDER
GINGERBREAD COOKIE MURDER
ENGLISH TEA MURDER
CHOCOLATE COVERED MURDER
EASTER BUNNY MURDER
CHRISTMAS CAROL MURDER
FRENCH PASTRY MURDER
CANDY CORN MURDER
BRITISH MANOR MURDER
EGGNOG MURDER
TURKEY TROT MURDER
SILVER ANNIVERSARY MURDER
YULE LOG MURDER
HAUNTED HOUSE MURDER
INVITATION ONLY MURDER
CHRISTMAS SWEETS
CHRISTMAS CARD MURDER
IRISH PARADE MURDER
HALLOWEEN PARTY MURDER
EASTER BONNET MURDER
IRISH COFFEE MURDER
MOTHER OF THE BRIDE MURDER

Published by Kensington Publishing Corp.

A Lucy Stone Mystery

MOTHER OF THE BRIDE MURDER

LESLIE MEIER

Kensington Publishing Corp.
www.kensingtonbooks.com

KENSINGTON BOOKS are published by

Kensington Publishing Corp.
119 West 40th Street
New York, NY 10018

Copyright © 2023 by Leslie Meier

All Kensington titles, imprints, and distributed lines are available at special quantity discounts for bulk purchases for sales promotion, premiums, fund-raising, educational, or institutional use. Special book excerpts or customized printings can also be created to fit specific needs. For details, write or phone the office of the Kensington Special Sales Manager: Attn. Special Sales Department. Kensington Publishing Corp., 119 West 40th Street, New York, NY 10018. Phone: 1-800-221-2647.

Library of Congress Control Number: 2022950823

The K and Teapot logo is a trademark of Kensington Publishing Corp.

ISBN: 978-1-4967-3376-4
First Kensington Hardcover Edition: May 2023

ISBN: 978-1-4967-3378-8 (ebook)

10 9 8 7 6 5 4 3 2 1   33614083165893

Printed in the United States of America

For Matt, Andy, and Emmy

Chapter One

The little bell on the door of the *Courier* newspaper jangled and part-time reporter Lucy Stone looked up to see who was coming in. Identifying the visitor as Janice Oberman, Lucy glanced at Phyllis, the receptionist, meeting her eyes and letting out a long sigh that was almost a groan. Catching herself, as Janice marched into the office, she rearranged her features into what she hoped was a welcoming smile as she prepared to face the usual onslaught.

"Hi, Janice," said Phyllis, peering at the newcomer over the bright-green cheaters that were perched on her nose and had been chosen to match her neon-green tracksuit. "What can I do for you?"

"You won't believe it," began Janice, who was quite obviously gloating over the news she was about to impart. A rather stout woman, dressed in the Tinker's Cove, Maine, spring uniform of windbreaker and duck boots, her double chin was quivering with excitement. "You won't believe it but it's another engagement announcement!"

"Wow," said Phyllis. "That's the second one this month."

"I know, and it's so exciting coming so soon after Morgan's engagement," said Janice.

"Who's the lucky girl this time?" asked Lucy, who knew that Janice was the proud mother of four daughters, all in their twenties. The oldest, Taylor, was married and Morgan was already engaged; that left Chelsea and Jordan.

"It's Chelsea, and she's got herself quite the catch," said Janice, emphasizing the fiancé's catchiness with a nod. "He's a doctor," she reported, with another nod and raised eyebrows, "finishing up his residency at MGH—that's Massachusetts General Hospital."

"I suppose Chelsea met him at work," offered Lucy, who knew Chelsea was a nurse at Mass General.

"All part of the plan," began Janice, launching into a favorite theme. "I told my girls, if you don't want to be old maids, go into something where you'll meet eligible men. Nursing is ideal, men always fall for nurses and hospitals are filled with eligible young doctors. But, of course, not everyone can be a nurse. Taylor, for instance, was never good at science, so she became a flight attendant. She figured out right away that the most eligible men are in business class, so she got herself that gig and, well, it was less than a month before she snagged Warren. He's a lawyer, you know, and doing very well." She paused for breath, and gave a smug little smile. "She's expecting a little boy, due in June, so I'll be coming in with a birth announcement before too long."

"Can't wait," said Phyllis.

"Morgan, on the other hand, well, you know she was quite the athlete. All-State in field hockey, but of course you don't meet many men playing field hockey so she switched to lacrosse in college and that's how she met Henry. Henry Wentworth. His family is loaded, absolutely loaded. Old money, if you know what I mean. They live in Fairfield County, that's in Connecticut, and happens to be the county with the highest median household income in the entire country."

"Henry does sound like quite the catch," said Lucy, trying not to sound sarcastic. "Highest median household income in the country, you say?"

"Well, one of the highest, anyway. And as you say, quite the catch," cooed Janice. "Just adorable, and he has the loveliest manners. He'll be going into the family business, stocks and bonds and things."

"Your girls have certainly done well for themselves," offered Phyllis.

"What about Jordan?" asked Lucy, naming Janice's youngest. "Has she hooked any prospects?"

"Scads, Lucy, she's fighting them off. And if you ask me, your girls could take a page out of her book. She's still in college, of course, but she's been taking classes in business and accounting, that's where the best prospects are."

"Well, my girls are out of school now . . ." said Lucy, dismissing the idea.

"That's true, they are getting on, aren't they," mused Janice, with a sad sigh. "Not getting any younger, that's for sure. I suppose your oldest . . . what's her name? I forget?"

"Elizabeth. She lives in France now."

"Well, she must be close to thirty. Is she getting nervous?"

"I don't think so. She seems quite happy with her life in Paris." Lucy's oldest daughter was a concierge at the tony Cavendish Hotel, and from all reports enjoyed a lively social life.

"Ooh la la," said Janice, with a touch of snark. "I suppose it's all fun and games now but before she knows what happened she's going to discover that men aren't interested in an older woman whose biological alarm clock is ringing." She paused to pull a folded sheet of paper from her shoulder bag and passed it to Phyllis. "All the details of the engagement are here," she added, pointing to the paper. Turning to Lucy, she asked, "And what about your Sara?"

"Sara works at the Museum of Science in Boston. She loves her job there."

"But what about men? Has she got a steady boyfriend?"

"I don't really know," admitted Lucy. "She hasn't mentioned anyone in particular, but she does meet a lot of scientists, after all."

"Oh, scientists," groaned Janice. "Always got their noses in nasty specimens, their minds on some theorem or other. I don't mind telling you that scientists do not make good marriage prospects."

I'm sure you don't mind in the least, thought Lucy.

"But Zoe, mmm, didn't I hear she's working for the Sea Dogs? All those eligible young baseball players, now that's what I call a brilliant move. Maybe she'll catch the next Ted Williams." She paused. "Of course, they can't all be superstars, now can they?"

"I do believe she's enjoying herself in Portland," said Lucy.

"Well, I wouldn't be surprised if she's the first of your little birds to fledge and fly off into matrimony even though she's the youngest. . . ."

"I suppose you have a lot to do," said Phyllis, coming to Lucy's rescue. "What with two weddings to plan and all."

"You are so right," exclaimed Janice, her voice soaring to new heights. "Dresses and table settings and flowers and DJs, it's quite a lot. Taylor is helping, she's been a bride so she knows all about the planning and what to avoid. She's even thinking of becoming a wedding planner, she enjoyed hers so much." Janice was quick to reassure her listeners that Taylor's decision was purely optional. "As a part-time sort of hobby thing, it's not as if she needs to make money, Warren's perfectly able to support her. In style, which is wonderful since she'll be able to stay home with the baby. Warren's a lawyer, you know."

Lucy did know; she'd heard all about the wonderfulness of Taylor's husband many times. "Well, we'll make sure Chelsea's announcement runs in this week's paper," she said, pointedly turning to her computer screen and opening a file.

"It's a lovely picture of the two of them," added Phyllis, tucking it away in a manila folder. "I'll mail it back to you," she added, hopefully dismissing Janice.

"Well," sighed Janice, realizing that she'd lost her audience. "As you know, I have an absolutely huge to-do list. . . ."

"Have a nice day," said Lucy offhandedly, her focus still on the computer screen.

"Take it easy," added Phyllis, as Janice yanked open the door and departed to the tune of the jangling bell, no doubt plotting her next attack.

"Oh, God, who'll be her next victim?" asked Lucy, rolling her eyes.

"Probably the post office. I noticed she had some unstamped letters poking out of her bag."

"You know, I wouldn't find Janice so upsetting if I didn't in my heart of hearts wish my girls would settle down and start producing grandbabies. I'm ashamed to admit it. . . ."

"There's no shame in it," said Phyllis, offering consolation. "It's natural."

"I don't understand these modern girls. I mean, I know Janice is some prehistoric throwback straight out of a Jane Austen novel, but it almost seems like girls today, my girls anyway, positively resist entanglements. They want to be free as birds, hooking up when it suits them and moving on when it doesn't."

Phyllis smiled naughtily. "Kids, today."

"Nothin' new, hunh," chuckled Lucy. "What goes around, comes around. I know I certainly gave my parents some bad moments."

"Didn't we all?" added Phyllis, who was flipping through some press releases. "That reminds me, the school department is starting a series of parenting workshops. Might be worth a story."

Lucy got up from her desk, stretched, and ambled over to Phyllis's reception counter. She was looking over the workshop press release when her cell phone rang and she pulled it out of her pocket. Glancing at the screen she saw that the caller was Elizabeth, video phoning from Paris. She immediately swiped and saw her daughter's face appear, magically, on the little screen. "Hi!" she exclaimed, raising the phone to capture her face and smiling broadly. "What's up?"

"*Beaucoup!*" replied Elizabeth, whose suppressed smile indicated she had some exciting news to impart.

"You look like the cat who got the cream," said Lucy, taking in Elizabeth's chic cropped hair, her sculpted French face that was all cheekbones, and the finger she was waggling in front of that face, the finger that was adorned with an enormous diamond. "Oh my God!" shrieked Lucy. "You're engaged!"

"You bet I am!" chortled Elizabeth. "To the absolutely most wonderful, *magnifique,* handsome, charming, genuinely adorable man in the whole of France, in the whole world!"

"That's *fantastique*," crowed Lucy, a bit floored by this

hoped for but entirely unexpected news. "How come I haven't heard about this amazing guy until now?"

"Well, you know how it is," began Elizabeth. "I had a feeling this could be really serious, like he was *the one*, and I didn't want to hex it. I kind of hugged it close to my heart, in case it all fell through."

This made sense to Lucy, who knew only too well how private her oldest daughter tended to be, and she herself had often been reluctant to share certain matters until she was ready. "Like when I was pregnant, I always waited until I was at least three months along before telling anyone, except your father, of course." She paused. "So how long have you known him? And what's his name?"

"Jean-Luc Schoen-Rene. And actually, it's all been kind of sudden. Six months, I think, since we got serious. I've known him forever, because his family has been coming to the hotel since long before I started working here so he was sort of part of the woodwork. But he never seemed to notice me."

"But you noticed him?"

"Mom, like I said, he's very good-looking. Of course I noticed him."

"So what made him suddenly notice you? You took off your glasses and let down your hair?" asked Lucy, thinking of the cliché move in romantic comedies.

Elizabeth chuckled. "Actually, it happened when he was here without his parents, which was unusual. He was checking in, he looked at me and I looked at him and something must've clicked because he asked me out to dinner that night." She smiled. "The rest is history."

"So what's he like? What does he do?"

Elizabeth thought for a minute. "He's very French, very elegant and well-mannered, a bit reserved. He dresses really well, when he wears jeans they're always freshly pressed and he wears cologne and usually throws on a scarf. He's thirty-seven, he's close to his family . . ."

That gave Lucy pause, but she kept her thoughts to herself as Elizabeth continued. "He's involved in the family business, they have a big château where they hold special events like conferences and weddings."

"That will be convenient," said Lucy. "Have you set a date?"

"We have! It's going to be this June at the château, of course. There's room for the whole family to stay, it's going to be amazing."

Lucy ventured a guess. "It sounds like the Schoen-Renes are pretty well off?"

"They're nobility! His father is a count and I guess Jean-Luc will be one, too."

"I thought they had a revolution and chopped off all those noble heads."

"They did, but a few years later they had a restoration, and the ones who didn't get their heads chopped off got their titles back. And sometimes their estates, and from what I can see the Schoen-Renes were able to do very well for themselves. You should see this place, Mom. It's absolutely beautiful."

"Well, I guess I will see it, in June." Lucy paused. "You're sure they'll want all of us to stay? I don't want to impose. . . ."

"Mom, the château has something like eighty-plus rooms, maybe more. Jean-Luc's mother, Marie-Laure, told me she would be absolutely devastated if the whole family doesn't come and stay with them."

"Well, I certainly wouldn't want to devastate the poor woman."

"Good choice. You know what they say, that French-women rule the country, and Marie-Laure is the definition of *formidable*," said Elizabeth, laughing. "So are you happy for me?"

"Over the moon, darling," said Lucy, crossing her fingers. "Over the moon."

Lucy was about to settle in for a long mother-daughter chat to discuss all the fascinating details, but Elizabeth was brusque as ever. "I've got to run, *à bientôt*," she said, and her face vanished from the screen. Lucy stared at the phone, feeling a bit let down.

Phyllis, who had been listening to the entire phone call, was beaming. "Congratulations, Lucy. That's wonderful news."

"I can't believe it. I can't wait to tell Bill and the kids. We'll have to do a Zoom tonight, with everyone."

"Personally, I can't wait to tell Janice Oberman," confessed Phyllis.

Bill didn't share Lucy's enthusiasm, when she called to tell him the good news. A skilled restoration contractor, he was at a jobsite, working to convert an old barn into a spacious summer home. From his tone, she knew she'd caught him at a bad moment.

"I gotta go, Lucy, the HVAC contractor messed up the vents. . . ."

"Aren't you excited about Elizabeth?" she asked, somewhat deflated.

"Well, sure, Lucy, but you know Elizabeth. I'll be amazed if she actually makes it down the aisle. Something will come up, it'll turn out that this guy eats meat or votes conservative or doesn't use organic toothpaste." He paused to shout something to the hapless contractor. "Like I said,

I gotta go. But I'm with you, I hope she's found the love of her life and will live happily ever after." He sighed. "I just don't quite believe it."

Despite herself, Lucy admitted she had a few misgivings as she ended the call. Elizabeth had always been the most challenging and headstrong of her four children and she suspected Jean-Luc would have his hands full. Nevertheless, she was determined to hope for the best, believing that Elizabeth was one young woman who truly knew what she wanted in a husband and that Jean-Luc was that man.

That evening after supper Lucy and Bill set Lucy's laptop on the kitchen table and opened the virtual family meeting, amazed at the ease of seeing their children's faces appear. Sara was finishing her dinner, chomping on a big salad which she proudly displayed on the screen, reporting that she'd lost five pounds. Zoe was adorable in a Sea Dogs cap, seated at the retro dinette set that came with her attic apartment in Portland. Son Toby wasn't able to join the Zoom, due to the time difference between Maine and Alaska he was still at work, but his wife, Molly, and son, Patrick, beamed in moments after Patrick got home from school.

"What's the big news, Mom?" asked Sara, getting right down to business.

"Your sister Elizabeth is engaged to be married!" declared Lucy, getting right to the point. "His name is Jean-Luc Schoen-Rene, his father's a count and the wedding is this June at the family château. We're all invited to stay at the château! In France!"

"Wow, count on Elizabeth," muttered Zoe, a touch of envy in her tone. "She always manages to outdo everybody."

"Is it true?" asked Sara. "We're all invited to France to stay at a château?"

"That's what she said," asserted Lucy. "She says there's plenty of space and the place has over eighty rooms."

"Wow," said Molly: "I wonder how many bathrooms."

"She didn't say," offered Lucy, smiling at the patchwork of young faces on the computer screen. "Do you all think you can come? Especially you, Molly. Do you think Toby can make the trip?"

"He's awfully busy at work," said Molly, "but a trip to France would certainly be educational for Patrick."

"Is a château like a castle?" asked Patrick. "With knights and stuff?"

"Probably," said Bill, beaming at his grandson. "There might even be a moat."

"I'm sure it's very grand, but that's just the icing on the cake," said Lucy. "I'm so happy for Elizabeth—she's getting married!"

"Personally, I feel for Jean-what's-his-name. You have to wonder if he knows what he's getting into," said Sara.

"If you ask me, it's terribly romantic," opined Zoe. "Like a Lifetime movie. I imagine he's very handsome. . . ."

"Well, he's rich, which is even better," said practical Sara.

"Yes on both counts," said Lucy, "at least that's what Elizabeth says. I hope you guys will call her and congratulate her. . . ."

"Absolutely, Mom," said Zoe. "Can't wait to hear all about it, especially if Jean-Luc has any eligible guy friends."

"I wonder if we're going to be bridesmaids," said Sara.

"Oh, I hope not," moaned Zoe. "Those dresses are always hideous."

"Maybe Patrick can be a page. . . ." suggested Molly, with a touch of mischief in her voice. "In white satin knee breeches."

"No way!" protested Patrick.

"I think you're getting ahead of yourselves, we don't know all the details yet," cautioned Lucy. "But it's a wonderful opportunity for us all to be together as a family. That would make me so happy—it would be the icing on the cake!"

"And on that note," said Bill, abruptly reaching for the mouse, "let's sign off until next time. Stay well, kids."

After the screen went blank, Lucy sat for a moment, staring at it and wondering why Bill had suddenly decided he'd had enough. "Wouldn't it be great, Bill? A dream vacation with all our kids. It's been such a long time since we were all together."

"I know, babe, but don't get your hopes up. Just getting to France will be expensive, especially for Toby. He might not be able to swing it."

"We could help. . . ."

Bill stiffened beside her. "I've gotta pay Uncle Sam first, April fifteenth is coming up fast. You know the song: 'I owe, I owe, it's off to work I go.' "

"Well, taxes come every year. What's the problem this year?"

"The IRS has discovered some sort of error and they say I underpaid last year so I have to make it up this year," he said, rolling his eyes, "with penalties."

"Well, I'm not giving up hope," said Lucy, setting her chin stubbornly. "Miracles can happen."

"That's what it'll take," grumbled Bill, pushing away from the table and standing up. He glanced at the clock. "Just in time, Bruins are playing the Islanders."

Lucy smiled indulgently. "I think I'll just do a bit of Googling, check out the Schoen-Renes and their château. And maybe take a peek at some bridal gowns . . ."

Bill bent down and kissed her head, then shrugged.

"What is it about women and weddings?" He headed for the family room, pausing at the door. "I'm not gonna have to wear a tie, am I?"

Lucy was still poring over wedding dresses at ten o'clock, much too excited to think about going to bed, when Toby called, just home from work. "Hi, Mom. Molly tells me that Elizabeth's finally landed a guy. Good for her."

"She sounded so happy, so excited," said Lucy.

"Molly says he's quite the catch, got a château and everything."

"So she says, and we're all invited to stay at the château for the wedding. I looked it up on the internet and it's a sort of fancy conference center now."

"That sounds expensive," said Toby, sounding concerned.

"Not for us. They've issued an invitation. This is social, not business, and we'll be their guests. I'm really hoping you can all come, it would be so nice to have the whole family together again." She paused before adding a giant guilt pill. "And it's been so long since I've seen Patrick."

"Aw, gee, Mom, I think we're going to have to settle for sending a nice present. We're country folk now, we wouldn't be comfortable hanging out with a bunch of stuck-up Frenchies."

Lucy's heart sank. "But it would be such a wonderful opportunity for Patrick, to visit a foreign country. And he's my only grandchild."

"I know, Mom, I know, but travel is not a priority right now. Molly's started a new job, I have a new supervisor, it's not a good time to take a vacation. You know how it is."

"I do," said Lucy, sadly. "That I do."

Ending the call, she couldn't help feeling terribly disappointed, but she also understood Toby's decision and trusted that he knew what was best for his family. She'd just have to make do with virtual visits.

Lucy couldn't wait to share the good news with her friends, who gathered regularly every Thursday morning at Jake's Donut Shack. The group, which included Pam Stillings, Sue Finch, and Rachel Goodman, had adopted the weekly meeting when their children went off to college and they no longer could count on casual encounters at school and sports events. The breakfasts had become a weekly ritual, offering the four women a chance to catch up with each other and to share advice and support through life's challenges.

As she expected, they were all thrilled for Elizabeth, whom they'd known since she was a cranky, colicky baby. "Imagine, Elizabeth finally settling down," said Pam, who was married to Lucy's boss at the newspaper, Ted Stillings. "Hold the presses!" Pam was a free spirit and former cheerleader who still wore the ponytail and poncho she'd adopted in high school.

"And in France," cooed Sue, who was the fashionista of the group and had a penchant for anything and everything French. "So romantic!" As always, she was perfectly turned out, thanks to monthly touch-ups at the Kut'n'Kurl and frequent shopping trips to the new outlet mall that promised designer clothes at bargain prices.

"Elizabeth's very grounded," observed Rachel, who majored in psychology in college and never got over it. "She's been wise to take her time, to get to know herself and also her new environment in France. I'm sure she's given this marriage serious thought, she's not one to rush into something."

"I don't know about that," said Lucy, remembering her

daughter's enthusiasm and excitement. "She seems pretty smitten with Jean-Luc, she said he was *magnifique.* Or maybe it was *fantastique?*"

"Well, any guy who comes with a château is pretty fabulous in my book," said Sue. "Are Zoe and Sara excited about the wedding?" Lucy paused, seeing their server approaching with a loaded tray. Norine had big hair and a big attitude and was a fixture at Jake's. "What's this I hear about a wedding?" she asked, plunking down a Sunshine muffin for Rachel, a yogurt granola parfait for Pam and hash and eggs for Lucy. Sue, who never had anything more than black coffee, got a disapproving scowl and a promise to return with the coffeepot for a refill. "Someday we're gonna run out, what're you gonna do then?"

Sue merely smiled sweetly. "I'll take my chances. Just like Lucy's daughter Elizabeth."

"She's the one who moved to France?" Norine tucked the tray beneath her arm.

"That's right. She's getting married in June."

"Well, good luck to her," said Norine. "I'm in favor of marriage, I've been married four times."

"I'm hoping once is enough," said Lucy, picking up a toast triangle and poking it into the egg yolk. "It was for me." She smiled, then took a bite. "Mmm."

Norine beamed at Lucy, snorted in Sue's direction, and headed back to the kitchen.

"So is everybody going to the wedding?" asked Pam. "A family reunion in France?"

"That's the plan," said Lucy. "Bill's worried about money, but I'm pretty sure we'll manage. It's really a bargain trip since we can stay at the château; there's just airfare. The girls are thrilled, of course." She stared down at her plate and poked the hash with her fork. "Toby didn't seem too interested, he says he wouldn't be comfortable hanging out with fancy French people."

"What?" exclaimed Sue as Norine returned, as promised, with the coffeepot. "She's his sister, after all."

"It would be very educational for Patrick, being exposed to a different language and culture," offered Pam.

"I'd just love to see all my kids together for once," admitted Lucy, watching as Norine filled Sue's mug, and went on to top off the others.

"Is that what he said?" asked Rachel. "That he'd be uncomfortable?"

"Yeah," nodded Lucy.

"Toby never struck me as being insecure," said Rachel, picking at the top of her muffin. "Rather impulsive and sure of himself, that's my impression anyway."

"He didn't hesitate a minute before marrying Molly," recalled Pam. "They were barely out of high school."

Lucy found herself defending her son, in spite of herself. "Well, he says they're country folk now, and I imagine the Alaskan lifestyle is a far cry from the French."

"Family is family, wherever you are," said Sue.

"You betcha," exclaimed Pam. "Elizabeth is his sister and blood's thicker than water, thicker even than this coffee."

"Sue's right," agreed Rachel. "Maybe that boy needs to stretch a bit and step out of his comfort zone."

Maybe, thought Lucy, maybe he did.

Chapter Two

That evening, after Bill went to bed, Lucy popped the DVD of *Something's Gotta Give* in the player and settled in on the couch with Libby the dog to wait a couple of hours until Toby was home from work and had a good dinner under his belt before calling him. She dozed off, of course, and woke up when the grandfather clock bonged eleven times. Lucy grabbed her phone and hit Toby's contact listing, waiting impatiently for him to answer. She was beginning to think she'd have to leave a voicemail, or send a text, when she heard his voice. "Hey, Mom, what's up?"

"Um, I'm sorry to bother you," she began, already regretting making the call. She didn't believe in laying on the guilt with her kids, at least that's what she frequently told herself. "It's just that I, well, I know you're busy and all but it would mean a whole heck of a lot if you guys would come to the wedding." She exhaled, reaching for Libby's head and scratching her behind the ears. "So I'm asking you to reconsider."

"Oh, gosh, Mom. I know you must be disappointed, but it's really not in the cards right now."

"Is it money?" she asked, wishing she could afford to pay for three round-trip tickets.

As the chief breadwinner, Toby took offense. "I'm doing just fine on that score, Mom."

"Of course you are. It's just that sometimes unexpected expenses can play havoc with the budget. Your dad's worried he's going to owe the IRS this year."

"Nope. We're doing fine. I already got a big tax refund and bought three ATVs, secondhand, got a good deal. Patrick loves going off-road, we're all into hunting and fishing. And believe it or not, Molly's become a terrific hunter. She's got a great eye. We mostly eat game these days."

This news about Molly didn't actually surprise Lucy; she'd long suspected her daughter-in-law had a keen killer's instinct. "Saves on grocery bills," said Lucy.

"That's not why we do it," explained Toby. "We're trying to become more self-sufficient. Up here we can see firsthand how the glaciers are shrinking, climate change is real and it's happening fast. A crisis is coming, things will get violent, and we want to be ready. We've filled the cellar with nonperishables, all sorts of food and fuel, and we've got weapons, too, to protect ourselves."

"Really?"

"Yeah. I'm thinking of getting an AR-15, before they ban them. We all go practice shooting together. The family that shoots together stays together. Patrick's quite the sharpshooter."

"My goodness," said Lucy.

"I know you probably don't approve, but believe me, the writing's on the wall and we're going to be ready." He paused. "So that's why I don't think we're gonna fit in with those Frenchies, prancing around with their scarves and stuff."

This was a lot of new information and Lucy wasn't sure

how to respond, but decided to try to find some common ground. "Hunting's popular in France, you know, and people are people, the world over. But the people I care about are you and Molly and Patrick and I don't think it's a very big ask to expect you to join the rest of the family at Elizabeth's wedding." She took a moment to catch her breath, realizing her tone had become a bit harsh, then added, "Blood is thicker than water, you know."

"No, Mom, I don't know." He snorted. "I never knew what that meant, but I do know that I love my family, all of us, and I'm doing everything in my power to keep this planet livable and, worst-case scenario, increase our chances of surviving. This is it, after all, we've only got this little tiny planet in a giant cosmos. And you've gotta know that air travel, all those jets, contribute in a major way to climate change."

That was all true, no doubt, but sounded like a lot of exaggeration as well as a convenient excuse to Lucy, who was beginning to lose patience. "Well, kiddo, I hate to inform you that all those jets are going to be flying whether or not you're on them. So if I were you, I'd book my tickets while the going is still good. After all, you never know what the future will bring and your father and I aren't getting any younger. It's my dearest wish to see all my kids together, celebrating Elizabeth's big day. It's not like any of us are jetting around willy-nilly, destroying the ozone layer. This is a once-in-a-lifetime opportunity, we may never be able to be together as a family ever again."

There was a long silence, and Lucy feared she'd gone too far. Finally, Toby spoke. "Wow, Mom, this really means a lot to you."

"It really does—and it's a great opportunity for Patrick to experience another culture. See a bit of the world—before it implodes."

Now Toby was laughing. "Okay, okay. I'll see what I can do."

"Good. Give my love to Molly and Patrick, and save some for yourself, too."

"Will do. Love you, Mom."

Now that they were empty nesters, Lucy and Bill had begun marking the end of the work week with a Friday night date. It was never anything too fancy, maybe taking advantage of happy hour at the Cali Kitchen restaurant down by the harbor, or catching a movie at the indie cinema in the long-shuttered old movie house on Main Street that Bill had helped restore to its former gilded glory. This week they went a bit farther afield, driving up Route 1 to Rockland to try a new bistro that had been getting rave reviews.

Once settled in a booth in the trendy restaurant, which featured exposed brick and copper-topped tables, Lucy sipped a glass of chardonnay while Bill attacked a glass of local IPA and they both perused the menu. "What is a *soubise*?" asked Bill. "And do I want it on my pork chop?"

"I haven't the faintest," confessed Lucy. "I guess you could ask the server."

"Or maybe I'll just order a burger and fries."

"Truffle fries?"

"Sure. How much can they mess up fries?"

"Good point," agreed Lucy. "I'll have that, too."

That important matter settled, and their order placed with the server, Bill sighed deeply and reached across the table to take Lucy's hand. Not a good sign, she thought, bracing herself for trouble.

"Lucy, I know how much you want to go to France for this wedding . . ." he began.

Lucy withdrew her hand and lifted her chin, preparing to resist.

"But the truth is, I just don't think we can swing it. For one thing, we'd have to help the girls. I really doubt they can manage the airfare, what with their student loans and all."

Lucy felt a stab of guilt; she had already heard from both Sara and Zoe, who had asked for loans to cover the cost of plane tickets but hadn't mentioned it to Bill, who'd figured it out on his own. You didn't have to be clairvoyant to figure that two young women starting careers after college would be struggling financially.

"It's only money, Bill," she protested. "We have resources, we could use the home equity line, or even charge the tickets and pay them off gradually." She took a big swallow of wine. "We'll never have an opportunity like this again, we've got free room and board at the château, our only expense is the airfare." She paused, eyeing the remaining half-inch or so of wine in her glass. "I think you're being penny-wise and pound-foolish."

Bill grinned and raised his arm, signaling the server for refills. "Lucy, think what you're saying. Do you know what the interest rate is on a credit card? I got a notice the other day, it's going up to fifteen percent! There's no way we can afford to run a balance. And as for the home equity, we need to keep that in reserve in case the well fails or we need a new roof."

"I think you might be being too cautious. . . ."

"Not at all. Staying at the château would be a big savings, but there will be other expenses. We'll need suitable clothes, probably a rental car, gifts, maybe even tips for the château staff. I finally heard from my accountant and he says the IRS found a mistake in the amount I claimed for a business vehicle last year. . . ."

"Well, isn't that his fault?" asked Lucy.

Bill took a long drink of beer. "It was my mistake, Lucy. I gave him the wrong figures and now the taxes we owe are going to wipe out my business account. . . ."

"But construction is due to take off. You'll have plenty of work coming up."

"And plenty of competition, too. I have to keep my prices in line with everybody else."

"Even though your work is higher quality?"

"People don't always consider that," he admitted, as the server delivered fresh servings of wine and beer, taking away the empty glasses. "They're concerned with the bottom line, they want the most they can get for the least money."

Lucy raised her glass and concentrated on the taste of the cool, buttery wine in her mouth, then swallowed. "I understand that the tax bill is a killer, but this is something I really want. I want our whole family together for Elizabeth's wedding."

"Well, maybe they can redo the ceremony here, in Maine. That might work."

"A redo?" scoffed Lucy, as the server returned with their burgers and fries. "What are you thinking?"

"People do it all the time. Couples elope, they get married quickly to make the baby legitimate, and then they have a big reception later."

"I never heard of that," said Lucy, taking a bite out of one of her fries, then grimacing.

"Not good?"

"Different," said Lucy, popping the remainder of the fry into her mouth and chewing thoughtfully.

Bill cautiously tried one of his fries, then laughed. "Maybe this place is overrated," he said. "It's certainly overpriced."

"Maybe we could economize for the few months," offered Lucy. "Instead of movies and dinners, we could go for long walks."

"The burger is awfully good," said Bill, smiling wickedly as a bit of juice trailed down his chin.

Lucy dabbed at his face with her napkin. "I'm not giving up," she told him. "I'll come up with something." She looked him in the eye. "We could cut the cable bill, for instance. That sports channel is pretty expensive."

"The Bruins look good for the Stanley Cup playoffs," he said, in a challenging tone. "Maye you could ask Ted for a raise."

Lucy savored that first bite of burger and smiled. "I don't know, we're so lucky. We have so much to be grateful for. How come we feel so poor?"

Again, Bill reached across the table and took her hand. "I know what I'm grateful for," he said, giving it a squeeze. "It's you. You're the best thing that ever happened to me."

"I know what you're after," said Lucy, with a knowing look. "And you might just get it."

Lucy woke up alone on Saturday morning, taking advantage of the extra space for a super-luxurious stretch. Getting out of bed and facing her naked self in the mirror, she smiled, remembering last night's activities with pleasure. She slipped into a robe and headed for the bathroom, then continued down the back stairs to the kitchen where the aged dog greeted her with a thump of her tail and the half-full coffeepot was waiting for her. Bill had already gone, but had tucked a slip of paper with a big heart drawn on it in her favorite coffee mug. She chuckled and removed the note, tucking it into the robe's pocket with a little pat, and filled the mug with black coffee. Then she sat down at the round golden oak table, savored that first big swallow of coffee, and stared out the window where she noticed with surprise that Bill's truck was still in the driveway, but her SUV was gone.

What was going on? She wondered, taking a few more swallows of coffee in hopes it would spark her brain into figuring out this puzzle. Why did he take the SUV? If he was going to his work site, that massive old barn he was rehabbing on Shore Road, he would have needed his truck. Same if he had gone to the lumberyard or the hardware store, which he often did on Saturday. Did he have a doctor's appointment that she had forgotten? Or worse, had he kept the appointment secret from her because he had some horrible symptoms and didn't want to upset her until he knew the awful truth? That was crazy, she told herself, last night had been proof positive that the man was healthy and still had plenty of testosterone surging through his system. She got up to refill her cup and popped an English muffin in the toaster, telling herself that all would be revealed in time. Meanwhile, she had some errands of her own and would have to take the truck.

After eating her yogurt and English muffin, Lucy loaded the dishwasher. Tossing her empty yogurt container in the garbage, she noticed it was full and removed the bag, tying it up and leaving it by the kitchen door so she wouldn't forget to take it out and toss it in the trash can. Then it was time for a quick shower, which always made her feel a bit weird now that the house was so empty. After so many years of kids coming and going and having to fight for time in the bathroom, not to mention waiting for the hot water to recover, she knew she ought to appreciate being able to count on a hot shower any time she wanted. But in her heart, she would rather have had the kids back home, even if it meant running out of hot water while her hair was full of sudsy shampoo.

Scrubbed clean, teeth brushed, and dressed in her Saturday outfit of old jeans, worn sneaks, and Zoe's abandoned, paint-stained Winchester College sweatshirt, Lucy let the dog out and followed with the trash bag, making a mental list of errands: post office, bank, grocery store, garden center, maybe even a splurge at the Saturday farmer's market for some early salad greens. She was thinking about the greens, and also some fabulous cinnamon buns, when she attempted to toss her trash into the bin and discovered it was packed full. If she tried to add this new bag, the top wouldn't close and that would mean a tasty midnight snack for the raccoons, and a big mess the next morning.

Suddenly, she wasn't thinking of Bill in quite the same way. Dump runs were his responsibility, not hers. Even worse, she had a sneaking suspicion that Bill had left her the truck for this very reason, shirking his manly duty and leaving her to take up the slack. Oh well, she could handle it, she'd done it before, but she'd be darned if she got any cinnamon buns for him.

She was climbing into the truck when she noticed Libby looking at her with her ears raised in a questioning expression. The dog often accompanied Bill in the truck and she clearly expected to do the same with Lucy. "Okay, c'mon," she said and Libby ran over and sat, waiting for her to open the door. When she did, she realized the elderly dog would need some help, so she climbed out and hoisted her rear, giving her a push into the seat. Libby rewarded her with a lick on the face, a doggy thank-you.

Once she was back behind the driver's seat, Bill's star

fell even further when she noticed a handful of lottery scratch tickets and even a few Mega Millions receipts stuffed in the central console. Lucy was shocked, she'd always thought Bill shared her deep disapproval of gambling in any form, and especially state-sponsored gambling which she believed took advantage of the people who could least afford to risk their hard-earned cash on a pipe dream. On the other hand, she suspected that his tax troubles had prompted him to spend a few dollars on the tickets in hopes of a win.

There was also, she noticed when she checked the gauge, very little gas in the truck, which explained why Bill had taken the SUV. The indicator was hovering close to "E," which meant her first stop was going to be at the Quik-Stop. She had to wait a bit for a pump, and while she waited she noticed a big sign in the window announcing the winning lottery numbers, including Mega Millions. Idly, since she had nothing better to do, she gathered up the scattered slips and checked the numbers. Most were old, dated weeks and even months ago, but one had been purchased days ago. She compared the series of numbers with the ones on the sign, and discovered that four out of five agreed. She didn't know the rules, not exactly, but she had heard of people winning small prizes with only a few matches.

Then it was her turn and she filled the tank, shocked at the total. It was a cool spring day with no danger that Libby would overheat, so she left the dog in the truck and hurried inside to pay, taking the Mega Millions receipt with her. She handed over her debit card, and then showed Ray her Mega Millions receipt.

"Wow, Lucy, this is a winner," he exclaimed, his face lighting up.

"Really?" Lucy didn't quite believe it.

"Yeah. Really. Four out of five gets you ten thousand dollars."

Lucy's jaw dropped, and she noticed some of the other customers were beginning to take notice.

"And it's even better because you've got a Megaplier of three, which means you've actually won thirty thousand dollars."

A small group had gathered around her, smiling and nodding. "Good for you!" said one man. "Congratulations," offered another.

Lucy was beginning to feel a bit unsteady and wavered a bit on her feet until the man standing next to her grabbed her arm. "The lady needs a chair," he said.

Next thing she knew she was sitting on a stool, sipping on bottled iced tea, and nibbling a chocolate bar. Her head clearing, she asked, "So do you give me the money now?"

That got a laugh. "No. Sorry. I don't have that much in the register," said Ray. "You have to make an appointment with the lottery commission. You take your ticket and they'll give you a check."

"A big check," added a man who was buying some night crawlers.

"So you better take good care of that receipt," added the man who had grabbed her arm.

"Yes," agreed Ray. "I've got a special envelope for you." He held up the envelope, and the receipt, making sure she saw him enclose the valuable slip of paper inside. Then he handed it to her, advising her to put it someplace safe.

"I will," she said, feeling much better thanks to the tea and the candy bar. She took the envelope and slid it into her purse, which she zipped right up. "Thank you," she said, standing up. Then she laughed. "You won't have to call the *Courier* with this news, 'cause I'm the reporter!" She then made her way through the happy little crowd, buoyed by their genuine joy for her good fortune, and climbed in the truck. "It looks like your daddy's tax problems are over," she told the dog, growing excited as an even larger possibility now opened before her, "and we can afford to take the whole family to France for the wedding!" Libby, however, was focused on some kids playing ball on the other side of the street and wasn't the least bit interested in the family's finances.

She pulled out her phone and called Bill, who was immediately apologetic when he answered. "I'm sorry about taking your car," he began, and Lucy let him explain. "I was in a hurry to meet a possible customer and knew I needed gas. I hope you're not too mad at me."

"I was kind of upset and then I found all these lottery tickets. . . ."

"It was the tax thing, Lucy. You know what they say, 'You can't win if you don't play.' "

"You know I hate gambling," she said, keeping him on the hook.

"I know. But Sid gave me a scratch ticket on my birthday and I won a few bucks so I used them to buy a couple more tickets. That's what I did, I only used my winnings, rolled them over to buy the tickets." He sighed. "You don't happen to know if anybody won the Mega Millions, do you?"

"Why would I know?" asked Lucy, unable to resist giggling.

"Well, it would've been on the news. . . ."

"Nobody won big," she said, intending to puncture his hopeful balloon.

"Oh, well, it was worth a try."

Hearing the disappointment in his voice, she couldn't keep his win a secret a moment longer. "Bill, you won thirty thousand dollars."

There was a long silence. "Are you putting me on?"

"No. It's true. They told me at the Quik-Stop."

"Wowee! I can't believe it! I won!" he crowed. Hearing his voice, Libby gave a little yip. "Wow, this is incredible. And, no more worries about those taxes!"

"And we can afford to go to France for the wedding."

Bill didn't seem quite as excited as he had been. "Oh, right, Lucy."

"And no more gambling, promise?"

"Yeah," he agreed. "France, hunh. Turns out winning isn't everything it's cracked up to be."

Chapter Three

The last week in June found Lucy and Bill debarking from a luxurious minibus parked in front of the Cavendish Hotel in Paris. Thanks to their lottery windfall, the tax bill had been paid and airline tickets bought for themselves and all the kids. In addition, the couple were dressed in brand-new clothes chosen for comfort on the overnight flight: stretchy black yoga pants and a white French terry hoodie for Lucy and a neat navy blue track-suit for Bill. Their suitcases were also filled with new clothes, carefully chosen according to Elizabeth's advice. "Most of all, good shoes," she'd advised. "French people are mad about shoes and never wear sneakers."

Their feet, clad in comfy camp shoes, had barely touched the ground when they were greeted by the doorman, dressed in a splendid uniform adorned with the Cavendish coat of arms, and a swarm of bellhops. "Do they do this for every-one?" asked Bill, under his breath.

"I s'pose so, it's a pretty fancy hotel," said Lucy, who was enjoying feeling like a celebrity.

Reaching the reception desk, they were warmly wel-comed by possibly the handsomest young man Lucy had ever seen. Checking his name tag, which read AHMED, Lucy took an inventory of his dazzling good looks: longish wavy black hair, cocoa skin, white teeth, tall and broad shouldered—it simply wasn't fair. "Welcome to the Cavendish," he said, with a smile that made Lucy's knees feel weak. "I see you are here for one night only."

"That's right, we're going on to our daughter's wedding in Saint-Quiriace."

"Well, it is certainly our loss, but you have my felicitations on such a happy event."

"*Merci,*" said Lucy, batting her eyelashes.

"Ah, it's been a long flight," said Bill, losing patience. "We'd just like to get to our room."

"Of course," said Ahmed. "I will need a charge card."

"No problem," said Bill, handing over his Visa.

"It will just be a minute," said Ahmed, consulting his computer. "Ah, I see you have a junior suite at a discounted rate. . . ."

"Our daughter works here. Elizabeth Stone," said Lucy.

"Ah, you're the *famille* of Elizabeth. *Enchanté,*" he added, beaming at them.

"Ahem. The key or the card, whatever it is . . ." suggested Bill.

"*Absolument,*" said Ahmed, with a nod, handing over a pair of key cards. "Your room is 411, and the elevator is just over there." He snapped his fingers and a couple of bellhops snapped to attention. "Take their luggage to 411," he told them.

Bill was ready to protest that they could manage it themselves, but Lucy gave him a look, and he desisted, unhappily joining Lucy in leading the little procession to the elevator.

When they arrived at the room, the junior suite, Lucy

stood amazed, admiring the plush carpet, lush drapes on the windows, the potted orchid on the coffee table in front of the curvaceous love seat, and the inviting, oh so inviting king-size bed. The bellhops whisked open the draperies, turned on the lamps, and consulted them as to where they would like their bags. They seemed ready to begin un-packing when Bill stepped in, handing each of them a cou-ple of euro coins and pointedly looking at the door. Taking his cue, they quickly departed, after inquiring most sin-cerely if there was anything else they needed.

Left alone, Lucy and Bill stared at each other as if in shock. "This was a great idea of Elizabeth's," said Lucy. "What a great way to rest up and gather the family before we head to the château." She sat on the love seat and pat-ted it. "I could get used to this."

"Well, don't," advised Bill, who was turning on the TV. "Even with the discount this place is going to cost us a for-tune."

"Which we can afford," Lucy reminded him. "So we might as well enjoy it."

Bill was flipping through the channels, finally settling on CNN and settling himself in a comfy armchair with a matching ottoman. "It's the only thing in English," he ex-plained.

"Well, we are in France," said Lucy, giggling with de-light. "In Paris!"

"I don't know why Elizabeth couldn't get married in Maine," grumbled Bill, yawning as he watched Israeli bombs fall on the Gaza Strip and Hamas rockets arc through the night sky aimed at Israel.

"You're just experiencing jet lag. We should freshen up and get out for a walk, that's what they say to do."

"I'd really like to take a little nap," protested Bill, yawn-ing again.

"Absolutely not. That's the worst thing you can do."
Lucy retrieved her toiletry bag from her suitcase and
headed into the bathroom, where she reached for the light
switch. The crystal chandelier came on, illuminating a
marble mini-spa complete with a soaker tub, gold-plated
faucets, and piles of fluffy towels on a gilt stand. "You
gotta see this," she screamed, and Bill came running.

"Oh, my," he said, gazing at the glorious *salle de bain*.
"I guess we're not in Maine anymore."

"No, we are not," said Lucy, taking his hand.

Sometime later, freshly showered and dressed in what
Elizabeth had promised them were appropriate street
clothes—slim Capri pants, ballet flats, and an embroidered tunic for Lucy; charcoal gray slacks (definitely not
chinos and never, ever shorts, she'd warned), a crisp pale
blue sports shirt, and highly polished loafers (no sneakers!) for Bill—the jet-lagged couple ventured out for a
leisurely tour of the neighborhood. They walked hand in
hand, which Bill would never do back home, under leafy
green trees past rows of tiny, parked cars, racks packed
with bicycles, and countless motorcycles tucked wherever
there was almost enough room. Lucy admired the pyra-
mids of blooming flowers set out for sale on the sidewalk,
the cafés with tables and chairs outside occupied here and
there by people watching the passing parade as they
sipped their morning café au lait, the charming boutiques
and tempting bakeries. Completing a circle of the block
they returned to the hotel, where Lucy had a déjà vu moment observing a much younger but practically identical
version of her husband.

"Toby!" she called, dashing and throwing herself into
the bearded man's arms for a huge bear hug. "You're
here!"

"We sure are," said Toby, indicating the sofa across the

lobby where Molly was sitting with Patrick, who had fallen asleep with his head in her lap.

Lucy was off to see her grandson, leaving Bill and Toby to do their male bonding thing of shaking hands and slapping each other's arms.

"Patrick didn't sleep on the plane, he's exhausted," offered Molly, "otherwise I'd get up and give you a hug."

"It's okay," said Lucy, plopping herself in the opposite sofa. "It's so great to see you. How was the flight?"

"Long, very long," complained Molly, with a sigh.

"It'll take a while for you to adjust to the time change," she advised. "Don't do like Patrick and go to sleep, even though it's what you want to do. You've got to bull your way through the day and get to bed a bit early."

"That's what I've heard." She looked down at Patrick, now a gangly, long-legged middle schooler, and stroked his head. "I'm afraid if he sleeps now he'll be up all night."

"Let's see what happens when you stand up, you can't sit here all day."

As if on cue, Bill and Toby joined them, commiserating about the hotel's rates. "If this is the employee discount, what do regular customers pay?" wondered Toby, clearly a chip off the old block.

"I can only imagine," grumbled Bill. "If you ask me, nobody really needs a chandelier in the bathroom. It's stuff like that that pushes up the price."

"There's a chandelier in the bathroom?" inquired Molly, perking up.

"In ours, anyway," said Lucy.

"Well, let's go see," suggested Molly, giving Patrick a gentle shake.

His eyes popped open, he saw his grandparents and sat right up, rubbing his eyes. "Hi," he said, sounding half asleep.

"Listen, Patrick," began Lucy, "when you're wide awake, we can go to the park. They've got a pond for sailing toy boats, and a merry-go-round."

Realizing that these attractions didn't impress him, Lucy raised the ante. "And they have the most delicious ice cream."

"Okay," he said, standing up.

"But first, I think we all need to wash up a bit," said his mother.

"What's your room number? I'll come by in an hour or so?"

Toby consulted the little paper envelope that contained their room cards. "409."

"You must be right next door to us," exclaimed Lucy.

"Shall we?" invited Bill, and they all walked together to the elevator.

"Where are our bags?" asked Molly, sounding panicked.

"Probably already in your room," advised Lucy. "Believe me, they take care of everything here before you even think of it."

"And you pay for the privilege," grumbled Toby, sounding just like his father.

An hour or so later Lucy knocked on the door of room 409, which was immediately opened by an eager Patrick. "Let's go," he said.

"Give me a tour first," requested Lucy, before noticing that Molly and Toby were both stretched out sound asleep on the bed.

"The bathroom has a tub and a separate shower," said Patrick, clearly impressed as he stepped aside so she could enter.

"You'll have to show me later," whispered Lucy. "Your mom and dad are asleep."

"They said it's jet lag," reported Patrick.

"Well, I see you're ready for action, so let's go. In French they say, '*Allons-y!*'"

"In Alaska, we say, 'Get a move on!'"

Lucy chuckled, imaging various scenarios in which Patrick had been advised to get a move on, and carefully closed the door behind them, leaving the sleeping couple to catch a few z's.

"This is a pretty fancy place," observed Patrick, as they walked down the carpeted hall, lit by crystal sconces, to the elevator.

"France is pretty fancy," said Lucy. "I bet the château will be even fancier."

"Really?" asked Patrick, as the elevator promptly arrived.

"I wouldn't be surprised," said Lucy, as they stepped inside and descended.

Crossing the lobby, Lucy asked the doorman for directions to the Jardins du Luxembourg, and was pointed in the right direction. "It's a fine day for the park," he said, giving Patrick a salute.

The park was only a few blocks from the hotel, and Patrick kept up a steady stream of chatter as they walked along. The flight had been long, but he liked the food they served on a tray, and seeing the clouds outside the window. Paris, he decided, was okay, but he was eager to see the château which he hoped had a moat like a real castle. "But Mom says I'm going to have to wear white satin pants for the wedding. Do I have to?" he asked, appealing to what he hoped was a higher authority.

"Sorry, Patrick, it's not up to me."

"Shit," he said, causing Lucy to widen her eyes in shock and surprise.

"Uh, Patrick, in France they say *merde*, but it's only for adults. Promise me you won't use potty talk, okay?"

"Sorry. I'll try."

"We want to make a good impression, we're visitors here."

"Is that the park?" he asked, spotting the gate across the street.

"Yes, it is. *Allons!*" Instinctively she grabbed his hand and looked both ways before crossing the street, amused when he pulled away and darted ahead of her through the gate.

He'd only gone a few steps before he pulled up short and turned to face her, demanding, "What kind of park is this?"

Lucy took in the neatly defined gravel path lined with statuary, the perfectly clipped grass, the flower beds packed with colorful flowers, the scattered green chairs for visitors, and the enormous Luxembourg Palace which dominated the scene, realizing it was a far cry from an American park. "It's a French park," she said, pointing to the carousel. "Shall we?"

"Yeah!"

Several turns on the carousel completed, they watched kids sailing boats on the pond, caught a puppet show in which they didn't understand a word, but joined the raucous crowd in laughing at the antics of the French version of Punch and Judy. Then it was time for a pick-me-up and they headed for the ice cream stand where Lucy opted for *fruit de la passion* and Patrick, somewhat dismayed that they didn't have cookie dough, settled for *chocolat*.

"How's the ice cream?" inquired Lucy. "As good as cookie dough?"

"It's pretty good," admitted Patrick, who had already eaten most of his.

"Time to go back to the hotel," she said, with a sigh. "They'll be wondering what happened to us."

June in Paris was much warmer than June in Maine or Alaska, and Patrick and Lucy were feeling the heat even as they walked along the shady boulevard. Stepping inside the hotel, they both breathed a sigh of relief, feeling the cool, lightly scented air conditioning. They were crossing the lobby, headed for the elevators, when Lucy heard someone call, "*Maman!*" She turned, just in case she was the intended *maman*, and saw Elizabeth waving to her from the seating area, along with Sara and Zoe.

Grabbing Patrick's hand, she pulled him along and dashed across the gleaming marble floor dotted with several plush rugs and attempted to embrace Elizabeth. Elizabeth, however, gave her the traditional French greeting of air kisses, or *bisous*, first on one side and then on the other. Taking a step back, Lucy examined her oldest daughter, noticing first that she had a new hairdo. The very short, spiky do Elizabeth had long favored was gone, replaced with a sleek bob. The black nail polish was also a thing of the past, replaced with the palest pink, and she was wearing a charming, flowered dress instead of the tight jeans and moto boots she'd previously favored on her days off. "Wow, you already look very bridal," said Lucy, watching as Elizabeth instructed Patrick in the art of a proper French greeting.

"We hardly recognized her," said Zoe.

"She's taking us out to lunch," said Sara. "Do you want to join us?"

Lucy was tempted, but noticing that Patrick was rubbing his eyes, she declined. "I think I'll bring Patrick up to our room and let him rest a bit," she said. "His parents were out like lights when we left and I don't want to disturb them."

"What about Dad?" asked Zoe. "I bet he's asleep."

"We won't bother him. We've got a suite with a living room and a bedroom . . ." began Lucy, only to be interrupted by Zoe. "Ooh la la," she crooned, "a suite!"

"It's gorgeous, you'll have to see it," said Lucy. "But for now Patrick and I can have some quiet time in the living room."

"Good idea, because I have a big evening planned," said Elizabeth. "I've arranged for dinner *en famille* in one of the hotel's private dining rooms. It's going to be fabulous—we'll gather here in the lobby at seven o'clock."

"That late?" inquired Lucy, who always served dinner at six o'clock.

"Mom, this is France, where people eat dinner at ten. Seven is the earliest I could arrange."

"Oh well," said Lucy, exchanging parting *bisous* with her daughters. "Enjoy your lunch."

The girls departed, chattering as they went, and Lucy took Patrick upstairs for the quiet time they both needed, which would be followed, she decided, by a room service lunch with Bill. He'd grumble about the extravagance, of course, but in the end would come around and enjoy spoiling his only grandchild. And, of course, they'd need something to tide them over until seven.

Lucy could hardly believe her good fortune when she and Bill stepped out of the elevator at the appointed hour and found her entire family gathered in the lobby. Her fondest wish had come true and she felt like pinching herself, to see if perhaps she was dreaming. Toby's booming voice made it clear, however, that this was real life. "So what's for dinner?" he demanded. "Frogs' legs?"

"Yes," teased Elizabeth. "Frogs' legs are a must at every French meal."

"Really?" inquired an alarmed Patrick.

"And snails, too," said Elizabeth. "And children don't get any dessert unless they eat their snails."

Noticing Patrick's rather green face, Lucy decided it was time to intervene. "She's teasing you, Patrick. Elizabeth is a great tease."

"Busted," chorused Sara and Zoe, as Elizabeth led the way to the private dining room where the family was soon settled at a beautifully set table. Printed menus at each place listed the courses in English, beginning with foie gras, followed by a salad of artichokes and goat cheese, cream of watercress soup with caviar, sole meunière with potatoes and petite peas, and strawberry tart for dessert. Suitable wines accompanied each course, and the meal would end with a traditional selection of cheeses.

"My God, this is gonna cost a fortune," mumbled Bill. "I bet each of these wines is a cool hundred dollars."

"You mean euros, Dad," advised Toby.

Elizabeth, however, was consulting with a gentleman in a black suit, who Lucy thought had the look of a maître d' or perhaps even the hotel manager. Taking Elizabeth by the hand, he stood by the table, clearly wishing to make an announcement. Lucy tapped one of her many glasses with a spoon, and they all fell silent.

"I am Robert Loiseau, manager of the hotel, and I wish to welcome you all here," he began. "We are very sorry to lose our lovely Elizabeth, but we wish her much happiness in her marriage and know she will be a great success at whatever challenges she undertakes in the future.

"All of us here at the Cavendish are honored with your presence, the family of Elizabeth, and this dinner is our parting gift to her and to you. I would begin by raising a glass of champagne to our very dear, very lovely Elizabeth."

Several servers immediately appeared bearing trays filled with glasses of champagne that they distributed. When everyone had been served, Loiseau raised his glass. "To Elizabeth. *Salut!*"

He promptly downed the champagne, then winked at Elizabeth. "Now I will leave you to enjoy your dinner. Bon appétit!"

"Feel better, dear?" Lucy asked her husband, who had promptly emptied his glass and was signaling a server for a refill.

"It's okay so far," he admitted, with a sly smile, "but I was hoping for some of those calves' brains I had last time I was here."

"No *tête de veau*, for you," said Lucy, shaking her head. "Some people are never satisfied."

Chapter Four

There was a bit of an awkward silence while the foie gras was distributed; Lucy put it down to the fact that the various family siblings, some of whom hadn't seen each other in years, were taking time to size each other up. It was her job, she decided, to get things rolling. "So, Elizabeth," she began, "tell us all about Jean-Luc."

"Yeah," chimed in Sara. "How did you meet?"

"Here at the hotel," said Elizabeth, picking up her knife and spreading a dab of pâté on a triangle of toast. "He often came with his family; they always stay here when they're in Paris."

"At these prices?" Bill was shocked.

"Dad," Elizabeth began, in that patient tone of voice grown children use to edify their uninformed parents, "they're really, really rich." She picked up the toast. "You'd be surprised how many people are," she added, then took a bite.

"Okay, so he's rich," said Zoe. "What other qualities does he have?"

"And why isn't he here tonight?" inquired Toby. "I thought we'd meet him."

"You will, Toby, you will," promised Elizabeth. "I thought it would be better if tonight was just family, let everyone clear the air and get reacquainted."

"What do you mean? *Clear the air?*" asked Bill, getting a look from Lucy.

"Oh, nothing. Family stuff. You know, tensions, old resentments, all that stuff. I thought it would be better to get the snarky stuff over before we meet the Schoen-Renes."

"Well, I'm the mom and I'm warning you all: There will be no snark. We are going to be an ideal, perfect family for the duration. Agreed?"

The kids all laughed and nodded.

Molly, bless her, broke the ensuing silence. "So Elizabeth, what attracted you to Jean-Luc?"

"Jean-Luc is everything a girl could want. He's rich, handsome, and attentive, plus he has a charming family and a château."

"That's all very nice, but are you in love?" asked Zoe.

"Of course," replied Elizabeth, actually blushing, which was something Lucy hadn't seen her cool, calm, and ever-so-collected daughter do in years.

"Well, that's wonderful," said Lucy, beaming with pleasure.

Bill had polished off his foie gras and his champagne. "I thought I heard that manager guy . . ."

"Monsieur Loiseau," volunteered Elizabeth.

"Yeah. Him. He said they were sorry to lose you, does that mean you quit your job?"

Elizabeth took a sip of champagne. "I'm going to be working at the château. It's not just a home, it's a business. They host all sorts of events for paying guests who want to pretend they were to the manor born: weddings, hunts, carriage races. It's a busy schedule and I'll be helping out."

"That sounds ideal, given your experience here at the hotel," said Sara.

"Sounds like a good deal for this guy's family," said Bill. "They not only get a daughter, but a worker, too."

"Dad, it's not quite like that. This sort of thing is very usual in France, where businesses are often family operations." She rearranged the remaining pieces of toast on her plate. "I'm excited about this. I'm getting the man of my dreams and the job of my dreams, all wrapped up in one really hunky package."

That got Sara and Zoe laughing. "Hunky, hey?" asked Molly.

"Decidedly. He's tall, well built, he has the cutest dimple in his chin . . . and he loves me."

"I'll drink to that," said Toby, raising his glass. "To love."

They all raised whatever they had in their glasses, champagne or water, and toasted Elizabeth. "To love."

But as she drained the last swallow of Veuve Clicquot, Lucy wondered if life at the château as the Schoen-Renes' daughter-in-law would truly be the ideal situation Elizabeth was expecting. To her, it seemed a bit of a risky proposition, like putting all her eggs in one basket, but she hoped with all her heart that she was wrong.

The goat cheese and artichoke salad came next, accompanied by a white burgundy. "I think you'll find this wine delicious, it's what we call a big white," said Elizabeth, showing off a bit.

Toby, as her older brother, felt the need to take her down a peg. "I dunno, Elizabeth. Can a fellow get an IPA around here?" A question that got a round of chuckles from the table.

Elizabeth was not to be bested, however. "Of course. The hotel caters to all tastes, including those of uninformed, unsophisticated Americans. You can have anything you want, even a Bud."

"That won't be necessary," said Lucy, glaring at Toby, who promptly turned his attention to his salad.

"This is delicious wine," said Molly, apparently used to smoothing over her husband's rough edges. Noticing that Patrick was digging into his salad with some enthusiasm, she asked, "How do you like the salad, Patrick?"

"It's really good," he said. "It's got cream cheese."

"Actually, it's go . . ." began Zoe, only to be quickly cut off in mid-noun by Molly.

"Really good cream cheese," she said, giving Zoe a warning glance.

Once the salad was cleared away, the cream of watercress soup was served, with a dollop of whipped cream and a dab of caviar floating atop the green puree. Patrick was definitely suspicious of green soup, and curious about the caviar. "What is this stuff?" he asked his father.

"Caviar."

"What's caviar?"

Sara was quick to answer. "Fish eggs," she said, in a teasing tone.

Patrick wasn't convinced. "No, really?"

"It's considered a great delicacy," said Lucy.

"But it's really fish eggs?"

Lucy gave him an apologetic nod. "Yup."

"Well, I'm not eating that," declared Patrick, shoving the bowl away and slopping the green soup onto the pristine tablecloth.

"Oh, Patrick!" exclaimed Molly.

"You better behave yourself," warned his father.

"Really, it's no problem," said Elizabeth, signaling to a server to attend to the mess.

The server smoothly removed the empty bowl, and covered the stain with a clean napkin, then awaited instructions.

"Patrick, is there something else you would prefer?" asked Elizabeth.

"I want a hamburger, right now!" demanded Patrick.

"I don't think so, buddy," scolded his father. "I think you can eat what you're given and be grateful. Your aunt Elizabeth and her friends here at the hotel have gone to a lot of trouble. . . ."

"It's no trouble, Toby," said Elizabeth. "I want everyone, including Patrick, to enjoy this meal."

"Well, I expect my son to behave himself and show his good manners," growled Toby.

"It's not a big deal, Toby," offered Lucy. "Boys will be boys, you ought to know that. You were far from perfect."

"He's my son and I expect him to do as I say." He turned to Elizabeth. "I don't like to reward bad behavior."

"Accidents happen," said Lucy.

"It was no accident," said Toby. "He was being rude."

"I think we all need to take a deep breath," said Bill. He looked at Lucy. "It's none of our business how Toby raises his son."

That got a grateful nod from Toby.

Bill continued, "But I think you can handle the discipline later." A server had arrived with a hamburger for Patrick, which Elizabeth had quietly ordered, and was standing by, awaiting permission to present it to Patrick. "Okay?" asked Bill, getting a nod from Toby.

The hamburger was placed in front of Patrick, who knew full well he wasn't off the hook. "Thank you," he said, in a meek little voice.

"You're welcome, Patrick," said Elizabeth, with a relieved sigh.

"But don't you dare do anything like that again," warned his father.

"This soup really is delicious," offered Molly, eager to move on. "We rarely get watercress in the supermarket."

"Maybe a bunch or two in the spring, that's about it," agreed Lucy. "If you're lucky."

"The whole food system is different here in France," said Elizabeth. "They have supermarkets but they aren't as popular as the open-air markets where farmers bring their produce. Those markets are very seasonal and people get excited when the first asparagus shows up, or the wild mushrooms. It's almost a ritual, every family has special recipes that feature the new crops."

"We do that, too," said Lucy. "Like when the first apples show up at the farm stand in the fall, and the cider."

"That's true," admitted Elizabeth, "but food is more important here than in the States. It's a big deal, and preparing and eating food is taken very seriously. There's no bingeing on potato chips an hour before dinner, and everything is cooked from scratch. No frozen pizza."

"It sounds a lot healthier than the usual American diet," observed Molly. "More variety, no preservatives. That's what Toby and I try to avoid, we've been keeping chickens and growing vegetables."

"Mom and Dad catch fish and hunt venison," offered Patrick, who had doubled down on his hamburger. "Sometimes he lets me kill a chicken," he added gleefully. "I chop off its head with my hatchet."

Greeted with a stunned silence, Toby was quick to explain. "If they stop laying, it's into the pot with them," he said.

"I think you will like the château," said Elizabeth. "They

have a farm and grow most everything they eat. And they breed game birds for shooting parties."

"Sounds like a gruesome sort of party," said Zoe. "Killing birds for fun."

"It is sort of fun," admitted Toby. "It's very satisfying to catch your dinner, whether it's hooking a wily old trout or tracking a big old buck."

"Or even cooking a chicken you've raised yourself," added Molly.

"Well, I'm thinking of becoming vegan," declared Zoe, just as the sole meunière was served. Sniffing the delicious, buttery aroma, she added, "That's if vegans eat fish."

The family members turned their attention to the delicious fish, which Lucy remembered had so impressed Julia Child when she first tasted it that she was inspired to learn about French cooking. Tasting the dish, Lucy had to agree with Julia. Fish was plentiful in Maine, but she'd never had any that tasted as delicious as this. Maybe she should take some French cooking lessons.

Zoe and Sara had both joined the clean plate club when they turned to Elizabeth, who was savoring tiny bites of fish.

"Wow, you really have changed," said Zoe. "Remember how you used to gobble up everything in sight?"

"Yeah, one night you ate an entire box of Oreos," recalled Sara.

"Here it comes," moaned Elizabeth. "I'm not going to be allowed to forget my misspent youth."

"None of you was exactly perfect," commented Lucy. "But you have all turned out pretty well." She beamed at Elizabeth, picturing her as a radiant, beautiful bride. Watching her wield her fish knife, she noticed the diamond on her ring finger sparkling, as she ate in the French manner using both hands. "Is your engagement ring a family stone?" she asked.

"You've got quite a rock there," said Zoe, eyeing the very large diamond.

"Is it real?" asked Sara.

Elizabeth put down her knife and fork and held out her hand, admiring the jewel. "It is rather nice, isn't it?" she said, with a smug little smile.

"You better be careful," warned Bill. "You shouldn't go traipsing around on the street with it. You could get mugged."

"It's insured, all five carats."

"But you might be hurt," said Lucy, fretting, "and there's always the sentimental value. You can't replace that, especially if it's a family piece that they've had for generations."

"Never fear, Mom. It's brand-new, from Cartier. Jean-Luc took me and asked me to choose something, that's how he proposed."

Lucy was shocked. "Couldn't you have chosen something smaller?"

"Oh, I did, but he kept insisting it had to be bigger, very big, like our love."

"Eeuw," groaned Sara. "You're making me sick."

"I suppose you're going on some fabulous honeymoon, too?" asked Zoe, rolling her eyes. "Not that I'm dying of jealousy or anything. I can take it."

"Relax. We're not doing anything right away. Jean-Luc wanted to go on safari. . . ."

Zoe was incredulous. "In Africa?"

"Yeah. He wants to stay at that treetop hotel Queen Elizabeth and Prince Philip stayed at way back when. It's still in business, but it's very popular, and he couldn't book anything until next year. So, we'll wait. Good things are worth waiting for, that's the French way."

"So you're not going away at all? Not even a couple of nights somewhere romantic? This is France, after all."

"It's fine, Mom. It's the busy season at the château. . . ."

Lucy nodded and pressed her lips together. She was beginning to think her fears that the Schoen-Renes were taking advantage of their daughter-in-law were well founded.

"Well, I bet if you were marrying that Secret Service guy who was so crazy about you . . ." began Zoe.

"Yeah. He'd be taking you to Disneyland," added Sara.

"Or maybe camping in some rustic cabin in the Rockies . . ."

"Yeah, he was a real red-blooded all-American guy," recalled Sara, turning to Elizabeth. "What was his name?"

"I don't know who you mean," protested Elizabeth.

"Of course you do. You were wild about him. He was here in France, wasn't he? Working for the American embassy or something?"

"Oh, you mean Chris. Chris Kennedy," replied Elizabeth, keeping her tone offhand and casual. "He's still around."

"Here in France?" asked Bill.

"Yes. He's in corporate security these days. Working mostly for American companies with offices and interests in France."

"Do you see him?" asked Lucy, remembering the handsome young Secret Service agent Elizabeth had first met one Christmas when she had her first job, working at a resort in Florida. He'd turned up again some years later, in Paris, where he had been investigating a currency violation, and had been instrumental in getting Lucy and Bill out of a tight situation in which terrorists had attempted to abduct Elizabeth. Since that fateful day the two had a long-standing on-again, off-again relationship, but that hadn't stopped Lucy from hoping they would eventually come to their senses and get married. In her eyes they were perfect for each other.

"Occasionally," said Elizabeth, with a shrug. "We're friends, that's all."

"He knows that you're getting married?" asked Toby.

"Sure. He's very happy for me."

Hmm, thought Lucy. Somehow that didn't sound at all like the Chris Kennedy she remembered.

"Will he be at the wedding?" asked Molly.

"Oh, no. It's going to be small and intimate. A real family affair, that's how the French do weddings."

"That's the best sort of wedding," said Lucy, as the servers began clearing plates in preparation for the dessert course. If Elizabeth said she and Chris were only friends, she had to accept it as fact, but she was relieved that Chris was not invited. The last thing a bride needed was an old flame showing up on her wedding day.

Chapter Five

That night, Lucy couldn't fall asleep until four a.m., which she suspected, after doing some fuzzy math, translated to her usual ten o'clock bedtime in Maine. The requested wake-up call at seven thirty was a rude awakening, after only a few hours of sleep. Bill, however, who had napped yesterday contrary to all the advice about coping with jet lag, had snored his way through a solid eight hours, which Lucy knew for a fact since she'd been lying beside him, awake, for most of them.

"Bone-joor, shari," he greeted her, with a dreadful French accent, wrapping his arms around her and snuggling close.

"I need coffee," moaned Lucy, stubbornly keeping her eyes closed.

"No can do, shari," Bill informed her, after checking all the drawers and closets for a coffee maker. "We'll have to go downstairs."

"Can't."

"Sure you can. Have a quick shower, it will perk you right up."

"I'm not opening my eyes until I smell coffee."

Bill was consulting the room service menu, shaking his

head. "This can't be right. Twenty euros for a pot of coffee."
The wheels were turning in his head, albeit somewhat
slowly. "Say? How much did that lunch cost us yesterday?"

"If you truly loved me you'd pay whatever they asked."
Lucy sighed dramatically. "And since we're getting coffee,
might as well add some orange juice and croissants."

"Really?"

"Wake me when it's here," said Lucy, rolling over.

It was close to ten when Lucy and Bill, freshly showered
and fortified by coffee and croissants, went down at the
appointed time to meet the rest of the family in the lobby.
Elizabeth, practiced in providing stress-free arrangements
for the hotel's guests, had organized a minivan to take the
entire family to the château, and it was already parked
outside. The family, however, was not complete: Sara and
Zoe were missing.

"I wonder what's keeping the girls?" asked Lucy.

"Thick heads," said Toby, with a knowing nod.

"What's a thick head?" asked Patrick, getting chuckles
from the adults.

"It's what happens when you have too much fun," explained his mother.

Patrick pondered this. "Fun gives you a thick head?"

"It's just a way of saying they drank too much wine,"
explained Lucy.

"There was a lot of wine at dinner, but they didn't seem
tipsy," said Bill.

"They went out afterward, to a club, with Elizabeth, for
a hen party," explained Molly. "They invited me, but I
was beat. All I could think about was bed."

"Maybe we should call their room?" suggested Lucy.

Bill indicated the elevator, where the doors had opened
revealing two rather disheveled sisters. Zoe's short hair

was sticking out every which way and Sara's shirt was only half tucked into her skirt, which was askew. Walking very gingerly, they approached their family.

"Big night?" asked Bill.

"Can we get you something? Coffee?" asked Lucy.

The two girls sank onto a sofa, leaning against each other.

"Nothing," croaked Zoe.

"Sara?"

"I want to die."

"The driver wants to know if everyone is ready?" asked the doorman, splendid as ever in his Cavendish uniform. "Your bags have now been loaded and he's ready if you are."

Bill glanced at his daughters, who seemed to be drifting off into dreamland. "As ready as we'll ever be," he announced. "Alley-oop!"

"I think you mean *allons-y*," said Lucy.

"Whatever." Bill shrugged. "Let's go."

Soon they were all seat-belted into the luxurious van, which was delicately scented with lemon verbena, and the doorman waved them off with a cheery "*bon voyage*." The driver hit the gas, the van zoomed into traffic and they were on their way. Traffic was still heavy in the city so there was much braking, sudden stops followed by short bursts of speed, but once they reached the highway it was smooth sailing. "We are leaving the city," he told them by way of explanation. "Everyone else is coming in."

Like all cities, the outskirts of Paris were filled with a variety of businesses providing support services: there were railroad tracks, gas stations, body shops, all sorts of warehouses, and numerous small contractors with fenced yards strewn with bits and pieces of machinery. But then, suddenly, they were in the countryside. They passed patches of forest, fields of rapeseed in golden bloom, meadows dotted with horses, cows, sheep, and goats. There were little towns, where the steeply roofed houses gathered around stone churches with tall steeples, and sometimes, in the distance, elegant châteaux were spotted.

"Do we have far to go?" asked Toby, checking his watch.

"About twenty more minutes," advised the driver. "Close enough to Paris, still in Île-de-France, but also far enough, eh?"

"Exactly," agreed Toby.

The driver was spot-on and they rolled through the château's gates exactly twenty minutes later. Tall trees lined the drive, creating a shady allée that concealed the château until they broke into the sunlight and it was suddenly revealed. Lucy gasped, taking in the enormous gray stone building which, as the little windows which dotted the steep tiled and chimneyed roof indicated, was at least four stories tall. The van continued over a little bridge which led over the moat into a graveled courtyard, embraced on both sides by columned extensions. Charming statues of plump children adorned the low wall that encircled the courtyard. The central block boasted two rows of huge windows with many panes, outlined in white paint, which flanked the central entrance door. High above, a triangular pediment contained a bas-relief sculpture of the family crest.

"We have arrived at Campanule," announced the driver.

"Wow," breathed Bill.

"Oh, it's just your normal château," said Elizabeth, nonchalantly.

"How big is it?" asked Lucy.

"I think Marie-Laure said there were eighty-six rooms, but don't quote me on that."

"How many bathrooms?" asked Sara.

"Plenty," replied Elizabeth, laughing.

They began gathering up their handbags and jackets, and filed out of the van, clustering together on the graveled courtyard. Bill tried to give the driver a tip, but he refused to accept it. "All taken care of," he insisted, then got to work unloading the bags. Moments later the monumental front doors opened and a man and woman stepped out, both smiling broadly and hurrying down the stone steps to greet them.

"*Welcome, welcome,*" trilled the woman. "Welcome to the beautiful Elizabeth's wonderful family. I am Marie-Laure, and this is my husband, Hugo. We are so pleased to welcome you to our home, which you must think of as your home while you are here."

Taking in the immense building, the rows of enormous windows, the climbing vines and the statues of playful children, Lucy thought the château was a far cry from her antique Maine farmhouse. "Thank you so much for having us," said Lucy, stepping forward and exchanging *bisous* with Marie-Laure and then, on tiptoes, with Hugo.

Hugo was immensely tall, and the very image of a country gentleman in a quilted vest, open-collared shirt, and gray trousers finished off with highly polished ankle boots. Marie-Laure was a picture-perfect lady of the manor, in a flowered, full-skirted shirtwaist dress, her gray hair styled in a perfect bob.

"Let me introduce my family," said Lucy. "This is my husband, Bill, our son, Toby, with his wife, Molly and son, Patrick." Much to Patrick's surprise, they were immediately showered with *bisous*, which sent him into a fit of giggles. "Our daughters," continued Lucy, "Sara and Zoe." More *bisous* were distributed, and then Jean-Luc appeared, with perfect timing. He was every bit as handsome as Elizabeth had promised, tall and dark and casually dressed in jeans and a pressed dress shirt, and the whole *bisous* process was repeated. Lucy noted with amusement that Jean-Luc's arrival seemed to have marvelous curative powers as Sara and Zoe were busily engaged in chatting him up, hangovers gone and now neatly pulled together with combed hair, slicks of fresh lipstick, and no more untucked clothing.

As if by magic, or perhaps some discreet signal, a woman accompanied by two young men appeared and stood by at the top of the steps, awaiting instructions. "Ah, this is Louise, our housekeeper," said Marie-Laure, indicating the smiling woman, dressed for action in a shirt and slacks with a big bunch of keys dangling from her wrist. "I know you must be tired, jet lag and all, so I will let you get settled," continued Marie-Laure, in perfect English. "Louise will show you to your rooms, and Jean and Jacques will bring your bags." She paused. "If there is anything you need, if something is not to your satisfaction, do not hesitate to let me or Hugo know."

This was Hugo's cue, and speaking slowly, in English with a heavy French accent, he said, "I am very happy that you are all here. I hope you have a very pleasant stay."

With that, Madame and Monsieur departed, leaving the family in Louise's capable hands. Jean-Luc lingered for a few moments with Sara and Zoe, but was soon sent on his way with a nod from Louise. "Come this way," she said, indicating a path leading around the side of the château. "I will give you a bit of a tour, while the boys deal with your bags."

They followed her through the grand entrance which led into a tiled oval foyer with a central table, a few stiff chairs sitting along the walls which were decorated with some rather fearsome medieval weapons, and an impressive staircase. French doors on the rear wall revealed a spacious lawn dotted here and there with enormous beech trees; their massive gray trunks reminding Lucy of elephants. Louise indicated the spectacular view with a wave of her arm, pointing out a terrace overlooking an elaborate formal garden with several sculptures, a spouting fountain, and in the distance, a lake shimmering in the sunshine. "The fountain is a copy of one at Versailles," she informed them. "It is supposed to represent the rising sun, which was the symbol of the king." Somewhat puzzled, since the fountain was composed of a charioteer rising from the water drawn by horses, they nodded in appreciation.

Then they were following Louise up the massive staircase, Louise maintaining a brisk pace, and down a very long hall, past the portraits of ancestors until she abruptly halted in front of a door. "This is the *chambre* for Madame and Monsieur Bill," she said, opening the door and stepping aside.

Lucy took the cue and went inside, Bill followed, and the door was closed behind them. She heard Louise trill, "Follow me," and then the sound of shuffling feet as the rest of the family continued on down the hallway to their rooms. "I guess we can say we've finally arrived," said Bill, gazing about the room in admiration and plopping himself down in a roomy upholstered armchair by the window. "This is something, hunh?"

"It's huge," said Lucy, surveying the spacious guest room, which had a curtained four-poster bed to the right of the door, with lamp tables on either side. A dressing table was placed in front of one of the windows on the opposite wall, and there were two armchairs in front of the second window. The bed curtains and window curtains matched, made of a pale green toile de Jouy, picking up one of the colors in the Aubusson rug that covered the floor. The wall on the left side contained an enormous antique armoire, which Lucy discovered upon opening the door already contained their suitcases, neatly stacked beneath a pole equipped with padded hangers. A highly polished dark wooden door next to the armoire led to the bathroom, all gleaming marble and shining chrome. Taking in the enormous soaking tub, the double vanity with its sconces and mirrors, the modern shower, and the tiny separate room that contained the WC, Lucy decided that complaints about French plumbing might have been true in the past but were now completely unfounded.

"I don't know why people think that Europeans don't have up-to-date bathrooms," she said to Bill. "This is at least as good, maybe better, than anything we've got in the States."

Bill yawned. "I'll reserve judgment until I learn if there's enough hot water."

Lucy sat down in the chair next to Bill's. "I'm pretty sure they've got that covered." She turned to look out the window, which overlooked the garden, and sighed. "It's like a dream, no wonder Elizabeth is smitten."

"Yeah," agreed Bill. "But the question is, is she smitten with the château or with Jean-Luc?"

"I guess we'll find out at lunch," said Lucy. "That's when we'll finally see them together." She leaned back in the chair and put her feet up on the matching ottoman. "What did you think of him?"

"Hard to tell," said Bill. "I didn't really like the way he was flattering the girls." He adopted a phony French accent. " 'You are every beett as beautiful as your seester.' "

"It's the French way. All women are beautiful, all men are accomplished. It doesn't mean anything."

"Tell that to the girls," advised Bill, "before they take one of these guys seriously."

"Not a bad idea," admitted Lucy, closing her eyes.

She was awakened an hour later by Bill. "It looks as though they're gathering for lunch," he reported, gazing out the window. "I guess we should go down."

Lucy would have preferred to go back to sleep, but duty called. After freshening up, the couple retraced the route along the hall and down the stairs to the foyer.

"Promise you'll be nice to Jean-Luc?" asked Lucy, who knew her husband was already finding fault with Elizabeth's fiancé and believed he would disapprove of any man who showed an interest in one of his daughters. She suspected he was having a bit of a difficult time accepting the fact of Elizabeth's marriage.

Bill answered with a grunt and Lucy took his hand, giving it a squeeze. They continued on through the French doors to the terrace, where Marie-Laure seated Bill beside herself and placed Lucy at the opposite end of the long table beside Hugo. Champagne flutes stood at each place, which gave Lucy pause: Did wealthy French people drink champagne at every meal? Two seats in the center of the table were empty, awaiting the arrival of the engaged couple, and when Elizabeth and Jean-Luc stepped onto the terrace they were greeted with applause.

Lucy studied Jean-Luc with interest, deciding that Elizabeth had not exaggerated his good looks, or his manners. He was tall and broad-shouldered and every bit as handsome as promised, right down to the dimple on his chin. He also behaved most politely and held Elizabeth's chair for her before seating himself.

"I think we will begin with a toast to the joyous couple," said Hugo, signaling to several servers who magically appeared with bottles of champagne and filled all the flutes. Patrick, seated between his parents, was given his own bottle of Orangina.

Raising his glass, Hugo began, "Today I am pleased to welcome the beautiful Elizabeth's wonderful family to our home, and to thank you for coming to share in this happy occasion. And now, I drink to the happiness of my son, Jean-Luc, and his bride, Elizabeth. *Salut!*"

"*Salut!*" Everyone stood up and joined in, smiling and clinking glasses and sipping the delicious wine. Then they sat down, bowls of cold vichyssoise appeared, and Marie-Laure began the conversation, politely asking Toby if there were really polar bears in Alaska.

"There are," he began, setting down his flute and climbing onto his soapbox, "but they're in trouble. The glaciers are melting, the ice is disappearing, and the bears' habitat is shrinking. It's a sad thing, we see these hungry bears living off garbage when they should be fishing and hunting. But their prey is also struggling to survive, there are not enough seals to sustain the bears who have to travel farther and hunt longer for their food."

"A sad situation indeed," agreed Jean-Luc.

"It's just the tip of the iceberg, pardon my pun," said Toby. "We'll be next, you know. The planet will become increasingly unlivable, there'll be increased migration, limited resources, violence will be inevitable as people compete for the necessities of life."

"My goodness, Toby, surely our leaders will come together to reduce carbon emissions," said Lucy, giving him a look that warned him to cease and desist. She wasn't happy with his attitude, or his beard and long hair which now seemed unkempt and grubby in contrast to Jean-Luc's polished appearance. He'd made an effort, donning a dress shirt, but it was a size too small, clearly pulled from the back of his closet. Molly and Patrick were almost as bad, she thought, comparing them unfavorably to the stylish Schoen-Renes. Molly had apparently gone natural and let her hair grow without benefit of an occasional trim, and looked uncomfortable in a long-sleeved polyester dress, probably the one she considered "best" and wore for important occasions, like funerals. Patrick had a fresh haircut, but Lucy thought his WILD, LIKE ALASKA T-shirt was perhaps a bit too casual.

"It's too little, too late," said Toby, ignoring her. "That's why Molly and I have decided to change our lifestyle. We've fortified our house, we're constantly stocking up on nonperishables, and I've been teaching Patrick how to hunt and also to shoot to protect himself."

"That is very interesting," said Marie-Laure, looking troubled and attempting to change the subject. "I hope you all like tuna, we are having salade Niçoise."

"That sounds delicious," volunteered Sara. "And your home is so beautiful."

"Everything is so lovely," said Zoe, surveying the table, which was covered with a pale pink damask cloth. Crystal bowls of white and pink roses were lined up in the center of the table, the silverware gleamed, the crystal sparkled, and the creamy faience plates had flowery borders.

"So, Jean-Luc, are you involved in helping here at the château?" asked Lucy. "It must require a great deal of work."

Jean-Luc had been gazing at Elizabeth and stroking her neck, which Lucy was surprised to see that previously stand-offish Elizabeth not only tolerated, but actually seemed to be enjoying.

"I am not here that much," he said, smiling as he tugged on Elizabeth's earlobe. "I travel a lot, representing the château."

"Internationally?" asked Bill.

"Sometimes," he agreed, taking Elizabeth's hand. "And also in France."

"Perhaps you will adjust your schedule to spend more time with your wife?" asked Lucy, who was worried that she might have to wait a long time before a second grand-child arrived.

"Of course," said Jean-Luc, lifting Elizabeth's hand and pressing it to his lips.

Glancing at Bill, down at the other end of the table, Lucy thought she detected a slight groan, but maybe it was simply the wind in the trees. She gave Marie-Laure a big smile, just in case.

"I am afraid this is the last day of freedom for Elizabeth," said Marie-Laure, beaming with pleasure at the amorous couple. "Tomorrow the preparations for the wedding begin in earnest and there is much to do. I hope you will all relax today, perhaps you would enjoy boating on the moat, or exploring the gardens."

"I'm sure Patrick would enjoy boating," said Lucy, "and I would love to see the gardens, especially the *potager*. I have a vegetable garden in Maine but it is difficult because the growing season is so short."

"There are also horses," offered Hugo. "I bet the boy would like to see them."

"I sure would," agreed Patrick, who was carefully avoiding all the vegetables on his plate but had consumed the hard-boiled eggs and tuna, as well as several big pieces of baguette. "Is there dessert?" he asked, getting a sharp look from Molly.

"Of course," smiled Marie-Laure, amused. "*Glace des fraises*, made right here with our own strawberries and cream."

Patrick looked a bit worried and Elizabeth was quick to reassure him. "It's strawberry ice cream."

"Oh, that sounds good," he said, obviously relieved.

Jean-Luc made his apologies as soon as the meal was over and departed. Lucy heard the zoom of his sports car as he sped off down the drive on the opposite side of the château. This was obviously the moment she'd been waiting for, when she could have some one-on-one time with her daughter, and she was quick to make her move. "Elizabeth, I'd love a tour of the garden, and maybe a bit of the château, too?" she asked.

Elizabeth didn't seem too enthusiastic about the plan, but it got a strong endorsement from Marie-Laure. "That would be charming, Elizabeth. And perhaps later you could show your father the *grenier,* how you say attic? It is most impressive."

"Okay," agreed Elizabeth, clearly willing to do whatever Marie-Laure asked of her.

Interesting, thought Lucy, as she and Elizabeth set off from the terrace and proceeded through the parterre, past carefully groomed beds of colorful annuals and perennials bounded by low boxwood hedges. "Lavender!" exclaimed Lucy, inhaling the heady scent and bending to pluck a budding stem. "I have one scraggly bush at home, nothing like this," she said, waving her arm at the large bed packed with the fragrant herb.

"That's how they do gardens here," explained Elizabeth. "Each of these little beds is planted with one kind of flower."

Reaching the tall hedge at the end of this section of the garden, Lucy spotted a stone bench in a shady nook and suggested they sit for a while. "I'm still a bit jet-lagged," she explained.

"But don't you want a tour of the château?" asked Elizabeth, glancing at her watch.

"Are you on a tight schedule?"

"Well, not exactly," admitted Elizabeth.

"You're just in a hurry to get away from me and my questions?"

Elizabeth looked startled, and immediately became defensive. "Of course not. Ask away."

"Okay, I will. So where will you and Jean-Luc live? Will you rent or buy?"

"We'll be living here at the château, we already have an apartment. It's quite common among French families. The château is both home and business, you see, and I will be organizing special events."

"And what about Jean-Luc?"

"He will continue with his current job, which is, well, I guess you'd call it sales. He attends travel industry shows, takes tour company execs out to dinner and talks up the château, that sort of thing."

"Will he be gone a lot?"

"About the same," said Elizabeth, sounding vague.

Lucy remembered the elephant trees she'd seen on arrival and smiled to herself, deciding to tackle what was to her the real elephant in the room, or the garden. This might be her only chance. "It does worry me a bit," she began. "It seems that you're taking on an awful lot. You're giving up a lot of independence, living with his parents and working for them, too. Marie-Laure has quite a strong personality and you're marrying her as well as Jean-Luc. In fact, it seems as if you'll be spending more time with her than with Jean-Luc!"

Elizabeth was gazing at the scene before them, the sparkling fountain, dazzling in the sunlight, and beyond, the fairytale château. "Don't worry, Mom," she said, standing up. "I know what I'm doing. Now, let's go see the château! I really want you to see the conservatory."

"All right," agreed Lucy, not putting her fears to rest but instead locking them away in a dark cell at the back of her mind.

That evening, however, when she and Bill were dressing for dinner, those troublesome thoughts burst out of their locked cell. "I'm worried Elizabeth is making a mistake," she said, as she tied Bill's necktie for him. "I'm afraid she's going to be dominated by Marie-Laure. It's not a good idea for your mother-in-law to also be your landlord and your boss."

Bill put his hands on her waist and pulled her close. "She's a big girl, now, and you have to trust her to know what she wants."

"But what if it's a big mistake and she's unhappy?"

"If you ask me, she seems pretty happy. And why not? Look at all this. Talk about a plum job, that girl has got it made."

Lucy wasn't convinced. "I hope she's got a good American-style prenup, that's all I've got to say."

"Good. Now it's time to shut up, face the music, and dance!"

Lucy raised her eyebrows in amazement. "Dance? What's got into you?"

"*La belle vie, bébé!*" he declared, taking her in his arms and swinging her around the room. "Do you think there will be more champagne?"

"I'm afraid so," said Lucy.

Chapter Six

There was champagne at dinner, of course, and also sauvignon blanc with the fish course, pinot noir with the beef and sauternes with dessert. Lucy had been invited to join Marie-Laure for an after-dinner tisane in the salon, but needed to find a *toilette* first and was having difficulty due to being a bit muddle-headed and blundered instead into the billiard room. There she found Toby, Jean-Luc, and his friends Claude and Jerry, who she was pretty sure had been invited to the festive dinner as escorts for Sara and Zoe. The guys, however, seemed to be more interested in their game than in the promised night out at a nearby club with the girls.

"So, Toby," Jean-Luc was saying, as he chalked a cue, "are you a frontier man in Alaska? Do you trap animals for fur, like the Quebecois?"

"I do a bit of hunting, but not trapping," admitted Toby, "and I'm actually a biologist working to manage the salmon fishery."

"And your wife? Does she work, too?" asked Claude, who was as tall as Jean-Luc, but had a more urban vibe going, with two days of stubble on his chin and a dashing scarf thrown round his neck.

"Is she also a scientist?" asked Jerry, who was shorter and stockier, brimming with energy.

"No. She's a social worker, she's helping the native population adapt to lifestyle changes necessitated by global warming. It's a tough job, there's a lot of depression and suicide."

Lucy hadn't been noticed and had been about to slip away, but fearing another sermon about global warming, she decided to intervene. "Ah, here you all are!" she began. "I thought you were going clubbing with the girls?"

"We are," said Jean-Luc, in a resigned tone, "but they are getting ready. It always takes Elizabeth a long time to get ready, to decide what to wear and to fix her hair and I don't know what all . . ."

"We are keeling time," said Jerry, seemingly pleased as punch with his mastery of English.

"Well, enjoy yourselves," said Lucy, reassured that the girls hadn't been abandoned. Back in the hallway, she tried a door opposite the billiard room and discovered it was indeed the room she needed. While there she cooled her wrists with cold water and had a big drink of water, too, hoping to dilute the effects of the wine. Feeling somewhat more clearheaded she made her way to the foyer, and from there found the salon. Or more likely, she guessed, one of the salons.

Marie-Laure was seated on a rather uncomfortable-looking sofa, done in the French style with a straight back and a minimally padded seat covered by shiny brocade set on skinny, curvy legs. A similarly delicate coffee table held a gleaming silver tea service. Looking up from her magazine when Lucy entered, she patted the seat beside her. "Do join me," she invited. "The tea has been steeping for a few minutes so it should be ready." She lifted the pot. "I asked for peppermint, I thought we needed something a bit perky after the dinner. Hugo insisted on the beef but I find it a bit heavy."

"Peppermint would be lovely," said Lucy, who felt she could certainly do with a bit of perking up.

"Sugar? Honey?" asked Marie-Laure, filling a fragile porcelain cup.

"A touch of sugar, please."

Marie-Laure obliged with graceful motions and passed the cup and saucer to Lucy, who was now perched beside her on the stiff sofa, feeling a bit as if she were back in the eighth-grade cotillion dance class she had hated so much, where she had to sit with one ankle tucked behind the other. Marie-Laure, she noticed, seemed perfectly at ease with her ramrod straight back and classic Ferragamo pumps lined up side by side on the gorgeous Aubusson rug.

"It was very thoughtful of you to invite Claude and Jerry," said Lucy, after taking a sip of the delicious mint tea. "My girls will enjoy a night out on the town."

Marie-Laure smiled. "Claude and Jerry are nice boys, well brought up. As a hostess, I want everyone to have a good time. And," she added, "these little arrangements can work out well. You introduce two nice young people to each other and sometimes"—she shrugged—"it works out."

"Is that what happened with Jean-Luc and Elizabeth? Did you introduce them?"

Marie-Laure sipped her tea, then replaced the cup on its saucer. "It wasn't necessary, they met during our frequent stays at the Cavendish Hotel. Business takes us to Paris several times a year, and we always stay there. Elizabeth was most impressive, she could find last-minute opera tickets, get us dinner reservations at La Tour d'Argent, even a private tour of the Picasso museum. And when I mentioned I wanted an appointment at Chanel but couldn't get it, she managed a fitting with Virginie Viard herself!"

"That must have been quite an experience," said Lucy, who didn't have a clue who this Virginie lady was.

"It was terrifying," admitted Marie-Laure, with a chuckle. "I was paralyzed while she poked me here and there with pins!"

"I used to hate it when my mother took up or let down hems. I would have to stand on a chair while she crawled around with a mouth full of pins. I was terrified she'd swallow one, but she never did."

"Your mother wanted you to be well dressed, that is admirable," said Marie-Laure. "And you have raised your children very well, I think."

Lucy drained her cup, and sighed. "I do feel I must apologize for Toby and Molly. They are very concerned about climate change and they tend to sermonize." She smiled. "They also could do with a visit to Dior, or Monoprix, which is more in line with their budget, to refresh their wardrobes."

"I find your Toby and Molly charming, and Patrick is adorable." Marie-Laure picked up Lucy's empty cup and refilled it, spilling not a drop. "You know, when we began this business at the château, Hugo and I made a decision that we would welcome everyone, from anywhere, and try to make them as comfortable as possible. Hugo's father detested the Japanese, you know, he was in Saigon when they invaded, before World War Two. Absolutely loathed them because of the suffering they caused. But Hugo and I find our Japanese guests are quite delightful, though I do wonder at their food choices. For breakfast they insist on miso soup," she said, pausing to shudder. "Why miso soup when you could have our lovely café au lait?"

"Why indeed?" asked Lucy, who didn't have the faintest idea what miso soup was, but was looking forward to café au lait in the morning. She felt the conversation had gone rather offtrack, and she still had questions about how Elizabeth and Jean-Luc's relationship developed. "So Jean-Luc took a fancy to Elizabeth when he met her at the hotel?"

"Not exactly," admitted Marie-Laure, with a little smile. "I may have given him a bit of encouragement. He wasn't a kid anymore, you know, getting close to forty and time to settle down. These boys, they want to be boys forever, but that's not how it works. Jean-Luc has responsibilities, a title, a family business, and Elizabeth seemed the perfect choice for him."

Lucy sighed. "So it wasn't love at first sight?"

"Perhaps not for Jean-Luc, but I could tell that Elizabeth found him attractive. She would smile and flirt with him, try to get his attention."

Lucy was beginning to feel rather hurt on Elizabeth's behalf. "But he wasn't interested?"

Marie-Laure rolled her eyes. "These boys! All they want is to zoom around in their fast cars and motorbikes, go to the races, go speeding in boats on the Riviera. Go to Prague for the best beer, go to Ireland for the horse races, Scotland for the golf, London for the tennis. It's go-go-go."

Hearing this, Lucy was increasingly dismayed. Was this Marie-Laure's plan? To have Elizabeth do all the work that was properly Jean-Luc's responsibility while freeing him to pursue his playboy lifestyle? Or was Elizabeth supposed to tame her wild party-animal husband and settle him into a dutiful domesticity? It all seemed a terrible way to start a marriage. "What changed? What made him notice Elizabeth?"

"Ah!" said Marie-Laure, raising a finger for emphasis. "Jealousy! He saw her leaving work one night in the company of a very handsome man, they were arm in arm, clearly, what you say? into each other. That caught his attention."

"I wonder who that was?" mused Lucy, picturing Chris Kennedy.

"Whoever it was, it didn't last. She seemed a bit sad the next day and Jean-Luc swooped in and swept her off her feet." Marie-Laure relaxed and leaned back, resting against the back of the sofa, as if she'd been relieved of a terrible burden. "It is going to be a great success. They have found love together, and they will have a strong partnership; they have different strengths and will support each other. Elizabeth is organized, careful, a planner. Jean-Luc is a dreamer, with big ideas, vision. Together they will make Campanule a five-star destination."

Aha, thought Lucy, so that was the plan. But Marie-Laure wasn't through, she was definitely looking ahead to the future. She leaned forward and pressed her hand on Lucy's arm, and spoke in a confidential tone. "I am sure, that you, as well as I, have hopes for grandchildren. And why not? This is the perfect place to raise a family!"

Lucy found herself smiling. This, at least, was one part of Marie-Laure's plan that she could endorse. But she had serious doubts about the rest of it, doubts that she carried with her as she made her way upstairs to join Bill, who had retired early. Elizabeth was no dummy, she reminded herself. As Marie-Laure had said, she was a planner, an organizer, and she certainly knew what she was getting into. She had even expressed enthusiasm about working at the château, she was excited about her new responsibilities. And the couple did seem very much in love, barely able to keep their hands off each other when they were together. But was it all a show, she wondered, for the benefit of their families?

Suddenly overcome by exhaustion, Lucy paused on the stair landing and leaned toward the open window, breathing in the jasmine-scented air. It was refreshing and she closed her eyes for a moment, savoring the lovely scent and the cool air. She felt herself drifting into sleep while standing on her feet and opened her eyes, shaking her head. She was about to turn and resume her climb when she heard a motor and looked out, over the drive, where she saw a long white stretch limo driving off. The kids, she thought, heading out for their night on the town. As for herself, she could think of nothing nicer than a night of slumber on those beautiful Yves Delorme sheets.

The sheets were indeed crisp and luxurious, but Lucy had another bad night and couldn't get to sleep even though she was terribly tired. She finally dozed off again around four a.m. and slept soundly until Bill woke her at eleven. "Time to rise and shine, sleepyhead," he coaxed, gently shaking her shoulder. "You'll miss the whole day."

"Is there coffee?" she asked, eyes still closed.

"Uh, no. You missed breakfast."

"Really?"

"Yup. But if you take a quick shower, you can make lunch."

"Oh, golly. What will they think of me?" she moaned, folding back the covers and sitting up. "I should be helping with the wedding."

"Probably best if we just stay out of the way," said Bill, who was looking out the window. "Trucks are arriving, probably for a tent. They're having a tent, right?"

"I guess so." Lucy was on her feet, heading for the bathroom.

"I think I'll take a gander around and see what's going on," said Bill. "I've got my phone, call me if you need me."

"Okay." Lucy was in the bathroom, closing the door. Time got away from her as she explored the bathroom's various options: the bidet, the shower that spurted not only from above but from sideways and below, in various strengths. She especially enjoyed the massage feature, and then there was the brightly lit mirror over the sink that offered frightening magnification options. Was that a hair sprouting from her chin? Were her teeth really that yellow? When she was finally plucked and brushed, moisturized and dressed, it was already past one o'clock and she was afraid she'd missed lunch. She hurried down, uncomfortably aware of her growling stomach, and was relieved to discover a buffet luncheon awaiting her on the terrace.

"Help yourself," advised Marie-Laure, who was just finishing her salad. "We are very informal most days, we offer the buffet from eleven to two and find it works very well. People seem to enjoy the freedom."

"It all looks delicious," said Lucy, helping herself to a ham sandwich, some tomato slices, and a little bottle of fizzy Perrier water. Marie-Laure was the only other person on the terrace, so Lucy joined her at her table, but Marie-Laure soon made her apologies.

"I am sorry to desert you, but there is much I must do," she said, with a sad smile. "I am sure you understand."

"Of course," said Lucy. "Do let me know if I can help."

Marie-Laure thought this over. "Perhaps with the flowers—some of the neighbors are arranging them today."

"Perfect," said Lucy. "I'm pretty good with flowers, if you like a natural style."

"Of course, and you will have lots of helpers," said Marie-Laure, apparently somewhat doubtful of Lucy's flower-arranging skill. She picked up her plate and carried it over to the waiting table, then disappeared inside.

Lucy applied herself to eating her sandwich, enjoying the crusty baguette and the spicy greens that accompanied the ham. It was lovely on the terrace, where the jasmine climbed the walls of the château and gave off a lovely scent in the sunshine. Not a bad life, she decided, savoring the moment, when her phone rang. Much to her surprise, it was a video call and the faces of her friends from home appeared on the tiny screen. "Sue, Rachel, Pam, what a surprise!"

"We're at Jake's for breakfast, and we decided to call you," explained Sue. "Is the château as fabulous as promised?"

"Just take a look," said Lucy, panning her phone around the terrace and the garden, then turning it back to her face. "What do you think?"

"Amazing," cooed Pam.

"I'm jealous as hell," admitted Sue.

"It's like a fairy tale," said Rachel. "How is your little princess doing?"

"Yeah," chimed in Sue. "And is Prince Charming really charming?"

"I think so," said Lucy. "I haven't seen much of him but he is gorgeous, and attentive to Elizabeth. They seem to be very much in love."

"Seem to be?" asked Rachel.

Lucy lowered her voice. "Bill thinks that Elizabeth is more in love with the château than with Jean-Luc, but he's probably just an overprotective father."

"What do you think?" asked Pam. "Any monsters in the moat?"

Lucy laughed. "No ogres, but Elizabeth will have her hands full with Marie-Laure, her future mother-in-law. She has a very dominant personality and she's going to be Elizabeth's boss at the château. She's the one who really runs the place."

"A typical Frenchwoman," said Sue. "They like to be in charge."

"You can say that again," admitted Lucy, with a sigh. "But Elizabeth is no pushover."

"Could be fireworks in the future," speculated Rachel.

Lucy was quick to reply. "Oh, there will be, professionally done of course, at the wedding."

"Let's hope they're just at the wedding," said Pam, laughing.

"Fingers crossed," said Lucy. "I hope Elizabeth will be happy but I worry it might be a big mistake."

"All moms feel like that," said Rachel. "You're not alone."

"We're all wishing Elizabeth the best," said Pam. "She's a big girl and knows her own mind."

"And put in a word for us with Marie-Laure," said Sue. "We'd love an invitation to the château with a friends and family discount, of course."

"Will do," promised Lucy, as the call ended and her friends vanished into the cloud. She put the phone down on the table and took a drink of Perrier, wishing with all her heart that they were here with her. She suddenly felt very alone with her worries and could sure use some friendly advice and support. Being mother of the bride was turning out to be harder than she'd expected.

Chapter Seven

Lucy had just finished the last bite of her delicious sand-wich when Elizabeth and Bill appeared; father and daughter had been observing the erection of the huge mar-quee that was underway on the side of the château.

"It's quite a project," said Bill, seating himself at the table, "but those guys know what they're doing."

"I've seen the plans and it's going to be gorgeous," added Elizabeth, resting her bottom on the stone wall that bordered the terrace. "The designer, Henri Bruneau, is putting up panels of wallpaper, even hanging paintings, so it will look like it's part of the house."

"Is the ceremony going to take place in the tent?" asked Lucy.

"Oh, no. There's a private chapel in the château. And first, we have to have the civil ceremony, which usually takes place in the town hall, but Hugo has arranged for one of his pals in the local government to do it here, in the library, just before the religious ceremony."

"Is it going to be a Catholic mass?" inquired Bill, who only reluctantly, and very occasionally, attended services at the Tinker's Cove Community Church, which combined the declining memberships of the former Unitarian and Congregationalist churches in an uneasy alliance.

"Of course," said Elizabeth. "But thanks to Marie-Laure, she somehow got the Pope to give me a special dispensation so I didn't have to convert. It seems they're old friends or something," explained Elizabeth.

"Really?" asked Lucy, amazed at Marie-Laure's apparent far-reaching powers.

"I bet a lot of money changed hands," speculated Bill. "A donation, of course."

Elizabeth shrugged. "I really don't know. She's one amazing woman. She's so gracious and calm and all the time she's making things happen, impossible things with a single phone call. Miracles." She smiled. "I asked her about renting the table linens for the reception and if Henri Bruneau had chosen a color, for example, and she just smiled. It wouldn't be necessary, she said, because she already has everything that will be needed. That's one hundred fifty napkins, not to mention tablecloths, crystal, china." She paused, and added with a little nod and a raised eyebrow, "Sterling silverware, antique, of course."

"That's a lot of silver," said Lucy, who had recently replaced a tablespoon missing from her prized service for eight and had been shocked at the cost.

"You said it."

"I guess they've had centuries to accumulate it all," said Bill.

"And they're titled," remarked Lucy. "Hugo's a count, after all."

"He is, but French titles aren't as prestigious as English ones," explained Elizabeth. "There's a lot more of them, for example, and a lot of them were actually purchased, not inherited. After the Revolution, I'm not clear on exactly when this happened, Hugo's ancestors emigrated to South America where they made a lot of money in coffee, or tin or something. His grandfather returned to France and bought the property after World War One, when he came to France as part of a church effort to assist refugees. He stumbled upon the château, which was in terrible condition. It had been deserted for years even before the war. Anyway, he fell in love with the château and France and devoted himself to restoring it and reclaiming his title. I think he may have been one of those émigrés who become more French than the French, if you know what I mean." She paused. "The French government even gave him a medal for his efforts. And now, of course, the family consider themselves thoroughly French, though they still have considerable financial interests in South America."

"I guess those interests would be considerable," said Lucy, glancing up at the château which loomed above them.

"Oh, yes. I believe the term is diversification."

"Well, however it was financed, it's quite a house," said Bill. "Say, I haven't gotten the full tour yet. Can you give me a quick look? I heard the framing in the attics is impressive, still solid after three hundred years, or so they say."

Elizabeth glanced at her watch. "Sure. I have a meeting with Henri in an hour." She gave a resigned shrug. "Not that anything I say will have the least effect. Marie-Laure and Henri have organized everything."

Lucy wasn't surprised, she'd guessed as much, but she was concerned for Elizabeth. In a bright tone, she made a suggestion. "I know you gave me a tour of the château's highlights but I'd love to see your apartment, where you and Jean-Luc will be living, if that's okay."

"Be warned, it's a mess, I haven't even had time to unpack. We'll start there and then climb up to the *grenier* for

Dad. Our rooms are on the second floor, which is the third in the US, so we've got a bit of a climb."

"No elevator?" inquired Bill, as they set off on the tour. "It's kind of odd in a place like this; they must get guests who have mobility issues. One of those towers on the back side would be perfect."

"They have a couple of suites on the ground floor for handicapped folks, but it doesn't seem to come up much. Fat Americans, mostly, and Marie-Laure certainly doesn't approve of people who let themselves get out of shape and have to use golf carts to get over to the pool."

"Funny," mused Lucy, as they trooped down the hall to the foyer and began climbing the stairs. "She told me that everyone is welcome, it's their official policy."

"Well," said Elizabeth, grinning, "let's say that some are more welcome than others. A fat wallet and a slim waist are most preferable."

"I guess that's the same everywhere," said Bill. "And with all these stairs you don't need a gym to keep fit."

"Oh, there's a gym, out at the pool," said Elizabeth, leading the way down yet another long hallway lined with portraits. "For Americans." She stopped suddenly in front of a door, threw it open, and announced, "Voilà! *Chez-moi.*"

As she stepped inside, Lucy's first thought was that this was certainly not what she expected, judging from the décor in the rest of the château. There, everything was light and freshness, neutral colors, classic forms, with plenty of space and light. This suite, in contrast, was small and crowded and dark. There were two rooms, a living room and a bedroom, plus a cramped, old-fashioned bathroom. Really old-fashioned, thought Lucy, guessing the toilet and tub to be originals installed when indoor plumbing first became popular.

"Pardon the mess," said Elizabeth, making a half-hearted attempt to gather up clothing that was strewn about the room, including some large shoes that Lucy assumed belonged to Jean-Luc. "We really don't spend much time here," she added, stuffing it all into an armoire.

"I can understand why," said Lucy, remarking on the truly dreadful wallpaper, which featured a somewhat frightening and oppressive design of brown climbing vines that crawled up the walls and was matched in somewhat faded and tattered chintz draperies as well as the hangings on the massive *lit à la polonaise* that took up most of the space in the bedroom. "This is a bit much," she added, in classic understatement.

"I know. I haven't had time to do anything about it but I really want to change it, get rid of all this creepy brown stuff." She shuddered. "At night, it's like being in a snake pit."

"Why don't you open the curtains?" asked Lucy, indicating the two windows that were covered with the tightly closed draperies.

"This is why," said Elizabeth, yanking one set open and sending out a cloud of dust that made them all sneeze.

Once the dust and sneezing subsided, Lucy noticed that the sunlight now streaming into the room seemed to make it appear more spacious.

Elizabeth also noticed. "This space wouldn't be half bad with some sheer voile curtains, to let in the light, and a normal-size bed. We could tuck some chests of drawers under the windows for more storage, and out in the living room," she continued, gesturing with her arm at the heavily carved Victorian sofa and chairs, "I'm thinking of a white or ivory sofa with a rattan chest for a coffee table, a place we could stow some of our stuff. And a nice leather armchair, a real man's chair, for Jean-Luc, so he can put his feet up."

"That sounds great," said Lucy, taking one last look before continuing on their way to the *grenier*.

"Since we're up here, let me show you the linen room," suggested Elizabeth, after they mounted two more flights of increasingly narrow stairs and found themselves in a dark hallway lit by one small window at either end. Opening a door, she led the way into a large, low-ceilinged space with several low windows. The windows were open, letting in a fresh breeze that enhanced the lavender-scented linens stacked on a large central table. With a wave of her hand, Elizabeth indicated the built-in cabinets that lined the walls of the entire large room, dozens of them. "The napkins!" she declared, indicating the cabinets.

"Oh, yes. Not only napkins, but tablecloths, sheets, and pillowcases, hundreds, thousands probably," said Elizabeth, opening one of the doors and revealing shelves filled with neatly stacked bedsheets.

"It's amazing," said Lucy, noticing that each shelf was labeled with a neatly printed card.

"Who does all this laundry?" asked Bill. "And where are the washers and dryers."

"The laundry is down in the basement, staffed with immigrants, mostly from North Africa. It's a hive of worker bees down there, what with the kitchens and the laundry. Upstairs, the housekeepers are mostly Middle-European, with some French."

"My goodness, I had no idea. Do they live here, too?" asked Lucy.

"Oh, no. Some are bused in early in the morning, before anyone's up. The shift changes in early afternoon, when guests are too busy to notice, and that shift departs after dinner. It's all very smooth."

"I'm sure," said Bill. "So where's this famous attic?"

"Through here," said Elizabeth, leading them back into the hallway to yet another doorway. When opened, it revealed a steep, narrow staircase, with a rope banister that enabled them to climb up. Reaching the top, they were greeted with a truly magnificent sight. Huge beams soared upward in a complex geometric arrangement that supported the many peaks and gables of the château's enormous roof.

"The roofing is tile?" asked Bill, his contractor brain busy computing weight and stress factors that the aged timbers supported.

"Slate tiles," said Elizabeth.

"Whew." Bill let out an impressed sigh. "And it's over three hundred years old?"

"Yeah," said Elizabeth, looking upward.

"I guess they don't make trees like they used to," observed Bill, examining one of the beams and patting it approvingly. "You couldn't do this today."

"Well," said Elizabeth, glancing at her watch. "Tour's over. I've got to go." When they had finally descended to ground level, she distributed parting *bisous* along with a recommendation. "You might take Patrick and Toby to see the horses and carriages in the stable," she said. "I bet they'd enjoy that."

"Good plan," agreed Bill.

"So you're off to see Henri?" asked Lucy. "Any chance I could tag along and get a sneak peek?"

"I don't see why not," said Elizabeth, with a smile. "To tell the truth, I could use a little moral support," she confided, as they made their way through the ballroom and out into the marquee. "Like I said, Marie-Laure and Henri, well, they're pretty much running the show."

"Well, I'm here for you," said Lucy, pleased by Elizabeth's admission. For so long she had felt estranged from her oldest daughter, who had seemingly left the family without a backward glance. Now, faced with a life-changing passage, she had discovered the value of a supportive, loving family.

"Ohhh, Henri," trilled Elizabeth, dashing off when they stepped into the marquee. "*C'est merveilleux, fantastique!*"

Or maybe she'd overestimated Elizabeth's need for maternal support, thought Lucy, following her daughter. Elizabeth was in animated conversation with a long-haired, very thin middle-aged man dressed in tight jeans, a tight T-shirt, as well as the necessary scarf. He looked to Lucy like a French version of Mick Jagger.

"Mom, isn't this fabulous?" asked Elizabeth, as Lucy joined the pair. "Oh, Henri, this is my mother, Lucy Stone."

"*Enchanté,*" said Henri, coming in for the obligatory two *bisous*, delivering air kisses on either side of Lucy's face.

"You are a miracle worker," said Lucy, indicating the marquee, where workers were busily erecting the promised wallpaper panels and hanging crystal chandeliers. Gilt-framed mirrors and paintings were propped here and there, awaiting installation.

"It's the flowers that will bring the space to life," said Henri. "Then it will be magical."

"What do you have in mind?" asked Lucy.

"I admit, I am a bit nervous," said Henri, in a low voice. "Marie-Laure insisted that she would take charge of the flowers. She's enlisted a group of neighbors," he added, rolling his eyes. "Ladies who enjoy gardening."

"Well, I'm sure they will be lovely, she has marvelous taste," said Lucy. Encouraged by Henri's gossipy attitude, she offered a confession. "I offered to help, but she wasn't encouraging. I don't think she believes my efforts would be up to her high standard."

"Nonsense. I am sure the mother of the charming Elizabeth knows how to arrange flowers," said Henri. "I understand they are being assembled now, if you would like to lend a hand."

"That's right, Mom," said Elizabeth. "They're actually members of the local garden club who have volunteered and are working in the basement."

"I'd love to help out," said Lucy. "Where do I find them?"

"That doorway, just over there," said Elizabeth, gesturing to a doorway set into the foundation some distance away. "You'll find yourself in a hallway, just follow it until you reach the flower room. You can't miss it."

"Great! I'm on it," said Lucy, who had figured out that Elizabeth and Henri did not need her hanging around as a third wheel. The pressure was on and they had the groom's mother to deal with; they didn't need her as well.

She had made her way out of the marquee and was about to follow the gravel walkway that ran alongside the château when she encountered a very worried-looking Molly. Whatever her concerns were, however, she forgot them to exclaim at the marquee. "Wow, this is really going to be over the top."

"You said it," agreed Lucy. "But is something wrong? You looked so worried."

"It's Patrick, I can't seem to find him anywhere. Ever

since we got here he's been running off on his own. Keeping track of him is a full-time job."

"Well, I think I know where he is," said Lucy. "Bill was going to take him down to the stables to see the horses."

"That's a relief," said Molly, letting out a big sigh. "Not that I think he'd get into any sort of danger, he's a smart kid, but this is an unfamiliar place and I like to know what he's up to."

"That's wise," said Lucy, taking her arm and drawing her aside as a worker was attempting to carry a stack of gilt chairs into the marquee. "You know, I'm sure that all the château employees have been thoroughly vetted by Marie-Laure, but there are going to be a lot of extra people around the next few days. You might just remind Patrick that he shouldn't go off with any strangers."

"Good point, Lucy. I think I'll meander down to the stables myself to give him a heads-up."

"Good idea," said Lucy, waving her arm in the general direction that Elizabeth had indicated. "I think the stable is that way, behind those trees."

Molly started off, when Lucy suddenly had a thought. "How was last night? Did you have a good time clubbing?"

Stopping in mid-stride, Molly turned back. "It was kind of a dump, a local sort of roadhouse place. There wasn't a band, just a jukebox. We girls danced a bit, but the guys were outside, playing some game with balls." She shrugged. "It was okay, I enjoyed catching up with Elizabeth. And I hadn't seen Sara and Zoe in quite a while, not since they started their jobs."

"Sounds nice," said Lucy, waving her off and continuing along the path, in search of the flower room. Imagine, a room just for arranging flowers! Boy, wouldn't she love something like that in her Maine farmhouse. But, she realized, coming back to reality, she didn't have the time or energy to maintain a huge cutting garden like the one at the château. She would have to be content with her meager assortment of reliable perennials: daffodils, lilacs, a few peonies, and plenty of day lilies, but day lilies weren't worth cutting because they only lasted for one day.

Chapter Eight

Lucy was temporarily blinded when she stepped out of the bright sunlight into the dim, cool basement. While she waited for her eyes to adjust, she became aware of a great deal of hustle and bustle. The basement was apparently a hive of activity as workers hurried past her, calling out to each other in a variety of languages.

Someone was speaking to her, saying, "Madame? Madame?" and she made an effort to focus, finally realizing the woman was Louise, the housekeeper.

"Ah, Louise," she said. "Perhaps you can help me. I'm looking for the flower room? I want to make myself useful, you see."

"The ladies have been working since early morning. I'm sure they would appreciate some help. Follow me, it's just along here."

Louise took off with some speed, and Lucy hurried to keep up. Then suddenly she braked and indicated a doorway. "Voilà!"

"*Merci,*" replied Lucy, with a smile, before stepping inside and inhaling the mixed scent of hundreds, maybe thousands of blooms, which were stuffed in buckets on the

floor and piled on a large wooden table. Lucy identified
roses in all shades, peonies, blooming branches, as well as
irises, poppies, snapdragons, sweet peas, baby's breath,
carnations, and foxglove, as well as masses of orchids.
Several women were standing around the table, snipping
and trimming the flowers, and they turned her way, offering polite but somewhat questioning smiles.

"*Je suis Lucy Stone, la mère d'Elizabeth and je voudrais
assister avec les fleurs,*" she said, attempting to explain her
presence.

"Welcome, welcome," said one of the worker bees, a slim
lady dressed in perfectly fitting jeans and a striped bateau
top. "We are grateful for your help."

Another woman joined in, speaking in heavily accented
English. "Yes, yes. Your Elizabeth is so charming."

"She will be a beautiful bride," added the first woman.
"Let me make introductions to Madame Stone." Hearing
her name, the four other women nodded and smiled en-
thusiastically. "I am Françoise," she began, placing her
hand on her chest, then pointing to the others one by one.
"This is Jackie, Christiane, Lourdes, and Aimée."

"It's lovely to meet you all," said Lucy, appreciative of
the fact that these women were volunteering their time
and talent. "I would like to help any way I can. I know
this is a big job and you are all working so hard."

Françoise promptly translated for the women who didn't
speak English; Lucy soon learned that Françoise was the
only fluent speaker of English, Jackie had some, and the others were soon chattering away to each other in a torrent of
French as they snipped and clipped.

"As you see," explained Françoise, "we are making a
variety of arrangements for the château. Some will go in
guest rooms, others in the salons and hallways. We need a

really big one for the foyer," she ended, indicating a massive blue-and-white Chinese fishbowl.

Staring at the big, empty bowl, Lucy was floored. How on earth did one fill that monster with an attractive arrangement? "Perhaps I should start small," she said, choosing a simple cream-colored pottery vase. Watching the others, she realized they began with a few filler pieces of greenery like ferns or branches, then added blooms in colors that enhanced the vase. A few more filler pieces were tucked in here and there, to finish the arrangement, and then they were on to the next.

"As you see, we are not too, what you say? Fussy? There are so many flowers and we want them to look natural if you know what I mean?" said Françoise.

Somewhat relieved, Lucy nodded. "I understand completely."

What she did not understand, however, was what the women were talking about. They spoke so rapidly, it was a ribbon of sound, and she could only pick up a word here and there. She thought she recognized *putain*, which meant whore; that definitely caught her attention. They couldn't be talking about Elizabeth, or one of her other daughters, could they? No, she told herself, she was being paranoid. No, she discovered, listening more closely, the *putain* apparently lived at the *ferme*, or farm. A little local business, she wondered, that catered to lonely farmers? That seemed possible, and surely forgivable, especially in France, right? But the ladies did not seem at all approving of the *putain*. Maybe she had an erroneous impression of French culture, which she'd always thought was more open to sexuality than her repressed and puritanical neighbors in Maine. Stepping back, she realized her arrangement was not really an arrangement at all but a mess, and decided to focus on the flowers instead of the conversation.

That concentration paid off as Lucy's arrangements began receiving approving nods from Françoise and the others, and she discovered she was enjoying the work, finding it a relaxing change. She'd been so wrapped up in traveling and keeping peace in the family and worrying about making a good impression with Jean-Luc's parents that she hadn't realized how tense she'd actually been. She felt her shoulders relaxing, and her breathing slowing as she concentrated on the flowers. Time flew by and she was surprised when a waiter arrived with refreshments for the workers, who stripped off their aprons, trilled au revoirs in Lucy's direction, and all trooped out to enjoy a break in the garden. Lucy wasn't inclined to join them, deciding that she really ought to check on her family.

They weren't hard to find, she discovered, walking down the hall that led to their rooms. Patrick's voice, raised in protest, was clearly audible through the closed door of his parents' room. She quickly rapped on the door, and when it opened, demanded, "What on earth is going on?"

"I won't wear them!" declared Patrick, whose face was beet red and whose legs were clad in sage-green satin knee breeches. White stockings and a blousy, ruffled shirt, along with a darker green cummerbund completed his outfit. A pair of patent leather pumps had clearly been flung in separate directions, one lying on a sofa, the other under a window. "I won't," he added, yanking the cummerbund off and flinging it in Lucy's direction.

"Patrick! Calm down!" demanded his mother. "You almost hit your grandmother!"

"You need to apologize," ordered his father.

Elizabeth, holding an empty Dior box, looked about to burst into tears.

Patrick offered a sullen apology. "Didn't mean to."

"I know, Patrick," said Lucy, giving him a hug. "You do look very handsome, you know."

"It's a girl's outfit," grumbled Patrick.

"It's a traditional page's outfit," explained Elizabeth, sniffing. "It's what boys wear who are attendants in French weddings."

"Well, I'm not French!" insisted Patrick.

"When in France, do as the French, that's how it is, buddy," said Toby. "So get out of those fancy duds before you wreck them and we'll go into town for a haircut."

Patrick exploded. "A haircut! I already had a haircut!"

"That's enough out of you, young man," said Molly, in a this-is-final tone of voice. "You can use a trim and your father definitely needs to get that beard of his under control. Now, do you want me to help you get undressed or can you manage it yourself?"

"I can do it myself," said Patrick, uttering the classic line, which caused Lucy to suppress a smile.

She knew it was wrong, but she did take a certain amount of pleasure in seeing her grown children deal with behaviors they'd indulged in during their childhoods. There was a certain justice in it, she thought. Elizabeth, however, seemed to be entirely undone, and had collapsed on the sofa, where she was studying the discarded patent leather pump and sniffling.

"It's going to be okay," said Lucy, seating herself beside her and wrapping an arm around her daughter's heaving shoulders. "He'll wear the outfit. He'll be perfect."

"It's all going wrong," sobbed Elizabeth.

Lucy's and Molly's eyes met. "Last-minute jitters, that's all," said Molly.

"That's right. It's going to be perfect," said Lucy, patting her hand. "Everything is going to be fine."

"It's just . . . it's all too much. . . ."

"I know, sweetheart, I know. But Molly's right. Brides always get nervous. I almost bailed on my wedding. . . ."

"I didn't know that," said Elizabeth, brushing away her tears.

"Well, I did. I was standing there on my father's arm, with that long aisle in front of me, and I started to turn, to run away. He grabbed me by the arm, started marching along, and whispered, 'It's too late now.' " She shrugged. "The rest is history."

Elizabeth sighed. "You're right. I'm being silly." She stood up. "And I've got lots to do. Marie-Laure is counting on me."

Always Marie-Laure, thought Lucy as Elizabeth hurried off. *Instead of thinking about her mother-in-law, Elizabeth should be thinking about herself and Jean-Luc, and their life together.* This was definitely not the best way to start a marriage.

That night, when they were all gathered once again at the dinner table, Marie-Laure apologized for neglecting her guests. "The wedding has kept me so busy," she said, pressing her lips together. "Normally I would be showing you the countryside, giving you a tour of our notable attractions. But instead"—she shrugged apologetically— "well, you see how it is."

"Not at all," Lucy was quick to say. "We're all having a lovely time."

"Why don't you all do a bit of exploring tomorrow?"

suggested Elizabeth. "I can give you directions to Saint-Quiriace, it's a lovely old town with a beautiful church."

Molly was quick to pick up on the suggestion. "We could have lunch out and make a little party of it."

"That sounds great, but how will we get there? Can we walk? Is there a bus?"

"No problem," said Elizabeth. "I'll arrange a van for you. I wish I could join you," she added, with a regretful smile, "but tomorrow is crunch time." She turned to Bill. "What about that, Dad? Do you want to lead an expedition?"

"Actually, I'm pretty interested in that attic," said Bill. "It's quite remarkable and I'd like to diagram those beams. . . ."

"No need," said Hugo. "The original plans are in the library. You can study them. . . ."

"Great!" said Bill. "That'll keep me busy tomorrow. What about you, Toby? Are you interested in sightseeing?"

Toby shook his head. "Patrick's persuaded one of the grooms at the stable to give him a riding lesson, and then we're going to do some fishing."

"Well, I guess it's just us girls," said Molly.

Next morning, the promised van was waiting in the driveway for them when Lucy finally rounded up Zoe, Sara, and Molly, who all took their time discussing outfits and fussing with hair and makeup. The driver, Michel, a remarkably handsome young fellow with cocoa skin and a head of curly hair, as well as a sparkling smile but somewhat limited English, made Lucy wonder if all French men were this handsome. She knew they weren't, they were a mixed bag just like at home, but since she'd entered the magical world of the château it seemed that everyone there was remarkably good-looking. Did they only hire attractive people, was it a condition of employment?

Looking out the window as Michel sped along the gravel drive, Lucy looked for the tree-lined allée but didn't find it. "When we came, we saw trees," she said, puzzled.

"We go diffayrent," explained Michel, with his thick French accent.

"Okay," said Lucy, eager to see more of the area. They were still on the château grounds, passing a farm area planted with produce intended for the kitchen: beans, tomatoes, squash, and plants she didn't recognize. Then there were animals; they passed a field with grazing sheep, pens with goats and chickens.

"Wow, this is quite an operation," said Molly, as they reached the main road and Michel accelerated, zooming along.

"Hold on to your hat," laughed Lucy, as the scenery whizzed by.

Approaching a charming little village, Michel whizzed right into the center of town and braked suddenly, by a covered market area. Somewhat shaken, they gathered their things and trooped off the van. Lucy paused to ask about *la retour* and he gave her a card with a phone number. She carefully tucked the card into her pocket, then joined the others on the sidewalk, where they were discussing a plan of action.

"Let's look at the market," urged Molly.

"How about lunch first?" suggested Sara. "I missed breakfast."

"Yeah, me too. And it's not like we need to buy veggies," argued Zoe.

"These markets have other stuff, too," advised Lucy. "Toys, soap, almost anything you can think of."

"Okay, but not too long," said Sara. "I'm starving."

The market was everything Lucy had promised. There were plenty of fruits and vegetables, piled high in colorful displays. There were lots of shoppers, too, with baskets over their arms, engaged in serious discussions with the vendors. Shopping in France was far different, thought Lucy, than dashing into the IGA and grabbing plastic bags of salad and fruit. Here each lettuce leaf, each strawberry was carefully examined for its suitability. There were also lots of other things offered for sale: lavender sachets and creams, shiny pots and pans, colorful Provençal dish towels and potholders, toys and puzzles. Molly was studying the puzzles, choosing one for Patrick, when Lucy spotted a stall selling baby clothes.

"Look," she cooed, grabbing Zoe's arm. "Aren't they adorable?"

"Mom, nobody's expecting," said Zoe, in a matter-of-fact tone of voice.

"Elizabeth could get pregnant," replied Lucy, in a hopeful tone of voice as she fingered a darling little smocked dress.

"So could I," declared Zoe, "but I don't plan to and I don't think she does, either. Not any time soon anyway."

The proprietor was giving Lucy a stare that said *don't touch unless you're buying*, and she removed her hand with an apologetic smile. "A grandmother can hope," she said. "Let's eat."

Of course there was a charming little café next to the market, with tables and chairs set outside in the plaza. They chose one with a big blue umbrella, and after they were settled and chatting quietly a waiter approached with a handful of menus. In French.

"Oh, my," said Lucy, studying the unfamiliar words, "menu French is different."

"Looks like they have salad," said Molly. "And what is 'croque monsieur'?"

"Grilled cheese. There's monsieur and madame, one has an egg but I can never remember which," confessed Lucy.

The waiter, however, did speak English and soon they had ordered glasses of what he promised was an exceptional rosé, salads, and sandwiches. Lucy sipped her rosé while she waited for her meal, listening idly to the girls' conversation and thinking she ought to be savoring this rare moment: time with her girls, the fabulous location, the sunshine, the truly delicious wine. But somehow she couldn't relax, she kept worrying. Something was nagging at her, preventing her from being in the moment, but she couldn't put her finger on it. Was she worried for Elizabeth? That was part of it, but Elizabeth was a grown woman, able to make her own decisions, and dealing with whatever the consequences of those decisions might be. Of course, concern for Elizabeth was part of it, she decided, but it was more the sense of unreality she'd experienced when she first arrived at the château. It was too perfect. That was to be expected of a place that catered to the public, promised every luxury and charged accordingly, but this was different. There was something off about it. It made her uneasy, she felt a bit as if she were in Oz and Marie-Laure was the wizard. What would happen if the curtain opened, revealing her hands on the levers? What would be discovered?

"Mom!" Sara's voice broke into her reverie, and she blinked, returning to reality. "The waiter wants to know if you want more wine?"

"Sure," said Lucy. "Why not? I'm not driving."

"You are tourists?" asked the waiter. "Staying at the château? I saw the van."

"That's us," said Lucy. "We're here for my daughter's wedding."

"Felicitations," said the waiter. "Is her fiancé French?"

"Yes. He's Jean-Luc Schoen-Rene," said Lucy, finding she enjoyed the unfamiliar pleasure of name-dropping.

The waiter's eyebrows shot up. "*Vraiment?*" he blurted out, in surprise.

"*Vraiment,*" replied Lucy, pleased as punch to participate in a French conversation, albeit a brief one.

The waiter departed, and Molly leaned forward. "That was odd, wasn't it?"

"Oh, I don't know," said Lucy, watching as he gathered with a couple of other waiters in a shady corner. "I suppose it is surprising when the son of the lord of the manor chooses a bride."

"Look at them," said Sara, indicating the waiters. "He's told them about Jean-Luc and they're laughing and joking."

"Maybe he has a bit of a reputation," suggested Molly.

"I wish I could understand what they're saying," fretted Lucy.

"Oh, guys are the same everywhere," advised Zoe, who was now exceptionally familiar with the opposite gender due to her job working for the Portland Sea Dogs baseball team. "Weddings, sex, it's always a big joke."

"I'm sure you're right," said Lucy, as the waiter returned with their fresh glasses of wine and promises that their meals would be ready shortly. He left, and Lucy asked the girls what they thought of Jean-Luc. "What do you really think of him?" she asked. "What was he like when you were all out the other night? Molly, didn't you say he didn't pay much attention to Elizabeth?"

"They were playing some ball game outside the café," said Molly.

"Mostly talking French," added Zoe.

"I think they're old friends, it had a stag-party feel," said Sara.

"What do you think, Molly? You're the married one, after all. Do you think he'll make a good husband?"

Molly took her time to answer. "He seems nice enough," she finally said, "and Elizabeth loves him. That's what matters."

"I hope you're right," said Lucy, as the waiter returned with their orders, swatting at a fly with one hand as he deftly managed the heavy tray with the other. That was the problem, she thought, there was always some fly in the ointment.

Chapter Nine

Returning to the château, Lucy was seated in the front passenger seat where she had a different view of the passing scenery; when leaving the château she'd been so glued to the window that she had missed the wider perspective. The countryside in France, she thought, was much more orderly than back home in Maine. Of course, French people had been working on their environment for much longer than people in Maine, but she also thought it betokened a different attitude. French people, it seemed to her, prized order much more than Americans. Trees were planted in neat rows, yards were enclosed with stone walls, houses and barns were scrupulously maintained. It was much different from the casual attitude back home, where toys and bicycles, campers, boats, and even discarded furniture and cars were often strewn about on front lawns.

She had just voiced this observation when the exception that proved the rule came into view: a very aged and dilapidated farmhouse where several scantily clad women were sunning themselves in a weed-filled, scrappy yard on a variety of chaise longues and plastic chairs that had seen better days. Even odder, they seemed to be relaxing under the watchful eye of a tough-looking guy.

"That farmer certainly doesn't keep his place in good order," said Sara.

"I wonder," mused Lucy, as a couple of the girls waved to them, "if this is the farm the flower ladies were talking about. I didn't understand much but they were giggling and rolling their eyes about some nearby farm."

"I hate to break it to you," said Molly, "but I don't think this is a farm."

"I don't see any sign of agricultural activity," said Zoe.

Lucy glanced at Michel, their driver, who seemed to be suppressing a smile while keeping his mouth shut and his eyes firmly fixed on the turn through the estate gate. Glancing back at the run-down farm, and the women outside, Lucy suddenly realized what she'd seen. "It's a brothel!" she exclaimed.

"I think you're right," said Molly. "I've seen similar establishments in Alaska, especially near the oil fields."

"Is that right, Michel?" Lucy asked the driver. "Is that sort of thing legal in France?"

Michel shrugged and shook his head. "I don't know anything about it."

"But it's so close to the estate. It doesn't make a very good impression. Why can't the Schoen-Renes shut it down? They're very influential, it seems crazy to have something like that practically on your doorstep."

"I think it's just a family, Gypsies maybe," said Michel. "They find empty places and move in."

"Really?" Molly sounded extremely doubtful. "Believe me, that's no family."

Michel stuck to his story. "No, it's true. Gypsies. People don't like them, but they're protected by the law. It's a real problem."

"Gypsies wouldn't operate a brothel," said Lucy. "From

what I understand, they have very strict rules about sex. That's why the kids get married at very young ages."

"See?" said Michel, eager to seize on support for his theory. "That is true. Sex, no, but when it comes to property, they, what you say? Pocket-pick?"

"Pick-pocket," said Lucy. "I was warned about them when we were in Paris years ago. At the Louvre. They had signs all over the place."

"Signs, yes. But do the police arrest them? Even just move them along? No," said Michel, pulling into the gravel area in front of the château. "So we have Gypsies. Big problem."

That wasn't the only problem, thought Lucy, taking in the scene as they returned to the château. There was barely room for the van in the courtyard, which was crammed with various vans and trucks, all making deliveries. One truck driver, frustrated because he was blocked in by the van, was yelling at Michel and gesticulating angrily.

"*Un moment, un moment,*" Michel was yelling back, giving as good as he got.

"We better hurry," urged Lucy, hopping out of the van.

Soon they were all out, waving goodbye to Michel, whose departure was quickly followed by that of the other driver. Turning to enter the château, they discovered the front door was blocked by a stack of audio speakers, probably intended for the DJ.

"Bummer," moaned Molly. "I don't want to have to walk all the way around to the back. My feet are killing me."

"It's so hot," complained Zoe, fanning herself with her hand.

"And we'll have to go around the tent, too," grumbled Sara, lifting her hair off her neck. "That will add another mile or two."

Hearing a familiar voice, they looked up and saw Elizabeth leaning out of a window. "I was watching for you, come around that side," she said, pointing to the side away from the marquee, "and you'll find a door. I'll meet you there."

Lucy smiled and waved agreement, then set off with the others. "I hope it's not far, I'm really feeling the heat."

"Maybe it's the rosé," said Molly.

Reaching a corner of the château, they slipped behind some pillars and discovered a shaded area, like one side of a cloister, that ran alongside the building and provided shelter from the hot sun.

"This is better," said Sara, with a grateful sigh.

"Now we just have to find the magic door," said Lucy, who saw lots of windows but no sign of a door. They trudged along, a rather bedraggled group, stopping abruptly at a mossy brick wall that blocked their way. There was no door in the side of the château, but there was a small wooden one in the wall. It opened and Patrick greeted them. "Boo!"

"Hey!" Lucy greeted him with a hug. "What are you up to? Staying out of trouble, I hope."

"Not quite," announced his father, who was right behind him. "So far he's frightened the horses, startled a gardener, and attempted to steal some peaches."

"Sounds like this young man is bored," said Elizabeth, also appearing in the magical doorway. "I've got just the thing. Come on through." She stepped back so they could pass through the wall, which quite surprisingly enclosed an exceptionally tidy, walled kitchen garden.

"Wow, this puts my pathetic little garden in Maine to shame," said Lucy, taking in the espaliered fruit trees growing along the wall and the neat beds of vegetables and herbs. No rickety wire tomato cages were in evidence here, she noticed, as the tomatoes were climbing charming willow *tuteurs*.

"Well, Mom, you don't have a staff of five professional gardeners, do you?" said Elizabeth, by way of consolation.

"I'm strictly amateur, just me, myself, and I," responded Lucy, who was studying the garden and taking mental notes, intending to adapt some of the pros' tricks of the trade. She could, for example, edge her garden with parsley and other herbs, as had been done here. And marigolds, too. But right now, all she could think about was getting out of the sun and having a big drink of water, and she wasn't the only one. The girls all seemed to have wilted, and Toby and Patrick were red-faced and sweaty.

"Well, come on inside," said Elizabeth, noticing the rather bedraggled crew. "It's cool inside, and I know Patrick is going to find the gun room fascinating." She led the way through a doorway, which opened directly into a large room stocked with rifles, neatly lined up along the walls.

As promised, the air was much cooler inside and Lucy noticed the girls were quickly reviving, looking about with interest. Turning her attention to the deadly array of armaments, which she found somewhat shocking, Lucy was somewhat relieved to see that each weapon was securely locked into place.

"This is quite a lot of firepower," said Toby, suitably impressed. "What's it all for?"

"Hunts," said Elizabeth. "The château hosts all sorts of hunting events for enthusiasts. They shoot birds, mostly, and deer, but the real attraction is the annual boar hunt every fall. There's a waiting list for that one."

"Are there really wild boars around here?" asked Elizabeth, somewhat disturbed by the idea. "Do they attack people?"

"There are boars, and from what I hear they can be pretty ferocious when they're threatened, but I haven't heard of any attacks," said Elizabeth, who was pointing out some rifles that seemed large enough to take down elephants. "These are the guns for the boars."

"Wow," said Patrick, suitably impressed. "Can I hold one?"

"Afraid not, kiddo," said Elizabeth, with a smile. "They're kept under lock and key."

"Good idea," said Molly, ruffling her son's hair. "If not, no one would be safe from this guy."

"The recoil would probably knock him into kingdom come," said Toby, who had been taking a close look at the rifles. "These are beautiful guns, though. I've never seen workmanship like this."

"As I understand it, they're not mass produced. They're bespoke, made by a master gunsmith especially for the château. He also maintains them, too. I guess some of these are actually antiques," said Elizabeth. "But the reason I brought you this way was to show you the fishing rods. I remember that you and Patrick want to go fishing."

"Where do we go?" asked Toby.

"Right here. We've got plenty of rowboats and canoes, and there are fish in that moat. Lots of carp, I believe."

"Sound good, Patrick?" asked Toby.

"Yeah. Can I row?"

"We'll see," said his father. "Anybody want to join us?"

"All I can think about is a cool bath and a big drink," said Lucy, exhausted from the heat and uncomfortable with all those guns. She knew they were intended for hunting, but there was no denying that a gun that could kill a boar could also kill a person.

"Well, off you go, then," said Elizabeth, opening a door that led into a hall from which she promised the foyer could be reached, although at some distance, if they simply kept turning right. "But you might want to spend some time at the pool; there's a fitness complex, you know. It includes a fabulous gym, as well as an absolutely gorgeous outdoor pool. It's not too far to walk, but we often whisk our American guests over there by golf cart."

"Not for me, thanks," said Lucy, intent on her bath. "But maybe the girls . . ."

"I'm in," said Zoe. "Me too," chimed in Molly and Sara.

"Okay. I'll phone for the cart, you can wait out back on the terrace. It will probably be waiting for you when you get there?"

"Don't we need to change into our suits here?" asked Zoe.

"If you want, but there are changing rooms there, as well as swimsuits, all sizes. A lot of our guests don't remember to bring their own."

"They really do anticipate everyone's needs here, don't they?" mused Molly.

"We sure try," said Elizabeth. "So guys," she said, speaking to Toby and Patrick, "they're going to go on to the foyer and out back to the terrace; we're going back out through the garden to the boathouse. Follow me." She paused a moment to make sure the women understood her directions, and getting nods, gave them a little wave. "À bientôt," she said, watching as they went on their way.

"Be sure to use sunscreen," advised Lucy, when the tired group finally reached the foyer after what seemed like miles of corridors. "This sun is very strong and if you didn't bring any I'll bet they provide it."

"I'm sure they do," said Sara. "Don't you love the little bottles of shampoo and stuff? It's much nicer than the stuff I buy at the drugstore."

"It's really nice, living like the one percent," observed Molly. "But I do feel guilty. Do you know that the top ten percent of the world's population causes ninety percent of global warming?"

"Well, that's not us," said Zoe defensively.

"If you make over forty thousand a year, you're part of the problem," said Molly.

"Really?" Sara sounded troubled. "I can barely make ends meet and I make more than that."

"Yeah, but think of the undeveloped world. People in some countries are lucky to have any cash income at all," said Molly.

"Well, I'm sure we'll all be more responsible in the future," said Lucy, "but we might as well enjoy this amazing, luxurious, very rare treat while we can."

"Hear, hear!" said Zoe, pausing at the French doors that opened to the terrace. That was where their ways parted, the girls trooping off outside while Lucy began the climb up the long staircase to her room.

Her legs felt leaden as she took the stairs slowly, one at a time, using the banister to pull herself along. When did she get so old, she wondered. Or was it just delayed jet lag? Feeling she couldn't go one step more, she paused by the window to catch her breath and rest her aching muscles. From there she could see Toby and Patrick, already sitting together in a little red rowboat, holding fishing poles. The greenish water was dappled with light, the gray walls offered a bit of shade, and that's where they had dropped their lines, thinking the fish might have sought cooler water. It looked, she thought, like an Impressionist painting she'd seen once: the sunlight and shade, the many hues of the water, the vibrant green of the bushes on the bank, and in the center the red boat. "It's like we're all in a painting," she thought, resuming her climb. "A beautiful painting."

Chapter Ten

Back in her beautiful room, Lucy freshened up in the luxurious bathroom, enjoying the lavender-scented soap. She was still coping with jet lag, so she decided to stretch out on the chaise in front of the open window, determined to begin filling in the empty pages in the journal she'd brought along to record the trip. When she bought the pretty little book, with its picture of the Eiffel Tower on the cover, she'd vowed to capture every detail of the trip and, most especially, Elizabeth's wedding. It would help her remember this special time and might eventually become something Elizabeth would treasure. She had a little notebook in which her grandfather had recorded dates and locations of his military service in World War II, but that was all he'd bothered to include and she'd always wished he'd written more. What was he doing in North Africa? Why was he promoted from private to sergeant in two weeks? How did he feel about it? It left her with more questions than answers and she didn't want to do that to Elizabeth. When she was no longer around in person, she wanted Elizabeth to know how proud she was of her and how much she hoped she would have a long and happy marriage.

A gentle breeze was coming through the open window, the sun was warm, and Lucy told herself she needed to count her blessings. Here she was in France, a pampered guest in a magnificent château, preparing for her lovely daughter's beautiful wedding. What could be better? She opened the little journal and stared at the blank page, wondering how to begin. At the beginning, she decided, remembering the phone call when Elizabeth announced her engagement. The words began to flow and she began writing, resolutely dispelling any doubts and negative thoughts and happily recalling pleasant memories. But as she wrote, her hand began moving slower and slower. Eventually her head fell back against the chaise, her hand went limp, and the pen dropped on the floor.

It was sometime later when she woke with a start, apparently roused by shouts from outside. Something was going on and, whatever it was, it didn't sound good. Her first thought was for Patrick, who had been in a tiny little rowboat, fishing with his father in the moat. Oh, no! Could he have fallen in the water? Was Patrick drowning?

She leaped from the chaise and ran to the window, but all she could see was a group of workers gathered around the little red boat, which had been pulled up onto the bank. Glancing around frantically she didn't see any sign of Patrick, or Toby. This was crazy, she thought, running from the room. They could both swim, they were strong swimmers. But people did drown all the time; the local evening news back home in Maine almost always reported a drowning: a toddler who fell into a backyard pool, boaters who capsized, foolish people who ventured onto the rocks at Pemaquid Point and were swept away by a rogue wave. But that couldn't happen to her son! Or grandson! They were skilled boaters and swimmers. But in the back of her mind as she dashed down the stairs was the oft-repeated warning that anyone could drown, even the best swimmers. Even professional rescuers sometimes drowned, attempting to save others. It happened. Cold water could cause muscles to seize up. A diver searching for someone could stay down too long and pass out. A swimmer could become entangled in water weeds, or submerged, discarded machinery. Who knows what might be in that centuries old moat? Maybe even some horrible huge fishy monster!

Visions of scaly, toothy giant moat creatures were swimming through her head as she ran through the foyer and fought her way through the piles of cartons and crates that blocked the front door. Sucking in her stomach and just barely making it through to the courtyard, she ran to the bridge that crossed the moat, where she paused to catch her breath. From that vantage point she was able to see Toby and Patrick sitting on the ground by the water's edge, safe and sound. She let out a huge sigh of relief and went over to join them. "So what's going on?" she asked, noticing that they were bone dry, but Toby had his arm around his son, who was looking rather ill, and was comforting him.

Toby looked up at her and smiled, then shrugged. "Patrick snagged something on his line," he said.

"Like what?" she asked, following his glance toward a shaded area where a group of workers were gathered, partially blocking her view of something that was lying on the ground. Something that looked like a body. "That?"

"Yeah," said Toby, giving Patrick a squeeze. "It's a woman. Patrick tugged on his line and she just popped up. Gave him quite a scare."

"I saw her face," said Patrick, with a shudder.

"How awful," said Lucy, sitting beside him and taking

his hand, giving it a squeeze. "It must have been terrible, but you have to put it out of your mind. Sad things happen but it's nothing to do with us." She'd no sooner said the words than she panicked, thinking of her girls. They were supposed to go to the pool but did one of them change her mind and decide instead to go for a walk after lunch? And did she somehow slip on the grassy verge of the moat and fall in? She turned to Toby. "Right? It's not? It's absolutely no one we know?"

"No, no," said Toby, shaking his head. "Definitely not."

"I didn't really think so," she admitted. "The girls were on their way to the pool when I went upstairs. I'm just upset." Lucy was watching that group of workers gathered around the body and discovered she wanted to know more. She was a reporter, after all, and had honed her investigative skills through the years. She couldn't ignore what was happening, she needed to know who this woman was and what she was doing, drowning in the moat. "I think you should take Patrick away from all this," she instructed her son. "Take him upstairs and give him something sugary. Find a distraction, so he can think about something else."

"Good idea, Mom," said Toby, getting to his feet. "Are you coming?"

"No, I think I'll stick around a bit, find out what's going on."

Toby's back stiffened. "Really, Mom? This is actually none of your business."

"Like it or not, we are sort of involved. You discovered this poor girl and I'm sure the police will want to talk to you, and Patrick. We need to be careful and the more we know, the better prepared we'll be," she said, somewhat defensively as she took his hand and let him pull her to her feet. "It's good to be informed, to get the whole picture."

"I think we'll be just fine," said Toby. "All we can do is tell the truth. I don't think we have to worry about getting involved, I think the problem is that you can't forget you're a reporter." He paused, meeting her eyes. "Dad's not going to like this, you know. He won't like you investigating. Especially not here. You're not on the job back in Maine, you know. This is France and they have different rules." He paused. "You might even get in trouble, impeding an investigation or something."

"I'm well aware that this isn't Maine," she responded, in a snappish tone of voice. She then caught herself, this was her grown son after all, and adopted a more reasonable tone. "But what if it's one of the workers here? Or a family member? I need to know so we can behave appropriately. Maybe the wedding will be called off. It's better to get one step ahead, be prepared."

Toby took Patrick's hand and gave his mother a disappointed look. "You're unbelievable," he said, shaking his head.

"Take care of Patrick," she said, with a little smile. "I'll give you a full report."

"Don't bother," said Toby, gathering up the fishing rods. "I hope you know what you're doing," he said, before leading his son back to the gun room.

Lucy watched them go, noticing that Patrick already seemed to be regaining his usual energy, marching along beside his father. She took a moment, thinking about Toby's warning, then brushed it aside and made her way over to the group of workers. They seemed to be shaking their heads sadly and gesturing excitedly as they discussed what to do and, finally coming to an agreement, sent one of their number off to report the discovery. Lucy picked up the word *couverture*, which she was pretty sure meant "a blanket," no doubt intended to cover the body. Of course, she thought, that's what people did. They covered the body and waited for the authorities.

Seeing her approach, they shook their heads and rattled off more French words, which she assumed meant she should go away. This was not something she should see.

"*Dommage*," she said, which she knew meant "sorry," and adopted a mournful expression. She added a shrug for good measure, and shook her head.

"*Oui*," said one of the workers, going on to say something about the dead woman being "*jeune*," or "young," and "*jolie*," which meant "pretty."

She nodded her head slowly in sad agreement. The girl was indeed young and beautiful, with long black hair. Her brows arched dramatically over eyes that were mercifully closed, her nose was small and straight, and her lips, slightly parted and bluish, were full. Now that she was closer, could see she was dressed for a party in a sexy little black dress. Even soaking wet she could see it was clearly a pricey little number with a complicated bustier effect that emphasized her generous breasts. Also pricey, she thought, was the jeweled necklace that still encircled her neck, now adorned with bits of water weed. Her fingernails, Lucy noticed, were long and painted bright red, and a strappy silver sandal dangled from one foot, the toenails also painted red.

More than anything, at that moment, Lucy wanted to snap a photo. She was a reporter, after all, and that's what reporters did. Unfortunately, she'd left her phone upstairs when she'd hurried down to see what was the matter. Perhaps it was for the best, she thought, realizing it would be in terrible taste. People wouldn't understand. She would have to make do by taking a long look at the body, trying to memorize every detail. There was no sign of a wound that she could see, though the water would have washed away any blood. The young woman's long dark hair could certainly conceal a wound, as could the black dress. And she could have a broken neck, a cracked skull, or been strangled. Those were definite possibilities, but could only be discovered by autopsy.

The one thing she was sure of was that the young woman hadn't been in the water for long. She'd been a reporter for a long time and she'd witnessed numerous recoveries of submerged bodies and was well acquainted with the damage water, tides, and aquatic animals could do to a corpse. She'd seen bloated bodies, bodies missing faces and fingers, torsos without arms and legs, and once even a dismembered head. No, the one thing she knew for certain was that this young woman had not been in the water for long.

The other thing that occurred to her was that she hadn't seen this person before, as she would have remembered seeing such an attractive person. She certainly wasn't one of the workers at the château, not dressed like that. She wasn't a guest, either. Maybe she was an administrative employee, a personal assistant or something, who had dressed for an evening out? But that jeweled choker and that dress indicated a much higher pay grade. Maybe she was involved with the wedding, a planner or designer of some kind, perhaps working with Henri Bruneau? That was somewhat more likely, but someone like that would have been dressed more casually, in clothing suitable for a busy day. The heel on that sandal looked to be four inches high, for goodness' sake, and even the most dedicated fashionista would have found such high heels problematic for walking on grass lawns and gravel paths.

Maybe this young woman was connected somehow to the boys, Claude and Jerry? A date, brought back to the château late last night? Or a friend? But they would certainly have raised the alarm if their companion had fallen into the moat. They would probably have jumped in to save her.

Perhaps, she thought, she was a friend of the family. Someone who had come a bit early to share in the preparations for the wedding. That would be terrible for the Schoen-Rene family, and terrible for Elizabeth as well. This death would cast a pall over the whole wedding; it might even be postponed.

It seemed to her that quite a bit of time had passed. Where was everyone? Shouldn't Hugo or Marie-Laure have been notified? And where were the authorities? There would be police of some sort, and certainly a *proc*, or *procureur*, which Lucy knew was the French equivalent of a district attorney in the US. The investigators would certainly want to question Patrick and Toby about the discovery of the body, that was a given. But a darker thought crossed her mind, a fear that as the outsiders in this little drama, her family members might very well come under suspicion. Much easier to blame the Americans, especially when dealing with a prominent and highly regarded family. They would have to be very careful, she thought, just as a distant siren signaled that the police were finally arriving. There was no time to lose, she thought, deciding to warn the others. The slightest misstep could be misunderstood and Lucy knew the French justice system had the reputation of being absolutely relentless. Visiting France was one thing; being detained in a French jail was something else entirely.

The siren was coming closer; she had no time to lose. She wanted to make sure that Toby and Patrick were prepared to talk to the police, she wanted to hear what they were going to say and make sure there was nothing at all that could be construed as the slightest bit incriminating. She hurried back to the château, looking up at the immense structure as she crossed the bridge over the moat. What was really going on behind that impressive façade, she wondered, thinking for a moment of Bertram's Hotel.

That hotel was the subject of a favorite Agatha Christie mystery, which she loved so much she'd read it several times. Bertram's, in the novel, was a British institution, embodying all that was best about a traditional London hotel. The afternoon tea was legendary, the service spectacular, but most importantly, the hotel re-created a bygone atmosphere that reassured folks struggling to adapt to changes wrought by World War II that absolutely nothing had changed. The Union Jack still flew over the Empire, the Nazis and Japanese had been soundly trounced, and everything would go back to the way it was.

It was all a grand pretense, of course; the war had changed the world and there was no going back. As for Bertram's, the hotel was actually cleverly created so no one would suspect the truth, that it was a front for a huge crime syndicate. Looking up at the massive stone château, topped now with festive, colorful pennants, Lucy wondered if something like that was going on here. Was the château, Campanule, a big fake?

Chapter Eleven

S he was so intent on her mission that she failed to notice Hugo until he practically bumped into her in the doorway. "They tell me someone has fallen into the moat?" he asked, looking perplexed. "This has never happened before."

"I'm afraid it's true," said Lucy, a bit out of breath. "It's a young woman."

"Is she all right? Should we call for an ambulance?"

Oh, boy, thought Lucy. It looked like it was up to her to break the terrible news to Hugo. "Um, it's a bit late for that, I'm afraid. She's, um, I'm so sorry. She's passed."

"She's okay? She's gone away?"

Clearly, there was some misunderstanding about American terms for death. "Permanently, I'm afraid. *Elle est morte.*"

Hugo's eyes practically popped out of his head and his jaw dropped. "*Mort? Mon Dieu!*"

"The police are arriving," said Lucy. "I heard the sirens."

"I thought it was a road accident," said Hugo. "They're here?"

"The body is in front, on the grass by the moat," she said, expecting him to immediately rush to the scene. She was wrong.

"I suppose I will be needed," he said, sounding unsure.

"I think the authorities will certainly want to talk to you."

He exhaled a long, deep sigh. "I think you are correct," he said, remaining in place.

"Perhaps you should go and take charge," suggested Lucy.

"Perhaps," he agreed, brightening a bit, as if he had an idea. "Perhaps Marie-Laure . . ."

"She may already be there," said Lucy.

"I don't think so," he said, scratching his chin. "She was down in the kitchen, meeting with the chef." He paused. "Consulting about menus. I doubt she would hear the sirens down there."

"Well, I think you should go," said Lucy, using her mother voice and stepping aside. "I need to check on my grandson now."

Hugo's eyebrows rose and he grabbed her hand, expressing concern. "Patrick was involved?"

"He was fishing in the moat with his father, they discovered the body."

"*Mon Dieu!*" He shook his head. "*C'est incroyable.*" He remained deep in thought, still holding her hand. She tried to withdraw it, desperate to go to Patrick and Toby, but his grip tightened. "Will you come with me?" he asked. "It would be better, I think. You could explain to the police."

Really? Really? thought Lucy, who wanted to get upstairs and warn Toby. Why did Hugo need her? Did he forget to put on his big boy pants this morning? She was curious, sure, but she didn't want to be front and center.

She'd hoped to do a little quiet investigating, remaining in the background. Her main goal was getting enough information so that she could protect her family. She'd been involved in a murder investigation years earlier, when visiting Paris, and she didn't want to repeat the experience. The police had demanded her passport then and she remembered how powerless she felt as the judicial system ground along, ever so slowly, until the case was finally resolved. She looked at Hugo, meeting his eyes, and saw a pathetic, weak man pleading for help. She sighed. "Okay, we'll go together."

"*Très bien, très bien,*" he said, squeezing her hand. "*Merci.* Thank you, it will be a big help."

So Lucy turned around and walked with him into the courtyard, from where they could see a number of official police vehicles filling up the grassy area in front of the moat. A small crowd of uniformed and plainclothes police were gathered around the body. Together, she and Hugo crossed the bridge. Hugo paused at the end to pull himself to his immense height and straightened his shoulders, then marched over to the group. Lucy followed, torn between her desire to learn more about the dead woman while wishing to remain an uninvolved observer.

Reaching the group, Hugo announced himself in a torrent of French and one of the men, a short, stocky fellow in a gray suit, stepped away from the others. He was sweating heavily and paused to wipe his face with a white cloth handkerchief, then replied, also in French. Lucy assumed he was the lead investigator, since the others seemed to defer to him.

Hugo and the investigator had a long conversation, punctuated with a lot of head shaking and hand gestures on Hugo's part, and a lot of nodding and hand gesturing on the investigator's part. Lucy wished she'd paid more attention in French class.

Suddenly the investigator turned to her. "I am Superintendent Javert of the OPJ, and I will be conducting the investigation into the death of this most unfortunate young woman. I understand you are visiting here at the château, that your daughter will soon be marrying Jean-Luc Schoen-Rene."

"That's correct," said Lucy. "Most of my family is here for the wedding, we are guests of the Schoen-Rene family."

As she dreaded, Javert produced a notebook. "Perhaps you will identify the members of your family, beginning with yourself."

Lucy gave her name, then went through the whole family, saving Toby and Patrick for last.

Javert noted it all down, asked how long they'd been at the château, how long they'd stayed in Paris. It was all very cut and dried, very factual, and Lucy was beginning to relax. Then he asked, "And so it was your grandson, this Patrick, who discovered the body?"

Lucy's heart dropped about six inches. "He was fishing with his father. They snagged the body with a fishing line and it popped up."

"That must have been very upsetting," observed Javert.

"Yes. He's just a boy, of course," said Lucy, intent on protecting Patrick. "A child."

"*Bien sûr,*" said Javert, with a kindly smile. "I will need to talk to him."

"Is that absolutely necessary?" asked Lucy. "He had nothing to do with this woman. . . ." A thought popped into her head and she decided it might be helpful, it might send the investigation into another direction entirely. "I think this woman, this girl, might be from that farm out by the road, the one that looks like a brothel. She might be a call girl, something like that. It would explain why we never saw her before."

Javert gave her a condescending little smile. "Madame, you are no doubt unfamiliar with the ladies of the night, but believe me, they do not dress in expensive clothes, they do not wear expensive jewelry. This woman was obviously wealthy."

Lucy followed his pointing finger and studied the body, noticing something she hadn't seen before. "But . . ." she began, only to be cut off.

"Those sandals, *par exemple*," he instructed her, in a condescending tone, "with the red soles, are Louboutins." He whistled. "Maybe cost a thousand euros." He shook his head. "No. She was not a low-class whore. And besides," he added, with a shrug, "I am not aware of this establishment you mentioned. Where exactly is it?"

"I'm not sure. We passed it this afternoon, out by the road. A run-down place, with several women outside, sunning themselves. There was a man, like a guard."

"Ah," said Hugo, who had been listening intently to the conversation. "*C'est fini*, they are gone."

"Gone?" Lucy was shocked. "It was there a few hours ago."

"Yes. But Marie-Laure, my wife, was not happy about it, the business they were conducting, and she demanded that they depart when their lease expired, which happened to be today." He shrugged. "My manager checked a short while ago and reported that they had gone. We have been planning for some time to renovate the farmhouse, for guests."

Wow, that was convenient, and fast, thought Lucy. Of

course, Marie-Laure might well have gone on the warpath against the brothel, especially with the wedding coming up. It gave a very bad impression; it was not the sort of thing any respectable person wanted on their doorstep. Although, it occurred to her, it might well have provided additional entertainment for the well-heeled gentlemen who attended the hunting events at the château. And the more she thought about it, the more she wasn't at all convinced by those fancy clothes and shoes that the dead woman was wealthy or well-connected.

"If you don't mind," said Javert, interrupting her thoughts, "perhaps you will take me to your grandson so I can question him?"

Seeing her alarmed expression, he was quick to reassure her. "It will be brief. I will take great care not to upset the boy."

As it happened, Patrick wasn't the least bit upset about being questioned. He examined Javert's credentials with interest and did most of the questioning himself. "What's it like to be a detective? Do you solve a lot of murders? Do you have a gun?" By the time Javert finished, the two were best buddies, and Patrick had been invited to the station to see the jail.

Closing the door behind him, Lucy leaned against it in relief. "Good job, Patrick."

"When can I go?" asked Patrick. "I want to see the jail."

"We'll see," said Lucy, falling back on that perennially useful phrase. If it were up to her, Patrick would never see a jail, not even out of curiosity.

"Well, I want to go soon," said Patrick.

"All in good time," said Lucy. "Why don't you go for a swim in the pool? Cool off."

"Good idea," said Molly, who had been silently observing the interrogation. "I could sure use a swim. Are you coming, Lucy?"

Lucy had something else in mind. "Toby, how about a little walk? I never get time alone with you anymore."

"Really, Mom? I'd like to swim, too."

"No problem. We'll just go the long way round to the pool. It would be a shame to miss the garden."

He shrugged. "Whatever," he said, giving Molly a resigned look. "Keep an eye on Patrick, don't let him drown."

"He's part fish, you know," said Molly, giving him a smile.

Lucy and Toby arranged to meet on the terrace in ten minutes, so Lucy hurried off to her room and quickly changed into her swimsuit, added a modest cover-up, stuffed her feet into a pair of espadrilles, and clapped a sun hat on her head. Considering herself prepared for the expedition she had planned, she skipped down the stairs and joined Toby on the terrace. "So what's this really all about?" asked Toby, furrowing his brow.

"I want to check out that run-down farm we saw earlier today. It was a brothel, I'm sure of it. There were several girls in skimpy clothes sunning themselves outside, overseen by a beefy guard. Molly said she'd seen similar setups around the oil fields. I think that girl may have come from there."

Toby was skeptical. "The dead girl?"

"Yeah. But just now Hugo said the place is empty, their lease expired today and the tenants have cleared out. Very convenient, don't you think?"

"Well, with a wedding coming up they'd hardly want a place like that on the château's doorstep," said Toby, as they headed into the garden. "But from what I saw, which wasn't much since I was focused on Patrick, that girl looked pretty high-class to me. Like a call girl, maybe, judging from those clothes, not a working girl catering to farmers."

"Look, they could keep the girls at the farm and dress them up so they'd fit in here at the château. I tell you, she was not a wealthy woman. Her teeth weren't right, the front ones stuck out, and she had those cheap stick-on plastic nails on her fingers. I could tell because a couple of them were broken."

Toby was thoughtful as they made their way through the garden and then followed a track circling a large field. "Do you actually know where you're going?" he asked, wiping the sweat off his forehead.

"Not specifically," admitted Lucy. "But I have a pretty good sense of direction and I sort of know where it is."

"That's not especially reassuring," said Toby, "especially when I could be floating around in that pool." He fell silent and trudged along for a bit, then spoke up. "Does Dad know about this?"

"I think he's been in the library all day, studying those plans Hugo told him about. He couldn't wait to take a look at them." Lucy sighed and marched along. It was certainly hot in this field and she wasn't at all as sure of their destination as she'd claimed. "Next thing you know, he'll be building châteaux in Tinker's Cove."

Toby snorted. "I don't think so." He fell silent and Lucy could practically hear the wheels turning in his head. "It's not so far-fetched, you know."

"Châteaux in Tinker's Cove?"

"No." He chuckled. "The brothel. Molly's right about the oil fields, there's plenty of entertainment available for the workers. They make good money and don't mind spending it. And I assume the same is true of these rich guys who pay a fortune to stay in a château and hunt boar or shoot quail. They probably like to party after a tough day out in the field."

"The Schoen-Renes leased the property to whoever ran the brothel. Hugo said Marie-Laure wanted it gone before the wedding, but it seems awfully convenient considering what happened with that girl."

"Probably just a coincidence, Mom."

"But it's been there for a while," said Lucy. "When I was helping with the flowers I think the women were talking about it. It seemed like it was common knowledge. Why would they decide all of a sudden to get rid of it? They weren't fooling anybody and they were collecting rent?"

"I don't like this," grumbled Toby. "Do you think Elizabeth knows who and what she's getting involved with?"

Lucy stopped in her tracks and faced Toby. "I don't know what to think. She's obviously in love with Jean-Luc, I guess love can make you blind. But she's been a concierge in a fancy hotel, she's been around a while, she must have seen call girls coming and going. Maybe it's the way of the world; maybe we're repressed New Englanders."

"I'm not against sex," said Toby, "don't get me wrong. But Molly's chewed my ear off talking about sex trafficking, the kidnappings, the drugs, and how these girls are abused. If they're too much trouble, they get killed."

"Even in Maine," said Lucy, remembering a shocking story she'd covered last year. "Look, I think the farm is just through that woods up ahead."

The path continued through the woods and it occurred to Lucy that this dirt road had seen a good bit of traffic. If in fact it led to the farm/brothel, it had seen plenty of com-

ing and going. It was cooler in the shady woods, which
was a relief from the heat in the field, but in a matter of
minutes they were back out in the sunlight, in the hard-
packed earth behind the derelict farmhouse. A few tum-
bledown sheds dotted the area, bits of fast food wrappers
blew around.

"Looks like nobody's home," said Toby, as they walked
around the house to the front. There the broken chaise
longues remained; strips of torn plastic webbing fluttered
in the persistent, hot breeze. The door to the house, a typical country farmhouse with stucco walls and a tiled roof,
was wide open. Lucy went straight for it, cautioned by
Toby. "Careful, Mom."

Peering into the dim interior, she saw an empty room. It
was silent, nothing stirred, so she stepped inside, followed
by Toby. Two doors led from the front room, one was obviously the kitchen, the other a makeshift bedroom, with
soiled mattresses covering the floor.

"I don't think they conducted business here," said Toby.

"Doesn't look like it." She bent down and picked up a
tube of mascara, missing its cap. "They slept here, and ate
here, judging from those wrappers. When I saw them, they
were sitting outside, watched by a tough-looking guy."

"Molly's told me about this sort of thing, but seeing
it . . ." said Toby, giving his shoulders a heave, "well,
it's a whole new perspective."

"Yeah," said Lucy. "Let's go for a swim and cool off before dinner."

"Good idea," agreed Toby, as they made their way out
of the farmhouse. "I could use a chlorine rinse."

"Me too," laughed Lucy, retracing their path through
the trash-filled yard. Even there, however, she noticed a
rosebush, clinging desperately to life and even producing a

few salmon-colored blooms. She paused to sniff them and noticed a scrap of newspaper caught among the thorns. She carefully removed it, noticing it was printed in a language she didn't recognize.

She called to Toby, who was a few steps ahead. "Look at this."

Toby took the paper and studied it. "Looks like some Slavic language, maybe even Russian."

Lucy glanced around, wondering what had gone on in the farmhouse. Had the girls been lured to France with promises of modeling contracts and high-paying jobs, only to find themselves trapped in the middle of nowhere, drugged, beaten, and forced to pleasure rich old men?

"This is a horrible place," she said, shuddering. "Do you think the Schoen-Renes were involved in more than collecting the rent? Do you think they actually participated in sex trafficking?" An even darker thought crossed her mind. "What does Jean-Luc do on all those foreign trips? Does he recruit the girls?"

Toby let out a huge sigh; he seemed to deflate like a balloon. "I hope not, I really do. But I gotta tell you, Mom, I've picked up a fair amount of French at fishery conferences. Not schoolbook French but I guess what you'd call gutter French." He looked off in the distance, then turned back to his mother. "I didn't want to tell you, but when I was at the barber shop with Patrick, I heard some disturbing stuff. There were a lot of jokes and snickers about the château, pretty ripe stuff. This place was no secret, you're right that everybody knew about it. And those so-called gentlemen at the château, well, they were interested in bagging something more than pheasants and boar."

Chapter Twelve

Lucy looked at her son with new respect, this younger version of his father, complete to the beard, broad shoulders, and huge feet. This kid who couldn't pass English in high school, much less French, was now a highly knowledgeable and respected member of the fisheries management community, attending international conferences and picking up colorful phrases in various languages. French? What about Icelandic? Maybe even Russian? The awkward boy from Tinker's Cove had grown into a smart, thoughtful man who operated in a highly competitive industry about which she knew nothing.

While she was covering selectmen's meetings in Tinker's Cove and interviewing ladies who made potholders for church fairs, he was hammering out deals with foreign governments specifying catch quotas, safety regulations, and, a top priority to him personally, environmental standards. She knew what he did, she'd known for years, but she hadn't really *known*. Toby, her Toby, was kind of a big shot, operating on a global stage. She was impressed.

"Mom," he was continuing, as they began walking back through the unkempt yard toward the woods, "I know you want to investigate this but that is definitely a bad idea. Believe me, the police, the local authorities, everybody knew about this place, that it supplied girls to the guests at the château."

"The head inspector, Javert, claimed it was news to him. . . ." said Lucy.

Toby snorted. "That's hard to believe. He's just covering his ass, pretending he saw nothing, heard nothing, knew nothing."

Lucy thought about Tinker's Cove, where everybody seemed to know everything about their neighbors, and nodded her head. "This is a small town, after all. You're right, people would know. It's not like they were keeping it a secret. Those girls were pretty obvious lounging out there in plain view."

"It goes on everywhere," said Toby. "I bet even in Tinker's Cove."

"Well, not out in the open, like here," she protested, unable to imagine that people in Tinker's Cove would have tolerated an establishment of that kind in their midst. "More like, under the covers," she said, making a little joke.

Toby smiled. "And that's where it should stay, Mom. It's none of our business, we don't need to get involved. You don't have to be a genius to realize that powerful interests are in play here, most likely organized crime."

In her heart, Lucy knew he was right. "But what about the Schoen-Renes? Do you really think they're involved with organized crime?"

"In some way or other, they probably couldn't avoid it. You know, 'an offer you can't refuse' kind of thing." He was thoughtful as they trudged along. "The Schoen-Renes probably run the town, they have contacts with important people throughout France, even Europe. They have a reputation to uphold. They certainly won't like you poking around, uncovering their dirty laundry."

"But what about Elizabeth? She's marrying into this family. Whatever they're involved in is going to involve her."

"She's a big girl, Mom. Like you said, she must have encountered this sort of thing at the hotel. Call girls, certainly."

They were entering the shady woods, but the temperature seemed to have risen and the trees no longer seemed to offer relief from the heat. The air itself seemed oppressive, Lucy felt as if it was crushing her chest, making it hard to breathe. "No, Toby. It's one thing to have a sophisticated, live and let live attitude; it's another thing entirely to be part of a sex-trafficking syndicate. We have to warn her."

"And what are we going to tell her? That we suspect her fiancé's family are a bunch of criminals?" argued Toby. "The less she knows about this, the better."

"Well, I don't know about laws in France, but in the US you don't have to know why you're waiting outside the bank with the engine running to be charged as an accessory. And there's a moral component, too. Does she really want to be part of a family that's up to their necks in corruption?"

"I don't know," sighed Toby, as they stepped out of the woods into the furnace-hot heat of the field. "But if it were up to me, I'd keep my mouth shut."

Maybe Toby was right, thought Lucy. It really wasn't her business and things had a way of working out. It was like that old song "Que Sera, Sera." Elizabeth had been on her own for a long time; she would certainly resent any attempt on her mother's part to tell her what to do. Maybe all she could do, she thought, was to cross her fingers and trust that Elizabeth was making the right choice.

They trudged on in silence; it was too hot to talk. The walk that had seemed endless when they weren't sure of their destination now seemed shorter on the way back, and they were only suffering from mild dehydration when they turned up at the pool. Toby greeted his wife and son with a wave, then ran across the deck and cannonballed into the pool, making a huge splash. Lucy entered the water more sedately, did a ladylike breaststroke across the pool, and climbed out, seating herself in the chaise next to Molly's. She had no sooner sat down than a waiter approached with a pitcher of lemon water and a couple of plastic glasses.

"Just what I need," said Lucy, as he filled a glass and handed it to her. "Brother, it's hot out there."

"Where were you?" asked Patrick. "You were gone a long time." His father was calling to him, urging him to jump into the pool, but he was waiting for Lucy's answer.

"Just a walk, Patrick. Go on, your dad wants to swim with you."

Patrick leaped into the water and was promptly caught by his father, who lifted him up and tossed him back in the water, getting shrieks of delight.

"It's nice to see them having fun together," said Lucy, drinking greedily.

Molly watched them for a moment, then sighed. "I hope Patrick doesn't have lasting effects from finding that body. He's just a boy, after all, and it would be traumatic even for an adult."

Lucy drained the glass while watching father and son racing each other across the pool. "He seems to be doing fine."

Molly wasn't convinced. "He gets bad dreams sometimes and wakes up terrified."

"Some warm milk and a bedtime story ought to do the trick," advised Lucy.

"I hope so, but it may not be that simple." Molly shifted her hips on the padded lounge. "So what were you and Toby really up to? Did you go to the farm?"

"Yeah," admitted Lucy. "It's deserted, nobody there. But we found this." She extracted the torn scrap of newspaper from the pocket of her cover-up and handed it to Molly.

Molly studied it, then gave a knowing nod. "Sex trafficking. They get these girls from Eastern Europe."

"I think Elizabeth needs to know," said Lucy, sending up a trial balloon, interested in Molly's take on the situation. "I want to warn her but Toby says she probably already knows all about it and I should mind my own business."

"Sounds like Toby," said Molly, chuckling. "I don't see what the harm would be if she already knows. She must have made her peace with it, right? But if she is truly unaware, well, if I were in her place, I'd want to know. Marriage isn't just tents and canapés and white lace, especially here where she's going to be deeply involved in the business of running the château."

"Do you think she would actually call the wedding off?" asked Lucy, well aware that things were moving fast. The rehearsal and celebratory dinner were tonight and the ceremony was planned to take place the next day.

"I would," said Molly. "For sure. But I eloped with Toby when I was only nineteen, for goodness' sake. Toby's the only man I've ever known; I'm not a sophisticated city girl like Elizabeth who knows the ways of the world." She sipped at her lemon water. "I think she really wants the marriage, maybe not so much for Jean-Luc but definitely for the job at the château." She smiled wickedly at Lucy. "She might want to make some adjustments in her job description."

"Good point," said Lucy. "I think I have to talk with her."

Molly turned to face Lucy and smiled. "You go, Supermom!"

"I sure don't feel like Supermom," admitted Lucy, getting up slowly from the chaise and slipping into her cover-up. Molly gave her the scrap of newspaper and she tucked it in her pocket as she shoved her feet into her espadrilles. But as she left the pool area and passed the discreet trash barrel near the exit gate, she was tempted to toss that scrap away. Just let it go, forget about the whole thing. She didn't, of course, but in the days to come she often wished she had.

After a bit of a search she found Elizabeth where she least expected: reclining on one of the chaises in a shady corner of the terrace. "I didn't know you were allowed to relax," she said, seating herself in a nearby chair.

"I've been ordered to relax by Marie-Laure herself," said Elizabeth. "She was worried that I might look too tense at the wedding tomorrow. I am instructed to empty my mind and take deep, cleansing breaths."

"And how's that going?" asked Lucy, noticing the little worry line between her daughter's eyebrows and the dark circles beneath her eyes that the carefully applied concealer didn't quite cover.

"It's making me tenser," declared Elizabeth. "I can't empty my mind. It keeps flitting around, stuff keeps popping up. Like did I order enough champagne? What about the trolley bringing guests from the train, did I double-check on that? Will there be enough servers at the reception?"

"I'm sure you've double- and triple-checked everything," said Lucy. That scrap of paper was practically burning a hole in her pocket, but she wasn't sure she should show it to Elizabeth. "Any progress on the dead woman?" she asked.

"No." Elizabeth shrugged. "Marie-Laure thinks it was a suicide. Says it's happened a couple of times before. Jilted lovers making a final romantic gesture and throwing themselves into the moat."

"Do you really think that's what happened?" asked Lucy, remembering Hugo's claim that such a thing had never happened before. Who was lying?

"Sad to say, I actually don't care." Elizabeth shrugged, then smiled. "When I'm not worrying about the flowers or the guest book I'm thinking deep, absolutely unclean thoughts about my delayed honeymoon." She sighed. "I wish we hadn't decided to wait, I wish we were flying off to Africa right after the wedding."

"As you should," said Lucy, laughing. And since Elizabeth had brought up the topic of sex, maybe this was the opening she needed?

But before she could speak, Elizabeth continued. "I mean, these things happen. It's nothing to do with me, so why should I dwell on it. Why should I care?" She sighed. "If anything, I'm ticked off at this woman. Why here? Why now, when we're having a wedding? My wedding. Darned inconsiderate if you ask me."

"It certainly is," agreed Lucy, "but I think you're involved whether you want to be or not. It seems likely to me that she was one of the girls at the farm." Lucy paused and locked eyes with her daughter. "I'm sure you know what I'm talking about."

"Oh, the farm," said Elizabeth, with a dismissive wave of her hand. "It's gone. For the time being, anyway. Marie-Laure insisted, she had her lawyer write a letter refusing to renew the lease." She flexed her feet and ran her fingers through her hair. "I don't know why you think that girl had anything to do with the farm. From what I heard she was dressed to the nines in very expensive clothes. Louboutin shoes."

"Yeah, but she wasn't a wealthy woman, underneath those obvious signs. She had cheap plastic stick-on nails, and she also had bad teeth."

"Oh, Mom, you're so American," chided Elizabeth, in a condescending tone. "Europeans aren't all hung up on perfect teeth, like Americans." She grimaced. "You must've really given that poor girl the once-over. How could you do it? Seeing her exposed and vulnerable like that. She was dead. It was indecent, you should have looked away."

Lucy felt as if she'd been slapped. She was stunned by Elizabeth's reaction. "I looked because her life was over and I wanted to understand why a young woman who could expect to live for many years had met such an abrupt and terrible death," said Lucy. "That young woman wasn't disposable, she wasn't a bit of disagreeable trash to wrap up and throw away. Whether it was by suicide, accident, or murder, her death needs to be acknowledged and understood. The dead deserve that much. It's a matter of respect for life, for personhood."

"Okay, okay," responded Elizabeth, in a shrill voice. "You're right and I'm wrong. I'm a terrible, selfish person."

"I don't think that," protested Lucy, unhappy with the way this conversation was going. "Believe me, I have your best interests at heart. I'm afraid that you might be getting involved in more than you bargained for."

"Rest assured, I know exactly what I'm getting into," declared Elizabeth indignantly.

"Love can make you blind, and I'm worried for you," said Lucy. "It's quite possible that the Schoen-Renes are more deeply involved in this than you realize. That farm was a sex trafficking operation, I found this scrap of newspaper there." She produced the bit of newsprint and held it out to Elizabeth. "It's some sort of Eastern European language."

Elizabeth did not take the proffered bit of evidence, but curled her lip in disgust. "So you've been digging around, looking for dirt. Can't you ever accept the idea that things are exactly what they seem to be?" She looked up at the château, towering above them, pennants flying in the sunshine. "The Schoen-Renes are lovely people, who've raised a wonderful son and have welcomed me into their world."

"A lovely family with a dead body on their hands," countered Lucy. "It's not like rain or snow, that happens to everyone. Trust me, dead bodies don't end up in your moat for no reason."

Elizabeth bounded to her feet and faced off squarely opposite her mother. "Trust you? Why don't you trust me? You're against me. The whole family is against me. You don't want me to be happy. You've never approved of my choices. Zoe and Sara have always been jealous of me, they think I've got it easy and don't understand how hard I've had to work." She pounded her fists against her thighs in frustration. "Why do you think I've stayed in France all this time? It's because my family has never been there for me. You've never supported my choices. You talk about that girl being discarded, well you guys tossed me out with the trash a long time ago!"

Lucy was absolutely stunned. Was this how Elizabeth truly felt? She watched her daughter begin to march off, then leaped to her feet and ran after her, grabbing her arm and pulling her into a hug. Elizabeth resisted at first, then allowed her mother to pull her close.

"I had no idea you felt that way," began Lucy, relaxing her grip on Elizabeth but reaching out and gently turning her face, making eye contact. "I hear you, and I'm sorry if you truly felt unappreciated. I've always loved you, you were my first little girl and that makes you special. I felt such intense love for you, when I first held you in my arms. You were red-faced and bawling then, and I have to say that was a pretty clear indication of how things would go. You were never easy, but I always, always loved you and I still do. I only want you to be happy."

All the steam, all the anger seemed to leave Elizabeth as she sank onto the stone wall surrounding the terrace. "I'm sorry, Mom. I guess I kind of got carried away." She sighed. "The truth is, I'm not really sure I'm doing the right thing, marrying Jean-Luc." She let out a long, long sigh. "My first thought when I heard about that girl was that she must be one of Jean-Luc's old girlfriends, someone he jilted who got desperate when she learned about the wedding and threw herself into the moat."

"That's not all that unlikely," said Lucy, considering this new possibility. She sat down next to Elizabeth and took her hand. "Have you asked him?"

"I'm afraid to," admitted Elizabeth. "It's too late now, it's gone too far. The wedding's tomorrow, it's like a big old train, rolling down the track. I can't get off, even if I wanted to."

"Do you?" she asked, squeezing Elizabeth's hand. "Do you want to get off? 'Cause if you do, we can all pack up and be out of here in a flash."

Elizabeth thought about the question, giving it some time. Finally she spoke: "No, I don't want to run away. I love Jean-Luc and that's what matters, none of the rest. I love Jean-Luc, he loves me, and we're going to be married." She smiled. "Tomorrow, I will be Madame Schoen-Rene."

It hit Lucy hard, the thought that in future, whenever she wrote to her daughter, she would have to stop a moment and remember to address the envelope to Elizabeth Schoen-Rene. Elizabeth Stone would be gone.

Chapter Thirteen

Lucy wasn't quite convinced by Elizabeth's protestation of love for Jean-Luc, even though she hoped that love would conquer all. She had to be satisfied with the fact that she'd been open with Elizabeth and voiced her concerns. Lucy had to accept the uncomfortable truth that this wasn't her decision to make. It was up to Elizabeth and she'd made her choice. Lucy hoped with all her heart that it was the right one and that Elizabeth wasn't making a big mistake.

She'd been understandably upset when Elizabeth claimed she'd been the unloved odd one out in the family, but figured that was a bit of an exaggeration. Elizabeth had always been better at offense than defense, often reciting that verse about eating worms and marching up to her room, inevitably slamming the door. And being a bride was stressful, even without the discovery of a body in your groom's moat.

"Okay," she said, patting Elizabeth's hand and standing up. "I'm glad we had this little talk. I needed to know how you felt." She glanced at the chaise Elizabeth had abandoned and gave a little nod. "I agree with Marie-Laure, the best thing right now is for you to relax and let go of your worries. So take a load off, put your feet up." She gave Elizabeth a little push toward the chaise. "Is there anything I can do that will ease your mind?" she asked. "Any last-minute stuff?"

"Actually, Mom, there is. I know they're putting the final touches on the chapel for the rehearsal tonight, but I haven't gotten round there to check on it. Could you just make sure everything's okay in there, that they haven't left any boxes or stuff lying around?"

"Sure," agreed Lucy, suddenly remembering she was still wearing her swimsuit, although with a modest cover-up. "Can I go like this? Into the chapel?"

"Sure." Elizabeth had seated herself and was unfolding her legs, stretching out. "Chances are nobody will be there."

"One more detail," said Lucy. "Where is the chapel?"

Elizabeth laughed, and it occurred to Lucy that she hadn't actually seen her daughter laugh for several days. "Through the foyer, on past the billiard room, turn right and it's at the end of the hall."

"Got it." Lucy gave her daughter a little salute, leaving her to her private thoughts. As she made her way to the chapel along the château's endless corridors, Lucy tried to remember how she'd felt on the eve of her own wedding to Bill. Her wedding hadn't been anything like Elizabeth's, she recalled; it had been a much, much simpler affair. She hadn't had much to do with the planning, either, since her mother had handled everything while she was supposed to be concentrating on finishing up her senior year of college. In truth, however, she'd spent most of her senior year in bed with Bill, in the shabby off-campus apartment he shared with some friends. Her parents had unfortunately discovered this arrangement during a surprise visit to campus and her father had followed up with a man-to-man talk with Bill about his intentions.

Lucy herself hadn't seen the need for a paper certificate validating their love, but much to her surprise, Bill had proposed a few days later, offering her his grandmother's diamond ring as a pledge of his love. So a wedding was planned the weekend after graduation, and Lucy had returned to the home of her childhood with her diploma in hand to discover an immense pile of packages awaiting her. "Who are all these people? And what am I supposed to do with all this stuff?" she'd wondered. Her mother had looked at her in some amazement. "Lucy, this is what people do. Family and friends send wedding presents. And," she'd added, in a no-uncertain-terms voice, "you must write thank-you notes to each and every one."

Working her way through the gifts, Lucy began to realize there was more to married life than shacking up in an off-campus apartment. Her parents had paid for her dorm room, which she had rarely used, and her dining card, which she did use, even while she spent her nights with Bill. Now, she was unwrapping pots, indicating cooking would be required, and fine china dishes on which to serve the food. Dishes that would have to be washed, but not necessarily by her. She wasn't going to be a housewife like her mother, oh, no, and Bill would have to do his part. Share and share alike, when it came to household chores. As she unwrapped some lovely new sheets, Lucy remembered thinking they would be a big improvement on Bill's thrift-shop bedding, but again there was the problem of washing them. It occurred to Lucy that they would need someplace for all these things, some place more permanent and private than Bill's shared apartment. And she was going to need a whole lot of thank-you notes.

It had been quite a surprise when Bill showed up for the wedding with a fresh haircut and missing his beard. He'd thought of everything: he'd found an apartment and a job, he was going to start in two weeks at a Wall Street brokerage. She remembered standing in the back of the church, seeing that strange man claiming to be her Bill, waiting for her at the altar, and wanting to run. If her father hadn't been holding her firmly by the arm, she sometimes thought she would have made a break for freedom and run away, like the bride in *The Graduate*. Just went to show, she thought with the benefit of hindsight, that sometimes parents actually knew best.

Finally reaching the chapel's double doors beneath a Gothic arch, she pulled one open with a loud creak and stepped inside, looked down the aisle with its white carpet, and smiled to herself. She'd walked down a similar white carpet, she'd said all the right words at the wedding ceremony, she'd danced at the reception, and as the early days of her marriage unfolded she discovered she'd most definitely made the right choice.

Now, in this French chapel, it was dim and cool, peaceful. Lucy found it a welcome relief from the busy activity outside, as well as the heat and dazzling light. Looking around, she decided it was rather overdone, at least in comparison to the simple, white-steepled churches in Maine. The chapel was full of gilt, it dripped from the walls and ceiling, and there were a number of religious statues. Mary, of course, and others she didn't recognize, although she thought the poor fellow bristling with arrows was St. Sebastian. If it had been up to her, she would have removed the unfortunate martyr for the wedding ceremony, but it wasn't up to her. Thanks to all that gilt, the chapel hadn't needed much in the way of decoration for the wedding, but small clusters of white flowers tied with white ribbons had been placed at the end of each pew and two large floral arrangements were placed on gilt stands beside the altar. A pair of prie-dieux with white satin cushions stood before the altar, and that was where Elizabeth and Jean-Luc would kneel and pledge their vows.

Everything seemed ready, decided Lucy, seating herself in one of the pews. Outside, she knew, the marquee was complete, the little gilt chairs were in place at the round tables, which were covered with damask cloths and ready to be set with the family's silver and crystal. The seating chart was already on the table in the foyer, the flower arrangements were all in place. Downstairs in the kitchen, the chef and caterers were working at a fever pace to prepare the food. As Elizabeth had said, it was like a train, thundering down the track, and as she had before her own wedding, she realized she wasn't ready. She wasn't ready to see her daughter marry Jean-Luc Schoen-Rene.

She grabbed the back of the pew in front of her and found herself lowering her head, resting her forehead on her hands. If this was prayer, it was wordless, just a letting go. What was that phrase that was so popular now? "All shall be well, all shall be well, and all manner of things shall be well." She'd thought it was pablum, a promise that could not possibly be kept. All too often in her experience things didn't work out, they didn't turn out well. But now, she found herself murmuring it, like a mantra, over and over. "All shall be well, all shall be well, it will all be okay."

Some minutes later, Lucy found she felt much better. Maybe, she thought, just maybe this marriage would be okay. She stood up, straightened her shoulders, and made a final tour of the chapel. It was, she had to admit, beautiful, in its way. And she had to believe the prayers uttered in this place through the centuries were lingering, floating about, bringing peace and comfort to all who entered, including Elizabeth and Jean-Luc. She was smiling at this rather fanciful thought when she left the chapel and practically knocked into a tall, young man. A young man she knew, she realized, recognizing the familiar face. The face of the last person she expected to see at Elizabeth's wedding.

"Chris! Chris Kennedy! What on earth are you doing here?" Lucy noticed he was dressed in a beautifully tailored business suit that was a far cry from the off-the-rack ones he had worn in his previous life as a Secret Service agent. His haircut was clearly expensive, just long enough to be fashionable but not too long, and he was sporting an equally fashionable stubble of beard. And on his feet, she noticed, highly polished tasseled loafers had replaced those sturdy Vibram-soled service oxfords. Oh my.

"I know," he admitted, giving her a hug and a couple of air kisses. "Old flame shows up at wedding."

"Are you planning to whisk Elizabeth away? Or stand up when the priest asks if there are any objections?" Lucy was joking, but the idea did have a certain appeal.

Chris smiled. "No. I'm definitely prepared to 'forever hold my peace.' As it happens, I'm here to meet with Hugo. He felt the need for more security at the wedding, something about a dead woman, and his lawyer recommended me. I've got my own security and investigative firm now. I work with a lot of American companies, as well as French companies doing business with Americans." He glanced around at the hall, with its endless carpet and rows of portraits hanging on the wall. "Elizabeth's done very well for herself."

"I could say the same about you. I'd never take you for an American, you look the very picture of a successful French businessman."

Much to her surprise, Chris blushed. "Oh, it's just part of the game. Down deep I'm the same Red Sox fan, straight out of Boston."

"But you've stayed in France?"

"Yeah," he admitted, nodding. "It sorta just happened. The Secret Service was transferring me back to the States and I was involved in some stuff here, so I decided to hand in my resignation and finish what I started. One thing led to another, I got a French partner, and here I am."

"So you're married?"

"Oh, no. I've got a business partner, a French guy." He stared down the hall. "Nope. I haven't found the right girl."

Lucy wondered if he just hadn't found a girl who compared to Elizabeth, but kept that thought to herself. "Well, I shouldn't keep you from your meeting," she said.

"Yup. Can't keep the client waiting." He started to go, but Lucy reached for his arm and he paused, giving her his attention.

It had occurred to her that Hugo might not be entirely forthcoming about the situation with the farm and the dead woman's possible connection. "There's something I think you should know," she began.

He glanced at his watch. "I've really got to run. Hugo's waiting for me." He scratched his stubbly chin. "I'd love to get your take on this. . . ."

"Things are really kind of a mess," she admitted. "Are you here for the night?" she asked, in a hopeful tone.

"Not here, here." He shook his head. "I'm at the inn in town."

"I'm tied up tonight, rehearsal and family dinner. Any chance we could meet in the morning, early, before the ceremony. There's a stable, that ought to be off the beaten track tomorrow."

"Okay. Sure. Seven a.m.?"

"Good. I feel better already, knowing you're here."

Chris smiled at her. "Lucy, I promise I'll do everything I can to make sure Elizabeth's day goes off without a hitch. Seven a.m., at the stable. See you then."

She watched as he marched off down the hallway on his long legs. If only, she thought, if only Elizabeth had had the good sense to fall in love with a man like Chris. A man who had once loved her, and Lucy suspected, loved her still.

Bill was reclining on the bed when she reached their room, watching a soccer match on TV. "This is a surprise," said Lucy. "I thought you hated soccer."

"Desperate times call for desperate measures," he said, with a shrug.

"Well, things aren't all that desperate," said Lucy, climbing onto the bed and stretching out beside him. "You'll never guess who I met downstairs."

"Nope, I won't."

"Chris Kennedy!" she announced, in a triumphant tone.

"Elizabeth's old flame?" He furrowed his brow in thought. "I don't see why you're so happy about it. Isn't this a problem?"

"Not at all. It's a good thing. He has a security firm here in France and Hugo hired him as extra protection for the wedding."

"Can't be too careful," he said, clicking off the TV.

"Stupid game, after nearly an hour of play the score is nil-nil." He stretched a bit, then pulled her close, slipping his hand beneath the cover-up. "This swimsuit thing is very silky. Sexy."

"It slips right off," said Lucy, shrugging out of the cover-up. "Want to see?"

"Sure do," said Bill, moving in for a kiss. "Sure do."

Sometime later, freshly showered, Lucy and Bill went downstairs for the celebratory family dinner, which they'd been told would be served on the terrace. Marie-Laure greeted the couple, who were holding hands, with a knowing smile and a raised eyebrow. "I trust you've had a pleasant afternoon?"

"Oh, yes," said Lucy, grinning and getting a warning tug on her hand from Bill. "Very relaxing, right, Bill?"

"I'm getting to like soccer," he offered. "Great game this afternoon."

"Well, I'm glad you are enjoying yourselves. Dinner will be more casual than usual, just panini," she said. "I'm sure you understand, the kitchen is busy preparing food for the wedding, and of course, we have the rehearsal after."

Lucy surveyed the terrace, where the long table was already set with colorful pottery and a parade of little vases filled with colorful zinnias. Toby and Patrick were sitting on the wall, talking with Hugo. Molly, Sara, and Zoe were standing together, holding glasses of rosé, and Jerry and Claude, along with Elizabeth and Jean-Luc, were gathered at the bar. "Do get yourselves something to drink," urged Marie-Laure. "Dinner will be served shortly."

She bustled off, intent on some errand, and Lucy and Bill made their leisurely way across the terrace to the bar, taking in the view of the garden where afternoon shadows were spreading across the lawn. "It's so beautiful here," said Lucy, positioning herself next to Elizabeth. She smiled at Jean-Luc and asked, "Are you ready for tomorrow?"

"I've been ready for a long time," he said, taking Elizabeth's hand and raising it to his lips. "But tomorrow Elizabeth will finally be mine."

"And you will be mine," said Elizabeth, radiant in the golden sunlight of a long June evening.

"Look at them!" teased Jerry. "The lovebirds!"

"A toast!" announced Claude. "A toast for the happy couple!"

Champagne was popped, glasses were filled, and Hugo provided the toast. "I wish you, darling Elizabeth and Jean-Luc, and along with everyone here, we all wish you every happiness in your marriage!"

"And don't forget grandchildren," added Marie-Laure, who had reappeared and was claiming her glass of champagne. "May there be many, many grandchildren."

"Maybe two, or three, certainly not many," cautioned Elizabeth, making everyone laugh.

"Well," replied Marie-Laure, with a shrug, "I will take what I can get. Now, *à table, s'il vous plaît.*"

While they had been chatting and toasting, platters heaped with panini had magically appeared, along with bowls of salad and many bottles of wine. They all found seats and Lucy found herself at the end of the table, sitting next to Claude and facing Jerry. Marie-Laure was at the very bottom of the table, opposite Hugo at the head.

Lucy chose a panini as the platter was passed, and added a healthful helping of salad, which she noticed included colorful nasturtium flowers. "Do we eat these?" she asked.

"Oh, yes," said Marie-Laure. "They are delicious."

Lucy was doubtful but popped one in her mouth, dis-

covering it was peppery, but also sweet. "This is a delightful discovery," she told Marie-Laure. Turning to Claude,
she asked in a teasing tone if he and Jerry had been keeping Jean-Luc out of trouble.

"Well, we tried," replied Jerry, also in a teasing tone.
"We did the best we could."

"We will make sure he gets to the church on time tomorrow," said Claude, in a solemn tone.

"It's a good thing you had the limo the other night," observed Lucy, taking a bite of crusty toasted bread filled
with ham and tomato. "I understand the law is very strict
about drunk driving here."

Jerry began to speak but Marie-Laure jumped in, cutting him off. "Yes, yes. The law is quite severe on anyone
who has drunk too much. The limits are quite low, lower I
think than in the US."

"It's true," agreed Jerry. "But we are always very careful, no need—"

"I'm sure Elizabeth and Jean-Luc are looking forward
to their honeymoon," said Marie-Laure, once again interrupting. "But that will have to wait. There is so much to
do here with the carriage races coming up."

"How soon are the races?" asked Lucy, surprised at
Marie-Laure's almost manic behavior. The wedding stress
must really be getting to her.

"Two weeks." Marie-Laure sighed. "And there is so
much to do. We have to meet the requirements of the or-
ganization, the FEI is very strict."

"FEI?" asked Toby.

"*Oui*. La Fédération Équestre Internationale."

"Ah, the carriage races!" exclaimed Jerry, raising his
glass.

"We always come," added Claude. "It's a lot of fun."

"Do you race yourselves?" asked Lucy.

"No. No. We watch."

"And party," added Jerry. "All our friends come. It is very social."

"It is very festive," agreed Marie-Laure, "but it takes a lot of hard work and planning."

"Well, Maman, you will have to give us some time off," said Jean-Luc, grinning mischievously. "If you want those grandchildren, that is."

"Oh, I want them," confessed Marie-Laure, going on to add, "But all in good time."

Thinking of the possibility that Elizabeth and Jean-Luc would be starting a family, Lucy wondered how they would manage with their small apartment. "I suppose they could move to a larger apartment, or perhaps re-model," she said, thinking aloud. "Or since the château is so large maybe they can simply add another room if they do have a baby, but that décor, those brown vines," she began, then caught herself before she made an insulting faux pas. "Well," she began, spearing another nasturtium with her fork, "perhaps something simpler and cheerier for a baby."

"Ah, but Lucy, that chintz is one of the château's treasures," said Marie-Laure. "It is an antique fabric, one of the first chintzes produced here in France. It dates from the late eighteenth century and we could not possibly change it. It would be a sacrilege."

"Oh, my, I hadn't realized," said Lucy. "It is certainly very remarkable. How could it survive all these years?"

"With care, my dear Lucy. In France we do not sub-scribe to the disposable culture of you Americans. Every year since it was put up that chintz has been gently brushed top to bottom to remove dust, and of course, the windows are kept closed, to keep out the sunlight."

"Remarkable, absolutely remarkable," said Lucy. "But there are only two rooms, where will the baby sleep?"

"Why, in the nursery, of course," said Marie-Laure, with a smile. "Up one floor, next to my room."

"Ah," said Lucy, reaching for her wine. "I see."

Chapter Fourteen

The wedding rehearsal, which took place after dinner, had gone off without a hitch, but Lucy wasn't reassured as she went through her bedtime routine. Bill snored away beside her all that sleepless night, but even the deluxe mattress and the luxurious Yves Delorme sheets couldn't overcome the disturbing thoughts that flooded her mind. One minute it was Marie-Laure, taking possession of Elizabeth and Jean-Luc's baby, her grandchild! And then it was an image of the dead girl, floating in the moat. In her worst imaginings, perhaps it was a dream, the corpse's face was covered with a wedding veil which floated away to reveal Elizabeth's face. Finding herself staring at the clock at a quarter to five, and noticing the sky was already brightening and the birds were calling, she decided she was far too restless to stay in bed a moment longer. She needed to move.

She eased herself out of bed and slipped noiselessly into the bathroom, where she dabbed some water on her face and brushed her teeth. Getting dressed presented a problem, as her clothes were all in an armoire in the bedroom and she didn't want to disturb Bill, who was still asleep. The château provided terry robes for its guests and those hung on hooks in the bathroom, so she wrapped herself in one and tiptoed out of the room, picking up the espadrilles she had left lying by a chair.

Once in the hallway she remembered the scrap of newspaper, which she'd left lying on the desk beneath the window, so she crept back in and found it, tucking it in the pocket of her robe. Then, returning to the hallway, she slipped into the espadrilles and made her way outside. Once on the terrace she felt better, she took some deep cleansing breaths of fresh morning air, then started across the garden. She wasn't exactly sure of the location of the stable, where she was supposed to meet Chris Kennedy in a little more than an hour, so she decided to find it, locate it firmly in her mental map, and then continue her rambles until it was time for the meeting.

A soft mist hovered over the garden, but the warming sun would soon dissipate it; a beautiful, sunny day was predicted for Elizabeth's wedding. Lucy smiled to herself, thinking that of course, Marie-Laure would have it no other way. Perhaps she'd requested her friend the Pope's intercession, or perhaps even the Creator would not dare to defy her wishes.

As it happened, the stable was much closer than she thought, discreetly screened by a line of evergreen trees. It was a handsome, half-timbered building with a steeply pitched tile roof, and Chris Kennedy was already there, dressed for the day in an inconspicuous gray suit, sitting on a bench and staring at his cell phone. "You're an early bird," said Lucy.

"Couldn't sleep," he said, with a half smile. "Thought I might as well do a little recon, get a look at the lay of the land. And you? Are you always an early riser?" He cocked his head and smiled. "Nice outfit."

"I couldn't sleep, either," said Lucy, sitting beside him.

"I had a bad night, I felt restless and I didn't want to disturb Bill so I grabbed this robe off a hook in the bathroom." She was dying to pour out all her concerns, especially Marie-Laure's comment about the nursery, but resisted the temptation. That was the sort of thing best shared with her girlfriends, and she suddenly realized how much she missed them. Pam, Sue, and Rachel would offer sympathetic advice and support, and would certainly disapprove of Marie-Laure, adding her to their list of terrifying mothers-in-law, pushy supermoms, and double-dealing lady bosses.

"Well, if you're worried about Elizabeth, you can be sure that she knows exactly what she's getting into," said Chris. "She's smart and capable and knows her own mind."

"I'm not convinced," admitted Lucy. "These days I look at her and wonder if some other person has taken over her body. She seems to be willfully blind, ignoring any and all signs of trouble."

"A château and a handsome, wealthy fiancé, I suppose it is all rather dazzling." Chris sighed. "Like a fairy tale."

"Yeah, and we know how those work out. There's a lot of trouble before the happily-ever-after part."

Chris put his warm, strong hand over hers. "That's why I'm here," he promised. "To make sure it all ends happily."

Lucy felt tears stinging her eyes and blinked furiously, holding them back. She heard a snicker and a neigh from inside the barn and managed a smile. "So what have you found out about the body in the moat?"

"Well," he began, "the medical examiner found that she was a female in her early twenties, there was vaginal tearing and scarring, indicating forced intercourse and earlier sexual abuse, most likely as a child. She was underweight, bruised from beatings, had TB, and had some very poor dental work, most likely in Eastern Europe. Her nails and jewels were fake, and cause of death was strangulation."

"It all fits in with what I've suspected," said Lucy, sadly. She wasn't naïve, back in Maine she'd covered plenty of cases of abuse, sexual and otherwise, but she'd never grown used to it. Every time she struggled with anger at the perpetrators who abused these girls, and tremendous sorrow for their suffering. Mostly she thought of the years they'd lost, the futures that had been stolen from them. "Did she have a name?" she asked.

He shook his head. "Not so far, and frankly, it's unlikely that she'll ever be identified."

"DNA?" she asked, hopefully.

"Maybe," he admitted, without much encouragement.

"Just one of the many," said Lucy, sadly.

"Yeah," agreed Chris.

After a moment, Lucy spoke up. "There was a brothel on the edge of the property here. She was probably from there."

"That's interesting." Chris's eyebrows rose, he scowled and began to chew his lip. "You said *was*? What happened to it?"

"Marie-Laure made them clear out, something about the lease expiring, conveniently just in time for the wedding. Toby and I did some exploring and we found this." She handed him the scrap of newsprint, now somewhat the worse for wear.

"Bulgarian, I think," he said. "Sex traffickers find vulnerable girls who've run away from abusive homes and lure them with promises of modeling contracts, they say they'll get them in the movies. It's all a lie, they drug them and when they wake up the girls find themselves at the mercy of organized criminals who hold them captive and force them to have sex with paying customers. The girls don't even see any of the money, they're lucky to get some secondhand clothes and crappy food. And the least signs of resistance get them beatings or worse."

"Like the girl in the moat?"

"It could be that she was a message to Hugo, an embarrassing little present on his doorstep, letting him know that their eviction was not appreciated." He paused, thinking. "The fact that she was sick, maybe she'd been troublesome, they probably wanted to get rid of her anyway."

Lucy shuddered, looking around at the cobbled stable yard, the charming outbuildings, and the perfectly mowed lawn beyond. "It's positively creepy," she said. "All this beauty and these disgusting rich men, overfed and drunk, forcing themselves on these girls. It's evil."

"Yeah, it's not exactly 'Cinderella.'" He scowled. "I'm glad you told me about the brothel, it puts a different spin on things."

"Organized crime?"

"I hope not." He gave her a reassuring smile. "Probably just a local entrepreneur."

Lucy wasn't fooled, she doubted a local madam would have international connections, but she wasn't about to argue the point. Chris was smart, he knew the score, but was trying to reassure her. "Well," said Lucy, standing up. "I guess I better sneak back into the house before somebody sees me in this robe."

Chris nodded. "Big day."

"But you'll be around? Keeping an eye on things?"

"Oh, yeah. Me and an undisclosed number of highly trained operatives. K and J Security guarantee safety and peace of mind."

"Well, I do feel better knowing you're on the job," said

Lucy, impulsively giving him a hug. He hugged her back, and she was reassured by his strength, his broad shoulders, his big chest. If only, she thought, if only Elizabeth had valued his goodness and wholesomeness, and had made a different choice.

"See you at the church," said Chris, releasing her.

"Right," said Lucy, immediately thinking she'd made a poor word choice. Nothing about this seemed right, it was all wrong.

She made her way back to the château, hurrying a bit in hopes of returning before anybody knew she had gone. That plan went awry as soon as she entered the lobby, where Marie-Laure was plucking a few droopy blossoms from the huge flower arrangement on the center table. She was dressed for action in a trim navy tracksuit, immediately putting Lucy to shame in the borrowed terry robe.

"Ah, Lucy, did you have an enjoyable swim?" she asked.

"Just out for a walk," said Lucy. "I didn't want to disturb my husband so I just put this on over my nightie."

"How very considerate of you." She adopted a concerned expression. "I suppose you are a bit anxious for your daughter on her wedding day."

"I suppose I am, a bit," admitted Lucy.

"You need not worry, everything has been carefully planned. All Elizabeth has to do is look beautiful, just be her lovely self."

For her part, Marie-Laure seemed her brisk and efficient self, emotions in check. "Aren't you a bit worried for your son?" asked Lucy. "He's the groom, after all."

Marie-Laure shrugged, then smiled. "Jean-Luc is what I think you call a 'cool customer.' He will be fine." She reached for Lucy's hand and gave it a squeeze. "Do not worry, Lucy. Their marriage will be a success." She gave a little nod. "I will make sure of it."

That's what I'm afraid of, thought Lucy, biting her tongue. "Well, I really need to put some clothes on and see if Elizabeth needs anything."

"I took her some breakfast, and got a peek at her dress," said Marie-Laure, with the air of someone confiding a secret. "I think you will be very pleased."

"I'm sure I will," said Lucy, feeling her dander rise. Why did Marie-Laure get to see the dress before she did? Wasn't she the bride's mother? And why did she feel so angry about it? She plastered a smile on her face and glanced at the stairs. Time to make her escape, she decided, before she lost her temper. "Well, see you in church," she said, by way of a goodbye.

"In the chapel," said Marie-Laure, making Lucy wonder as she began the climb whether Marie-Laure was simply agreeing with her, or correcting her choice of words.

When Lucy reached her room she discovered that breakfast had arrived and Bill was biting into a huge croissant. "Where've you been?" he asked. "When I woke up you were gone."

"Just out for a walk, I had trouble sleeping."

"Mmmm," he said, his mouth full of croissant. When he finally swallowed, he expressed a bit more sympathy. "Worried about Elizabeth? It's only natural."

Lucy plunked herself down on the side of the bed. "Like my dad told me, there's always divorce."

"I bet it's pretty complicated in France. Everything is, you know."

Lucy got back up. "You're not helping, Bill," she said. "Are you okay with the bathroom? Do you mind if I take a shower?"

"Don't you want some breakfast? It's delicious."

"Couldn't eat a thing," said Lucy, watching as he dropped a huge dollop of strawberry jam on the last bit of his croissant, popped it in his mouth, and reached for another.

"Okay if I eat yours?" he asked, holding it up.

"Bon appétit," she said, leaving him to his breakfast. A knot was beginning to form in her stomach and she had a bad feeling that it was going to grow as the day wore on.

She had styled her hair, applied some light makeup, and donned her wedding finery, a gold silk shantung suit, when she emerged from the suite and headed for Elizabeth's apartment. Zoe and Sara were already there, and were helping Elizabeth into the dress. Marie-Laure had not exaggerated at all, she decided; the dress was a triumph of simplicity, a strapless sheath with a little bolero jacket that would cover her arms and shoulders for the church service but would be removed for dancing at the reception.

"It fits like a glove," exclaimed Zoe, who was zipping up the back.

"Where did you find it?" asked Sara. "It's like it was made just for you."

"It was," laughed Elizabeth. "A designer I know made it especially for me, she even gave me a discount. I could never have afforded it otherwise."

"She must be a very good friend," observed Lucy. "Is she coming to the wedding?"

"No," said Elizabeth, admiring herself in the full-length mirror. "It's more a business kind of friendship, because as a concierge I could recommend her boutique to hotel guests." She sat down at her dressing table and reached for a lipstick. "It's like that in France, one hand helps the other."

Lucy made eye contact with her daughter in the mirror.

This was her last chance, she had to speak up and say what was troubling her. "You know, sometimes it seems to me that your marriage to Jean-Luc is more of a business arrangement than anything else. You seem to be marrying a business rather than a man."

Now that the elephant in the room had been pointed out, Elizabeth's sisters and mother braced for her reaction. Elizabeth wasn't angry, however; she just laughed. "That's not a bad thing, is it? If anything, it's a good thing for a husband and wife to share the same interests. We will work together and it will make our marriage stronger."

"There's such a thing as too much togetherness," said Lucy.

"And that mother-in-law, Marie-Laure, is pretty scary," observed Zoe.

"Not at all," scoffed Elizabeth. "I get along just fine with Marie-Laure. And for your information, I love Jean-Luc and he loves me."

Sara wasn't convinced. "Are you sure he loves you?" she asked. "If you ask me, he seems a lot more interested in Claude and Jerry than he is in you."

"That's crazy!" declared Elizabeth, eyes blazing. "It's always the same with you, all of you. You're jealous. You always want to spoil things for me. Heaven forbid you should be happy for me, you can't even manage it on my wedding day!"

Lucy stepped behind her daughter, placed her hands gently on her shoulders, and bent down to kiss the top of her head. "It's because we love you. We just want to make sure you're doing the right thing," she said, making eye contact in the mirror. "It's not too late to call the whole thing off if you've got any doubts at all."

Elizabeth shrugged her shoulders and wiggled out from

under Lucy's hands. "Get real, Mom. It's too late. Even if I wanted to get out of it, which I don't, I have to go through with the ceremony and the reception. The guests are arriving, the food is cooked, and there's nothing for it but to do it."

Lucy was about to offer some reassuring words, she wanted to let Elizabeth know that no matter what, she was her mother and she would support her, when the door flew open and Marie-Laure blew in, now dressed in a classic pink Chanel suit trimmed with black and white braid. "Elizabeth," she trilled, "it is time for the civil ceremony. Hugo has already gone down to the library to greet the *le maire*. Are you ready?"

Elizabeth stood up and Marie-Laure gasped. "*Magnifique!*" she declared, beaming with pleasure and grabbing Elizabeth's hand. "We must go, we must not keep *le maire* waiting," she insisted, pulling Elizabeth to the door. There she paused and pressed her hand to Elizabeth's cheek. "Elizabeth, you are not my *belle-fille*, you are more than a daughter-in-law. Today you become my *fille*, my true daughter, the daughter I always wanted but never had." And with that declaration, Marie-Laure whisked Elizabeth out the door, leaving a stunned silence behind.

Chapter Fifteen

"Well!" exclaimed Lucy, as the door closed behind Marie-Laure and Elizabeth. She shook her head. "All I can say is that woman has some nerve! Elizabeth already has a mother. I don't think she needs another."

"You know, for a little while, I was really jealous of Elizabeth," confessed Sara. "I mean, I'm barely making it from paycheck to paycheck and my love life is pretty much nonexistent, but it's my life. I get to decide things for myself." She shook her head. "I wouldn't want to be in Elizabeth's fancy designer wedding shoes for anything."

"Yeah," agreed Zoe. "She's letting Marie-Laure run her life." She was thoughtful. "I don't know why Jean-Luc doesn't stick up for her." She chewed her lip. "He doesn't seem the least bit independent. I think of the guys on the Sea Dogs team and how they're focused on the game and making it to the big leagues. He doesn't seem to have any, what do you call it, mojo or something."

"I think you mean backbone," offered Sara.

Lucy was moving about the room, tidying up, and stared at the big bed Elizabeth and Jean-Luc shared. The marriage bed. The ugly antique coverlet with its pattern of brown vines was rumpled, the bed left unmade, but only one side had been slept in. "Haven't they been sleeping together?" asked Lucy, smoothing out the sheets.

"Yeah, but last evening, when I was leaving the rehearsal I heard Marie-Laure say they should sleep apart. Something about him not seeing the bride before the wedding . . ."

Lucy finished making the bed and moved to Elizabeth's dressing table, where she replaced the cap on a lipstick and looked at her reflection in the mirror. She and Bill had been sleeping together for months before her wedding and she remembered how silly it had seemed to her that she had to pretend to be a blushing virgin in a white dress. "I thought that was a thing of the past," she said.

"Welcome to the past," said Zoe.

"Yeah, this place is like time travel," offered Sara. "Just look at the wallpaper."

"I'd rather not," said Lucy, tightening the cap on a bottle of foundation and setting it on the dressing table. "Let's go down and join the party."

When they descended to the foyer and proceeded down the hall to the library, however, it was clear something was amiss. Marie-Laure was standing in the library doorway, wringing her hands. It occurred to Lucy that this was one of the very few times she'd seen Marie-Laure express any emotion besides her usual smug self-satisfaction and control.

"Is something the matter?" asked Lucy, noticing that Elizabeth and Jean-Luc were standing in the library, along with Hugo, but the mayor was conspicuously absent. "The mayor . . ." she began.

"*Le maire* is not here!" exclaimed Marie-Laure, angrily. "He called! He is stuck in traffic. Stupid man. He should have left earlier. He could have stayed here last night, I invited him. But no, he could not leave his wife and the newborn baby. He would come in the morning, *pas de problème,* he said. As if there is no such thing as a road accident that holds everyone up for hours and hours."

"Why is it such a big deal?" asked Zoe. "They're getting married in the church anyway."

"French law doesn't recognize sacramental marriage, it has to be a civil ceremony," explained Jean-Luc. "Otherwise you're not married in the eyes of the law."

"The religious ceremony doesn't count?" wondered Sara.

"Only to religious people," said Jean-Luc, with a charming little smile. "It is, what you say? Ceremonial only. But lovely. And traditional. People enjoy it, like a bit of a show."

"What are we going to do?" demanded Marie-Laure. "Is there someone else? Another official? Hugo, you must know someone?"

"I don't think so," said Hugo, shaking his head. "As you know, the ceremony usually takes place at the *hôtel de ville.* Monsieur DuPont very generously made an exception for us."

"It wasn't generous at all," declared Marie-Laure. "He got paid very well for his flexibility."

"And he will get here," said Hugo, in a soothing voice. "I suggest we go ahead as planned, and when he arrives, he can perform his legal magic."

"But the civil ceremony is always before the sacramental . . ." protested Marie-Laure.

"It doesn't matter, Marie-Laure," said Hugo, in no uncertain terms. "They will be married in the eyes of God, after all, and as for the eyes of the Republic," he continued, with a shrug, "that will take place also. Hopefully sooner, rather than later."

"It had better be sooner," grumbled Marie-Laure, checking her tiny little gold watch. "Ah, well, the photographer should be here any minute. . . ."

And with impeccable timing, the photographer had appeared in the doorway and Marie-Laure acknowledged his arrival with a curt nod. "In the garden, I think, since Monsieur DuPont is absent," she suggested, gathering up Elizabeth and Jean-Luc and heading off with the little group to organize some casual pre-wedding photos.

Hugo retreated to the now empty study, shutting the door behind him, leaving Lucy alone in the hallway with Sara and Zoe. "Crisis averted, I guess," she said, laughing. "But I wouldn't want to be in Monsieur DuPont's shoes."

"That was some show," said Zoe, also laughing.

"I don't think the wedding can hold a candle to it," said Sara.

Lucy couldn't stop laughing. It wasn't just Marie-Laure's loss of control, it was the accumulated tension of the past few days, finding release. She collapsed on the stairs, holding her stomach, which was beginning to hurt from laughing so hard. The girls joined her, caught up in the contagious laughter, until they were confronted by Bill. "What's so funny?" he asked, checking his watch as he hurried down the hall to join them.

"Too bad you missed it," said Zoe, shoulders heaving with laughter.

He looked ashamed, as if he'd made a faux pas. "Don't tell me I missed the civil ceremony? Did I have the time wrong? I thought I was early."

"You didn't miss anything," said Lucy. "It didn't happen. The mayor is stuck in traffic."

"Marie-Laure had a fit," added Sara, wiping her eyes and getting to her feet.

Bill thought this over. "I would've liked to have seen that," he finally said. "C'mon, people are gathering. Let's join the circus."

Lucy smoothed her skirt, smiled at her husband, and realized she felt much better. If she could laugh, she decided, things really couldn't be all that bad. The laughter had been just what she needed; now she finally felt able to enjoy Elizabeth's wedding. The sun was shining, the birds were singing, and all the fabulous preparations were in place. She reached for Bill's hand and he clasped hers, giving it a squeeze. Together, they walked out onto the terrace, followed by the girls, and paused to take in the view. Beautifully dressed guests were arriving, enjoying the garden as they made their way to the chapel. The enormous white tent, pennants flying, provided a festive atmosphere, and in the distance in a far corner of the garden, Lucy spotted the wedding party, Elizabeth and Jean-Luc along with a half-dozen young attendants, including Patrick, posing for photos.

"I still don't understand why we're not bridesmaids," grumbled Sara.

"It seems that in Europe it's traditional to have children," said Lucy.

"Yeah, because the brides don't want any competition, they don't want to be upstaged," said Zoe.

"These French girls think of everything," added Sara, darkly.

"But at least we didn't have to buy some ugly dresses we'll never wear again," said Zoe, looking on the bright side and causing Lucy to smile.

"Let's go, Bill," she suggested. "We can use our phones and get some photos of Patrick."

"He'll never forgive us. I'm sure he doesn't want any photographic evidence of those fancy pants."

"So true," agreed Lucy. "We can use them for black-mail, in the future. . . ."

But when they reached the garden corner where the wedding party was posing, Patrick actually seemed pleased as punch with all the attention he was receiving. He, and the other young attendants, all looked adorable in their finery. Patrick and the other page were wearing matching white ruffled blouses, sage-green satin breeches, stockings, and black pumps, with wide silk sashes tied round their waists. The little girls, four of them, were similarly dressed in ballet-length sage-green satin dresses, white stockings, and Mary Janes, and also with matching forest-green sashes.

Lucy joined Toby and Molly, who were standing by proudly, obviously relieved by Patrick's change in attitude. "Things are getting off to a good start," said Toby, with an approving nod.

"Let's hope it stays that way," said Lucy.

Bill took her hand. "It's going to be great, don't worry," he said. "Just look, Elizabeth is so happy."

Lucy looked and had to agree. She had never seen her cantankerous, difficult daughter look so full of joy. Radiant, actually, as she posed for the camera with Jean-Luc's hands around her waist, her head turned as she gazed into his eyes. Lucy sighed and sent up a little prayer, a little wish that Elizabeth's happiness would last.

Then Marie-Laure clapped her hands, announced it was time to go to the chapel, and they all began a leisurely procession through the garden, past the little squares and triangles of colorful bedding plants, all neatly contained by low borders of clipped boxwood hedging. Reaching the chapel, they paused in the back of the church, where every seat, apart from those reserved for family members, was filled and a string quartet was playing the prelude. Jean-Luc planted a kiss on Elizabeth's cheek, whispered something into her ear, and made his way down a side aisle to his place in the front of the church, where his best man, Claude, was already standing. Jerry, the other grooms-man, escorted Zoe and Sara to their seats in the first pew. He then returned and offered his arm to Marie-Laure, and she proceeded gracefully down the aisle to her seat on the groom's side of the aisle. Jerry again returned to escort Lucy to her seat, opposite Marie-Laure's, and she took his arm, straightened her back, and set off. Behind them, she knew, the little attendants were lining up and Elizabeth was taking her father's arm, waiting to begin the walk down the aisle, into her future.

Lucy took her seat, beside Sara and Zoe, and Jerry went to stand beside Jean-Luc and Claude. The priest, splen-didly robed in embroidered silk, took his place and a string quartet struck the familiar strains of the wedding march. All heads turned to see the bride, but Lucy looked at Jean-Luc, eager to see his reaction as his bride ap-proached. She was not disappointed; Jean-Luc stood transfixed, as if he'd never seen anyone so beautiful. Her heart lifted at the sight and she turned to watch the bridal procession, led by two tiny flower girls, holding their rib-boned baskets of pink rose petals. Reminded by someone on the aisle, a relative perhaps, they each grabbed a fistful of petals and dropped it, all in a clump, and continued in that fashion, every now and then throwing a ball of mashed petals onto the white carpet. Somewhere, Lucy knew, their mothers were shaking their heads in embarrassment. The tiny girls were followed by the two pages, each carrying a velvet pillow with a wedding ring tied securely in place with a white ribbon. Good thing, because the boys were flipping the pillows every which way, as if preparing to drop and kick them onto a soccer field. Then came the older bridesmaids, two girls in their early teens, smiling self-consciously and holding their bouquets tightly as they stepped-and-paused their way down the aisle. And then, finally, there was Elizabeth, the beautiful bride, on the arm of her proud father. Lucy wished she could capture the image forever and then, remembering that she could, raised her phone to snap the photo. It was exactly at that moment when a single shot rang out.

There was a collective, horrified gasp. Zoe, who was seated next to her, immediately shoved her down between the pews, for safety, and she felt her heart pounding in fear. There were no more shots, just the one, so she cautiously raised her head by inches and peered over the back of the pew, allowing her instincts as a reporter and keen observer to kick in. Zoe and Sara, crouching beside her in the pew, were all right, as were Molly and Toby in the pew behind them. Bill had immediately shoved Elizabeth to the ground, and was crouched in a defensive posture above her. The attendants had been grabbed by nearby adults and pulled into the pews for shelter; the littlest girls were crying but Patrick was looking about with interest. Somewhat reassured, she surveyed the chapel, checking to see if anyone was hit. It seemed not, all the wedding guests seemed okay, she thought, with a huge sense of relief, noting that a few people were gradually peeking out from their sheltered positions between the pews. She then whipped her head around to see the front of the church where the groom was waiting for his bride. At that moment, she watched in horror as Jean-Luc collapsed, falling at the feet of the priest.

Most of the guests remained crouched like Lucy between the pews, but a few brave souls were on their feet, pointing up at the loft. Looking upward she saw the black-suited musicians were shocked into immobility, and the lady soloist was hunched over and hugging the railing for dear life. "The shooter! He was up there!" someone yelled, pointing. Already several men in gray suits, certainly Chris Kennedy's operatives, were charging out of the church, in pursuit of the shooter. Hugo was at his son's side, calling for a doctor, and Marie-Laure, hands trembling, was on her phone, calling for help.

Elizabeth! Lucy found her on her feet, midway down the aisle, shaking and sobbing on her father's shoulder. His arms wrapped around her, Bill helped her make her way down the aisle to her bridegroom. An embroidered white altar cloth had been wrapped around his chest as a bandage, already stained with a steadily growing patch of blood. Not a bad sign, Lucy told herself. If he was still bleeding he must be alive. Wounded but clinging to life. Some people were frozen in place, absolutely stunned; others were still crouching between the pews, fearing more shots. The parents of the young attendants were consoling their children; several guests who had medical training were attending to Jean-Luc, watched anxiously by Marie-Laure and Hugo. When Elizabeth and Bill joined them, Marie-Laure embraced Elizabeth and wiped her eyes with a handkerchief, which she pressed into her hand.

A commotion at the door announced the arrival of the ambulance team, who were rushing down the aisle with a wheeled gurney loaded with cases of equipment. There were three EMTs and they went into action right away, lifting Jean-Luc onto the stretcher and whisking him away. Hugo and Marie-Laure followed, their faces masks of anxiety. Lucy reached for Marie-Laure, hoping to give her a quick word as she passed, but she flew by, intent on accompanying her son.

Lucy then hurried over to Elizabeth, who was now sitting on the altar steps, slumped against her father. "I'm sure he'll be all right," said Lucy, who wasn't sure at all.

"Why? Why would somebody shoot Jean-Luc?" Elizabeth kept shaking her head, her face a mask of tragedy. "It's unbelievable. He wouldn't hurt a fly," she declared, as Sara and Zoe joined her on the steps, one on each side of their sister. "Honest, I've seen him carefully scoop up spiders and set them free outside. Why? And on our wedding day." She sniffed and brushed away a tear. "We were so happy."

Lucy had a few ideas: organized crime, perhaps? Like maybe the disgruntled tenants who'd been evicted from the farm? Marie-Laure could have made more than a few enemies in her relentless pursuit of success, enemies who wouldn't mind taking her down a peg. Jean-Luc himself was certainly mild-mannered, but what did he do on those business trips of his? He might well have got involved with the wrong people, buying or selling drugs, for example, or even sex trafficking. The one thing that stood out to Lucy was the fact that Jean-Luc was most certainly the intended target, and the shooting had been carefully planned. Almost as carefully as Marie-Laure's plans for the wedding and for the couple's future, a thought that gave Lucy pause. Did Marie-Laure orchestrate the shooting of her own son? She was stunned to realize it didn't seem all that impossible, especially if Jean-Luc had become a dangerous liability and she could replace him with capable Elizabeth. But no, Lucy wasn't going to go down that rabbit hole. She was going to focus on her daughter, on her family. They were her top priority, she had to help them deal with this shocking development.

She sat down on the altar steps, next to her daughters.

Toby and Molly joined them, both holding Patrick by the hand. Bill carefully picked up the bouquet that Elizabeth had dropped and held it.

"Everybody's okay, right?" asked Bill.

They all nodded. Nobody seemed to have anything to say, they simply gathered together, each member of the family trying to process what had happened.

It was Elizabeth who broke the ice. "Do you think I should go to the hospital?"

"Yes," said Lucy, seizing the opportunity for action, any sort of action. "Let's get you changed into something more comfortable, first."

"I'll drive her," said Bill, helping her to her feet. "I'm sure they'll let me borrow a car."

"We'll help her change," offered Sara. "Right, Zoe?"

"No," declared Elizabeth. "I'm going like this. Let everybody see what they did."

Lucy watched as Bill and Elizabeth retraced their steps down the aisle, where the white carpet was now rumpled and smudged. She remembered she'd been taking a photograph at the very moment the shot rang out, so she checked her phone. Sure enough, she hadn't had time to frame the photo properly and she'd captured only Elizabeth's and Bill's heads, cutting off their bodies. But she had caught the loft and in the very top of the photo, standing behind the musicians, was a figure in a dark suit, with a scarf pulled up over his face. He was holding what looked to Lucy like an assault rifle, aimed downward toward the front of the church. She had caught the shooter in the act.

Looking up, she spotted Chris, passing them in the aisle, and hurried to meet him, phone in hand. "I got a picture of the shooter," she told him.

"Let me see," he said, taking the phone. "He got away, probably blended in with the crowd, I guess. He was dressed appropriately enough, certainly a pro, he wouldn't have aroused any suspicion."

"What about the gun?"

"Left in the stairs to the loft."

"Fingerprints?"

"Not a chance," said Chris, indicating the black gloves pictured in the photo. "Can you send this to my phone?"

Once he'd received the photo, he reached for her arm. "Are you all okay?" he asked.

"Pretty shaken up, like everyone."

"What about Elizabeth?"

"She doesn't understand why anyone would shoot Jean-Luc," said Lucy. "She's on her way to the hospital, Bill's taking her."

He nodded. "People are gathering in the tent, Hugo sent word that the luncheon should be served and the guests accommodated, given whatever they need, while they wait for the police to interview them."

"I need a stiff drink," said Lucy, getting a smile from Chris as a siren was heard, distant at first but coming closer.

"Police are arriving, so I should meet them." Chris seemed reluctant to leave her. "Be sure to let Elizabeth know that she can count on me. I will get this creep, I'll get to the bottom of this."

Lucy smiled. "I'll tell her." She squeezed his arm and gave him a little shove. "Go get 'im."

He saluted, and Lucy watched as he marched off. Then she joined her family, Sara and Zoe, Molly and Toby, who were still sitting on the altar steps, forming a circle around Patrick. "Word is, we're supposed to go to the tent. They're serving food and everyone has to wait there for the police."

"Are they going to question us?" asked Molly, wrapping a protective arm around Patrick's shoulders.

"I don't know how they do it in France, but in the US with so many witnesses they'd most likely just check everyone's ID and take down contact info to follow up later," said Lucy, suddenly feeling wiped out. "I don't know about you, but I'm done in. I could use some food, and drink."

"Me too," said Sara, looking pale and shaken.

"What a shocker," said Zoe, taking her sister's hand.

They got up and began walking together toward the side door of the chapel, which led to the tent. As they went, Toby bent down and asked her a question. "Who was that guy you were talking to?"

"Security," said Lucy.

"Well, he did a lousy job," said Toby.

"He's American. Used to work for the Secret Service, but now he's got his own firm. Quite successful, I gather." She paused. "He also happens to be one of Elizabeth's old boyfriends."

"Chris is here?" asked Sara, surprised.

"Ooh la la," said Zoe.

"Well, that does put a different spin on things," said Toby. "Maybe his heart wasn't in the job."

Chapter Sixteen

That was something to consider, mused Lucy, as they made their way to the tent. Was Chris himself the killer? Every fiber of her being resisted the notion, but it kind of lingered, hovering out there as a possibility. She tried to think it through, figure if he could actually have done it. The killer, she knew from the photo, was in a black suit, while Chris was wearing gray. He wouldn't have had time to change, for one thing. And he was certainly busy during the ceremony, supervising his operatives and making sure the security plan was running smoothly. But what about those operatives? Could one of them been the shooter? Either working for Chris, or for someone else?

"Toby to Mom, Toby to Mom, the spaceship has landed, we're back on earth."

"Sorry. I was just thinking," she said, quickly, with an apologetic smile. They were just outside the tent, where guests were huddled at the tables, conversing in quiet tones. Uniformed police were moving among them, checking IDs and filling notebooks with contact information.

"So, what's the plan?" asked Toby. "Do we just sit down somewhere?"

Lucy glanced around the tent, so beautifully decorated with flowers and crystal chandeliers, the fabric walls disguised with wallpapered panels and displaying paintings from the family collection. A harpist was seated on a raised dais, playing some sort of New Agey tune. Under normal conditions, she probably wouldn't have been heard over the celebratory din, but today no voices competed with her plaintive notes.

"I guess we should follow the seating plan," suggested Molly.

Lucy noticed that the head table, where she would have been seated, was empty. Toby's family, she knew, had been assigned to a nearby table, which was also empty. "Let's all sit together," she said, impulsively, leading the way. "I don't want to be all by myself."

They'd no sooner seated themselves than a server appeared, advising them that they could either have the full meal prepared for the reception, or if they preferred, could request something lighter. This simple choice completely flummoxed Lucy; she didn't know what she wanted. "I'll have a whiskey," she said, "and whatever's easiest for you."

"Same for me," said Toby. "White wine for my wife . . ."

"Us too," said Sara, speaking for herself and Zoe. "Large ones."

". . . and how about a Coke for my son?" finished Toby.

"Can I have French fries? *Frites?*" asked Patrick, taking advantage of his distraught parents, who normally strictly limited such unhealthy food. As he'd suspected, they raised no objection.

"Absolutely," said the server. "I will bring *frites* for the young gentleman, and a selection of hors d'oeuvres, also. Then, if you want something more, just ask. I am happy to oblige."

The drinks came, and the promised hors d'oeuvres and *frites*. Lucy sipped her drink and nibbled on savory petits fours, feeling numb. That's how it was after a shock, she thought, you just had to let it all sink in. Images flitted through her mind: the photo of the shooter, Elizabeth's horrified expression, the crouched and frightened people. She hoped Jean-Luc wasn't seriously wounded and would recover. She hoped the shooter would be caught. She hoped Elizabeth would . . . she wasn't sure what she hoped for Elizabeth, except that she wanted her to be happy. And then she realized she needed to find a ladies' room, rather urgently, in fact.

"Anybody want to come with me?" she asked, standing up. "I'm going to the loo."

"I'm okay," said Molly, who was somewhat scandalized, watching Patrick tuck into his fries with gusto. Sara and Zoe shook their heads, well into second servings of sauvignon blanc.

"And it looks like Patrick is coping with shock quite well, if his appetite is any indication," observed his father.

"I'll be right back," promised Lucy, winging off like a homing pigeon fixed on reaching its coop. Mission completed, she dallied as she wound her way through the tables, eavesdropping as she went. Several guests, those confident of their English, stopped her as she passed and offered their sympathy.

"Such a shame," said one lady, clasping Lucy's hand in hers, which Lucy couldn't help noticing was adorned with at least a five-carat diamond ring. A bunch of gold bracelets jangled on each wrist and a large gold cross hung from her neck, mingled with several pearl necklaces. "Such a beautiful couple." She met Lucy's eyes. "I am praying for them."

"Thank you," said Lucy. "Please, if you noticed any- thing at all, do tell the police. Will you do that?"

"Of course," said the lady, releasing Lucy's hand with a sad smile.

Another guest, an older gentleman with a neatly clipped mustache, rose as she passed his table. "Madame Stone, please allow me to offer my services," he said, taking her hand and kissing it. "If there is anything I can do for you, do not hesitate to ask."

Somewhat taken aback, Lucy tried to think of a polite way to inquire as to precisely what services he was pre- pared to offer. Realizing her hesitation, he was quick to apologize.

"Ah, madame, of course, you don't know who I am. I am Benoit Espinasse, the minister of defense."

Somewhat awed, Lucy smiled at the minister. "I appre- ciate your offer, but I don't think we will need to call out the troops."

He patted her hand. "Probably not, but there are other things I can do." He produced a card and gave it to her. "Don't hesitate to call me," he said. "I am at your ser- vice."

"Thank you so much," said Lucy, moving on, catching scraps of conversations, words here and there. Several words seemed to be on everyone's lips: "*filles*," which she knew meant girls, "*putains*" or whores, and "*gitans*," or Gypsies. It seemed everyone had heard about the brothel, despite Marie-Laure's efforts to eliminate it. But why were they talking about Gypsies? Lucy knew that Gypsies, or Roma, as they preferred to be known, were a despised mi- nority in much of Europe, often suspected of crimes they didn't commit. Were Roma involved in the brothel? Or had something else happened, something people were gossiping about? Sometimes when she approached, people fell silent, other times they were so involved in their whispered conversations that they didn't notice her. "*Scandale*," she heard, and "*quelle catastrophe*." Marie-Laure's name was mentioned, heads were shaken, and tongues clicked. She was dying to know more, to ask questions, but doubted people would speak freely to her, a foreigner and by definition, a stranger, even if she could surmount the language barrier.

A slender lady in a flowered dress tapped on her shoulder, and turning, Lucy recognized one of the women she'd met when arranging the flowers, Françoise.

"*Désolé*," began Françoise, then switched to English, struggling to find the right words. "Very terrible for you, I am so sorry."

"Yes," agreed Lucy. "It is terrible. Unimaginable." She managed a rueful smile. "But I do think our flowers look very well."

The woman smiled and put her hand over her heart. "I hope, *je prie*, that we are not arranging flowers for Jean-Luc's funeral."

Lucy took her hand and gave it a squeeze. "Forgive me," she began, "but perhaps I can impose on your good will? I am an outsider here, and I have many questions."

Françoise nodded and pulled her away from the table, where other guests were observing their interaction. "What do you want to know?" she asked, leaning close and presenting an ear for Lucy's question.

"Do you think . . . do people suspect that Jean-Luc, or his family, are involved in . . . ?" She left off, not wanting to utter the word *crime*, finishing with a smirk and a shrug.

Lucy expected her friend to raise her eyebrows in shock

and pull away in disgust at this terribly inappropriate, probing question, but she didn't. Instead, she gave a tiny nod and said, merely, "Perhaps. Some people think so." Then she broke into a conspiratorial smile. "Others say Marie-Laure would never allow such a thing."

"What do you think? Is it something to do with *les gitans*?"

"Possibly," admitted the woman, stepping away and obviously uneasy with the topic.

"I'm sorry," said Lucy, "I didn't mean to make you uncomfortable."

"Not at all," said Françoise, clearly disinclined to continue the conversation and eager to join her friends at the table.

Lucy nodded in farewell and moved on, thinking about what the flower lady had said and wondering what the neighbors and locals really thought of the Schoen-Renes. Were they respected as gentry, upstanding folk above reproach, or were they believed to be involved with criminals? Maybe even organized crime? More and more, she thought, the château had been revealed as a fantasy, a Potemkin village, hiding a crumbling and corrupt establishment.

"But what is their choice?" a very British voice was heard to rise above the others. "You know yourself, Toby, it's beastly difficult to keep a place like this running. Roofs, drains, dry rot, there's always something. These châteaux absolutely eat cash."

When she approached her table she noticed a uniformed officer also approaching from the opposite direction. "I am Officier Lucien Laurent, with the OPJ," he announced. "Do you mind if I collect your personal information?" he asked Toby, speaking heavily accented English.

"Are you a gendarme?" asked Patrick. "I saw gendarmes in Paris."

"*Oui*. The OPJ, *officiers de police judiciare*, mmm, how you say? we are under the supervision of the *Gendarmerie*." He smiled at Patrick. "My unit is the *Section de Recherche*, we investigate the crimes local."

Taking her place with the others at the table, Lucy noticed that young Officer Laurent looked very dashing indeed in his dark blue uniform, which unlike American uniforms showed his slim physique to advantage. His nose, however, was a bit large. "Ah, madame," he said, removing his hat and respectfully nodding his head. "May I begin with you?"

"I am Lucy Stone. . . ." she began.

"*Mes condoléances, madame*," he said. "I understand you are the mother of the bride?"

"That is true," said Lucy, going on to give her address and phone number.

He then moved on to the others at the table, carefully noting down their information in his cell phone, double-checking Zoe's phone number. Hearing that Toby's family came all the way from Alaska, he seemed quite impressed. "Is it true, there are polar bears in Alaska?" he asked. "And is it very cold all the time, even in summer?"

"We have summer," offered Toby, "but it isn't very hot and doesn't last very long."

"The days are long in summer?"

"Yes," said Molly. "And very, very short in winter."

"And the bears? Do you see them?"

"Not in Anchorage, the city where we live, but my work takes me into the country and I have seen them there. They dig into people's trash."

The gendarme shook his head in amazement. "I have

seen them in the *parc zoologique*. They are in danger," he added, pronouncing it dahn-jaire."

Toby couldn't resist raising his favorite topic: "As are we all. We're all in danger from climate change."

"I agree most strongly," said the gendarme, indicating Patrick. "We must preserve the environment for the children. So they will have a future." Then, recollecting his job, he nodded and gave Zoe a big smile before moving on to the next table. Before he could leave, Lucy asked if he'd gotten any information about the shooting from the other guests.

"They were very upset, very shocked," he said, speaking in a serious tone. "The bride, so beautiful, the event so *élégante*, they were most pleased when the family invited them to partake of the *déjeuner*." He paused and lowered his voice, sharing a confidence. "Many said the wine is absolutely spectacular."

Lucy was charmed and amused by this young officer's account, but he wasn't telling her what she wanted to hear. "That is very good to know, but I was asking about the crime, the shooting. Did anyone recognize the shooter? Did anyone suggest a motive? We can't understand why anyone would shoot Jean-Luc."

"The investigation is just beginning," he replied. "All will be revealed in time."

"I have heard rumors about the château and the family," said Lucy, persisting. "Some people seem to think there are connections to organized crime. . . ."

The gendarme's eyebrows shot up. "*Le Milieu?*"

"If that's what you call it," said Lucy. "Organized crime, gangs. There was a . . ." She paused, mindful of Toby's big ears. "*Une ferme, avec les putains*," she said, unsure she was getting it right.

From the gendarme's expression, she thought she had. He was retreating into his official role like a turtle withdrawing into its shell. "I do not know, madame, but I can assure you that the investigation will be most thorough."

He suddenly snapped to attention, saluting, and Lucy realized that a more senior officer, in plain clothes, had arrived. "Allow me to introduce myself," he began, with a genial smile. "I am Pierre St. Martin, the *procureur*. I understand you are Americans?"

"Yes," said Lucy, taking in his short gray hair, substantial girth, and well-worn suit that had given up any pretense to tailoring and had long ago yielded to his bumps and bulges. His expression was kind, his eyes sympathetic, but Lucy wasn't entirely fooled. The *procureur*, she knew, was responsible for the investigation, similar to an American DA, but with greater authority.

"My role is to oversee the investigation into this deplorable event," St. Martin said, shaking his head. "The officers will compile a *dossier*, which we will present to the *juge d'instruction*, and *le juge* will create a *reconstitution*, which will be a complete explanation of the crime." He paused, checking to see if they understood. Getting nods, he continued. "I wish to assure you that as *parties civile*, you will have complete access to the investigation as it proceeds. And now, if you do not mind, I must request your passports."

Lucy had been down this road before, on a previous visit to France when the chef for a cooking class she was attending was killed. She remembered spending long weeks in Paris, without a passport and unable to return home. "Our passports? Is that absolutely necessary?"

"Yes. We will keep your passports for the duration of the investigation. It is the law."

"How long do you expect the investigation to take?" asked Toby.

St. Martin shrugged. "As long as it takes."

"But I have responsibilities at home. We all do. We must get back to our jobs."

"That's right," said Sara. "We can't stay here indefinitely."

"In America, I understand, you must work all the time, not like in France." He shook his head, then brightened. "But your accommodation is happily not a problem," St. Martin informed them. "Madame Schoen-Rene has agreed, in fact, Madame has said she will be most pleased to offer you accommodation here at the château for as long as it is needed."

"Excuse me," said Molly, a mother bear defending her cub, "but are you really saying that we must continue to remain in an actual crime scene? With our child? Among people who may very well be involved, are perhaps criminals themselves. People don't just get shot for no reason, you know." She narrowed her eyes suspiciously. "Something is going on here and it isn't good."

"At the very least," added Lucy, "Patrick has had a traumatic experience, that could have lasting effects."

St. Martin eyed Patrick, who had moved on from his fries and was systematically working his way through the remaining hors d'oeuvres. "The young man seems to be coping well. He has a good appetite, no?"

"An eating disorder!" exclaimed Molly. "He's eating because he's upset."

"Then, madame, I suggest you seek therapy for your son. It is widely available here in France, you will find it is part of our national health system."

"I think the best treatment for our son would be to get

him back home, into his familiar routine," said Toby, struggling to maintain a reasonable tone of voice. "We will be happy to stay in touch, we have computers and phones, we can be easily contacted whenever needed to answer any questions that come up."

"Alas, monsieur, the French legal system remains old-fashioned. We rely on people, not machines. The criminal, even, will be treated as a fellow human being." He chuckled. "Murderers, I must admit, are often not in the best frame of mind when confronted with their crime and the certainty of a long imprisonment. Our goal is to bring the criminal not only to justice, but to an acknowledgment and understanding of the crime. We wish to make not only the victims but also the criminal whole again."

"Well, that's all very well and good," snapped Lucy, "but I don't see what it has to do with me or my family. We want to go home."

"*Désolé*. That is not possible. I assume you do not have your passports with you? They are in your rooms?"

Reluctantly, Lucy nodded.

"I will have an officer accompany you and when you surrender your passports you will receive proper documentation. You will remain here, if you please, until the officer is made available to you. Do you understand?"

"What I understand is that we're being detained, not the criminal," grumbled Toby. "Apparently in France, everyone is guilty until proven innocent."

"Precisely," said St. Martin, with a condescending smile. "Precisely."

Chapter Seventeen

The *procureur* left to go about his business, leaving Lucy, Patrick, Toby, and Molly at the table. Lucy knew she had no choice but to be compliant but was seething with resentment.

"Honestly, who do these French think they are?" demanded Sara, apparently in agreement.

"They can't just keep us here, forever," added Zoe. "This investigation could take a long time, it doesn't seem like they're trying very hard."

It was true, thought Lucy, looking around the tent where a handful of uniformed officers were chatting pleasantly with the guests, now and then making a notation in their cell phones. So far there had been no sign of a forensic team, although there was crime scene tape around the chapel. She thought of the day the girl's body had been discovered in the moat and wondered if the investigators were making a connection. After all, there couldn't be that many police officers in a little country town like this; it must have occurred to the investigators that they were returning to the scene of a previous crime. A crime committed mere days ago. Wasn't that suspicious? Why hadn't they asked about it? But they hadn't posed any questions, they had only asked for identification and demanded their passports.

"I think we're going to be here for quite a while," said Lucy.

"No, an officer is coming our way," said Toby. "I think we'll be able to go to our rooms."

"That's not what I meant," said Lucy, practically snarling. "I mean staying in France. It looks to me like this investigation is getting off to a very slow start."

The officer, a genial middle-aged man, greeted them with a polite salute, and requested that they accompany him to their rooms to surrender their passports.

They got to their feet slowly, signaling with their body language that this was the last thing they wanted to do, and shuffled along, aware that they had become objects of interest to everyone in the tent. All eyes were on them as they made their way through the tables. "We're not the guilty ones," muttered Molly. "Why are they staring at us?"

"We're the foreigners, the Americans. The outsiders. Next thing you know, we'll be in jail," growled Toby.

"Do you have a jail?" asked Patrick, impressed by the gendarme's natty uniform. "Do you have a gun?"

The gendarme, who probably had kids of his own, gave Toby an indulgent smile. "Ah, yes. We have guns. We have a jail. But we do not like to use them."

"I would," declared Toby. "I'd shoot the bad guys and throw them all in jail!"

By now they had left the tent and were outside, following the path that led round the château to the terrace. The sun was still shining, the sky was blue, the garden continued blooming in neatly ordered squares and triangles, but to Lucy everything had changed. It was all very beautiful, but it was still a prison and she and her family were all prisoners.

She was in that glum mood when, much to her surprise, a couple of goats suddenly appeared in the garden, escapees from the château's farm. They all stood, riveted, watching as the goats began nibbling on a bed of blooming impatiens. "C'mon, Patrick," said Bill, "we better round up those critters. Okay with you?" he asked the gendarme.

The officer smiled. "*Bien sûr.*" Toby also decided to help out so off they ran, joining a couple of farmworkers who had now appeared, all hot in pursuit of the goats who were heading toward the swimming pool. Lucy, the girls, and Molly were left with the gendarme, who was apparently familiar with the château and had been advised of their room numbers and locations, and he led the way. Reaching the first room on his list, he waited in the hall with the others as Lucy retrieved her and Bill's passports from the mini-safe in one of the armoires. Giving them to him, she felt as if she was giving up part of herself: her freedom. She no longer felt like an American, she realized, and she certainly wasn't French. She was without a country, a displaced person. An alien.

After the others had departed with the gendarme, Lucy sat down on the bed, feeling very low. She had no energy, no ideas, nada. She was completely wiped out; she had nothing, she decided. No plans, no future except this horrid château. She was tired, so tired, but knew she was much too tense to even attempt a nap. Nevertheless, she flopped down onto the bed and pulled a pillow over her face, shutting out everything. Well, except her hearing, because after a few minutes she heard the door open and Bill's voice, talking to someone.

Someone's voice responded, saying, "First thing, you've got to contact the embassy."

Lucy removed the pillow and sat up, discovering Chris standing in the middle of the room with Bill. "Any news?" she asked.

"No. They took Jean-Luc right into surgery. I left Elizabeth at the hospital with Hugo and Marie-Laure and came back here where I ran into Chris. He's offered to help us, and says the first thing we must do is report our situation to the embassy."

"Good idea, but with what?" she asked. "They took our passports."

"Did you make copies?" asked Chris.

Lucy knew she should have, but hadn't. She'd been too busy finishing up her work at the paper and getting ready for the trip. That was one little detail she'd missed.

"Of course," said Bill, pulling his suitcase down from the top of an armoire and unzipping it. Once it was open, he unzipped the lining and produced several sheets of copier paper. "Passports, credit cards, PINs, bank accounts, it's all here," he said.

"All you need are the passport numbers," said Chris, producing his phone and hitting a speed dial number.

"The embassy wasn't much help before," said Lucy, remembering frustrating dealings with a very junior member of the diplomatic staff.

"Ah, yes," said Chris, identifying himself on the phone. "I have here an American family who are being detained relative to a crime and have been required to surrender their passports. I am going to put the head of the family, Mr. Bill Stone, on the phone."

He handed the phone to Bill, who provided his and Lucy's passport numbers, described the shooting and their current situation, listed the other members of the family, and promised to provide their passport information. He then made a writing gesture with his hand and Chris grabbed the notepad provided by the château, complete with crest insignia, and wrote down the embassy official's contact information.

"This fella seems on the ball," observed Bill, after the call had ended.

"Yeah. He's the ambassador's personal assistant," said Chris.

Maybe, just maybe, thought Lucy, things would be different this time. Now, it seemed, they had friends in high places. Even, she thought, fingering the card she'd tucked in her pocket, the minister of defense.

"So how long do you think this investigation will take?" Bill asked Chris.

Chris stared out the window for a long while before answering. "Like most everything in France, investigations are not rushed. They take as long as is considered necessary. Ideally, it's a truth-finding process, not adversarial, and the suspects are considered fellow human beings endowed with natural rights and are invited to participate in a search for the truth."

"Are you kidding me?" asked Bill.

"Yeah," chimed in Lucy. "I've seen these French crime shows, the movies. They don't seem all that different from American ones."

Chris smiled. "True, but remember, those shows are entertainment, and they're heavily influenced by Hollywood."

"So how long does a typical investigation take?" asked Bill, pressing the issue.

Reluctantly, Chris admitted the sad truth. "Sometimes, as long as two years."

"Two years!" exclaimed Bill.

"There's no way we can stay here for two years!" added Lucy.

"I don't think you need to worry," said Chris. "At this stage the police are simply checking identities, making sure you have no criminal record. Remember, you've also got the American embassy on your side, they can apply some pressure. Once you're cleared, they'll return your passports. I'm guessing two weeks, at most."

"But we're supposed to go home tomorrow," groaned Lucy.

"Think of it this way, two weeks is a lot better than two years," said Bill.

"And what about our plane tickets?"

"You better get right on that and change them. You won't have to make a reservation, you can leave the date open," advised Chris.

Bill went back to the suitcase, which he'd left open on the bed, and dug out the printouts he'd made of their tickets and began dialing the airline.

Lucy caught sight of herself in the dressing table mirror and realized she was still in her wedding suit, which hadn't held up well to the stress of the day. She was a wrinkled, crumpled mess, and the Spanx Sue had advised her to wear had scrunched up around her waist where it seemed to be interfering with normal bodily processes, like breathing. And her feet, in unaccustomed heels, were killing her. "Well, if you'll excuse me," she said, kicking off the shoes and gathering up some jeans and a shirt, "I'm going to get into something more comfortable."

"Good idea," said Bill, pulling off the tie which he had already loosened. He was still holding the phone to his ear, apparently on hold, and seated himself on the chaise, resigned to a long wait.

"Well, I'll leave you guys to it," said Chris. "I'd like to catch the *procureur* before he leaves, see how he thinks things are going."

"Thanks, Chris," said Bill, reaching out to grasp his hand and shaking it. "I really appreciate your help."

"It's my pleasure," replied Chris, with a serious nod, giving Lucy a little salute as he left the room.

While struggling out of the Spanx and the pantyhose, Lucy listened to Bill's negotiation with the airline representative. From what she heard, it seemed they would have to pay a hefty change fee, but the tickets would be valid for a year. "Not too bad," was Bill's verdict when the call ended. He glanced around and shrugged. "What now?"

"I don't know about you, but I feel all antsy. Let's go downstairs, get some fresh air," she suggested. "When I left, Patrick and Toby were chasing some goats that got loose."

"Fine," agreed Bill. "I'll get changed." He proceeded to get out of his suit, passing the pants and jacket to Lucy to hang up in the armoire. His dress shirt went in the hamper, and soon he was the same old Bill she knew and loved. Still more dressed up than usual, however, as he was wearing a polo shirt instead of his favorite Slack's Hardware T-shirt with his cargo shorts.

Finally ready to go, he grabbed Lucy's hand. "I'm all for checking on the goats, Lucy, but I'm not convinced you're really all that interested." He gave her a warning look. "I don't want you thinking you can start some sort of investigation of your own. We're in France, remember, not Tinker's Cove. The best thing for us is to lie low and keep quiet and stay out of the way. That way they'll soon realize we're not involved and let us go home."

Lucy stepped close and wrapped her arms around his neck. "Don't worry. I'll be good," she promised, giving him a quick kiss. Then, hand in hand, they made their way downstairs to the foyer, where they encountered Elizabeth, returning from the hospital.

She was a sorry sight, thought Lucy, taking her daughter in her arms for a hug. Her hair was mussed, her makeup smeared from tears, and her dress, that beautiful dress, was a mass of wrinkles. Her mood, however, as she pulled away from her mother, was joyful. "He's going to live," she exclaimed. "Jean-Luc was shot in the shoulder. He lost a lot of blood but no vital organs were hit. The main concern is whether he'll regain full use of his arm, they won't know about that for a while. But it's just his arm, and you know how they work miracles with physical therapy and all."

"That's great news," said Lucy, feeling a huge weight lift off her chest.

"Wow, he was lucky," said Bill. "He sure didn't look good when they took him away in that ambulance."

"I know," agreed Elizabeth, sniffling and wiping away a tear. "It was terrible."

Lucy wrapped her arm around her daughter's shoulders. "So what now? Change out of that dress? Get something to eat? Rest?"

"Food!" declared Elizabeth. "I'm starving."

"Stress does use up a lot of calories," said Lucy. "You'd think I'd be dropping the pounds, but no such luck. I guess it just makes me eat more."

"Well, I haven't eaten all day," said Elizabeth, "so let's go down to the kitchen and see what they've got."

"Good idea," chimed in Bill. "Those little sandwiches weren't very filling."

Elizabeth led the way through a series of hidden passages, cleverly designed so servants in the old days could come and go without disturbing their masters. And also, Lucy guessed, so those masters could secretly engage in romantic dalliances. Lucy found herself descending a steep, narrow staircase, so well worn that the treads dipped in the middle, and then entered a long utilitarian hallway devoid of any embellishment save a muddy-green shade of paint. Voices could be heard in the distance, growing louder as they advanced, and soon they found themselves in the middle of a very busy kitchen. Chefs, sous-chefs, dishwashers, all were scurrying back and forth, carrying out their various tasks.

No one noticed them at first, but then one cook exclaimed, "*La mariée!*" and everyone stopped in their tracks, concerned expressions on their faces. Silently, they waited to hear the news. Was Jean-Luc alive? Dead? In a coma? They all wanted to know, demanding answers in an assortment of languages.

Elizabeth smiled, and the tension in the room eased slightly. "He will be okay," she said, and they were all jumping and hugging and cheering.

This exuberant reaction surprised Lucy, who wouldn't have thought Jean-Luc was all that popular with the staff. Apparently, she was wrong. As she processed this her mind wandered to Hugo, and to Marie-Laure. She suspected Hugo was popular with his workers, but Marie-Laure? She seemed a stern taskmaster and Lucy suspected she was most likely resented. But now, in the belowstairs kitchen, it was all joy and rapture. There were pops as a couple of champagne bottles were opened, glasses were filled, and everybody toasted to Jean-Luc's health.

After she had drained her glass, Elizabeth asked if there was anything she could eat.

Immediately a table and chairs were produced, she was seated, and dishes began arriving in quick succession. Sandwiches? Quiche? Some soup? Can we cook something specially for you? What would you like?

"This is fine, more than I can manage," she said, greedily popping little toasts topped with pâté into her mouth, then moving on to a piece of sliced ham, which she rolled up and ate with her fingers. Lucy was a bit shocked by her daughter's lack of manners, but her appetite met with great approval from the kitchen staff, who nodded and beamed at her as they presented various dishes. They invited Lucy and Bill to partake, also, and they soon found themselves digging into the most delicious array of leftovers that could be imagined.

Lucy suddenly had a huge appetite, stress-induced, she told herself, and dived into a steaming bowl of delicious onion soup, a roast beef sandwich, and enjoyed a bottomless flute of champagne. Bill asked for, and got, a beer, and was chomping on a slim baguette stuffed with veggies and cheese. Then the desserts arrived, slices of wedding cake, but also little fruit tarts and flaky pastries, filled with cream.

Finally, stomachs stuffed, they had to stop. Tiny cups of coffee were provided, which they sipped gratefully, sated. It was then that Chris arrived, carrying a bottle of scotch.

"They told me you were here," he said, greeting Elizabeth. "I hear it's nothing but good news. Jean-Luc is going to be okay."

"That's what the doctors say. They wouldn't let me see him, but he was out of surgery and in recovery. His parents are there."

"I brought you this, I thought you could use a pick-me-up," said Chris, plucking a glass from a shelf and pouring in a finger of whiskey. He gave it to her, saying, "It's the Balvenie. I remember how much you like it."

Elizabeth stared at the glass, picked it up and took a sip, then let it drop from her fingers as she burst into tears. Floods of tears. Lucy reached out to console her daughter, take her in her arms, but Chris was ahead of her. He'd pulled Elizabeth to her feet, wrapped his arms around her, and held her close. Chest heaving she sobbed and sobbed into his shoulder, hugging him tightly for all she was worth.

Lucy's jaw dropped. Bill sat riveted by the spectacle. Then he turned and their eyes met. They were both thinking the same thing: What the hell?

Chapter Eighteen

Next morning Lucy woke up to the beeping of a reversing truck and the shouts of workmen. Tossing back the covers she made her way to the window, where she was just in time to see the tent collapse. The gleaming white marquee, supported by tall poles that raised the roof into two fairy-tale-castle points topped with colorful pennants, was now nothing more than a puddle of white plastic spread out on the ground. A fitting symbol, she thought morosely, for all their dashed hopes. Her hope for a fabulous family vacation, and more especially, certainly, Elizabeth's hopes for a happy marriage and bright future with Jean-Luc. She let out a huge sigh, which was caught by Bill, emerging from the bathroom.

"It's not so bad," he said, stepping beside her at the window and taking her hand. "So the fancy-shmancy wedding didn't happen, but Jean-Luc is on the mend. They can do the deed when he's better, maybe a smaller affair."

"I wonder if that will actually happen," mused Lucy. "She seemed awfully happy to see Chris yesterday."

"I think it was just a momentary thing, an emotional breakdown. A familiar face, relief over Jean-Luc, a shoulder to cry on."

"She seemed to recover pretty quickly, when he wiped her eyes with his handkerchief," said Lucy, recalling the tender scene. "You gotta love a guy who carries a big old clean white handkerchief in his pocket, just in case he encounters a lady in distress."

"Well, she's still wearing a big honking diamond on her finger," said Bill. "It took her long enough to make up her mind, and I don't think she's going to change it any time soon. Not if I know our Elizabeth."

"She is certainly stubborn, once she commits to something." Lucy raised herself on her tiptoes and gave Bill a peck on the cheek. "Might as well look on the bright side. It isn't what we planned, but it looks like we'll have a longer vacation than we expected."

"That's the spirit." Bill gave her a pat on the bottom. "I'll call for some breakfast, how about that?"

"Ask for extra coffee," suggested Lucy, heading for the bathroom.

Breakfast came quickly, and was just as quickly devoured, leaving Bill and Lucy with plenty of time on their hands. "We could watch the workmen," suggested Bill, and with nothing better to offer, Lucy agreed. The day promised to be bright and the garden was lovely as ever, there was always the pool, but Lucy was frankly bored with the château's attractions. Even the sight of the workmen, as they went about the process of dismantling the tent, wasn't all that interesting.

Sensing her lack of interest, Bill suggested walking around the moat and perhaps taking a paddle in one of the colorful little rowboats. "Okay," agreed Lucy, "but you have to row."

"Wouldn't have it any other way," joked Bill. "I've seen

how you handle the oars. Or, I should say, mishandle them."

"I do not."

"You catch crabs," teased Bill, meaning that her strokes were far from smooth and often resulted in splashes.

"I don't think there are crabs in the moat," she replied, coolly.

"Well, if there are, you'll certainly catch them," insisted Bill, leading the way to the little dock. But when they arrived, there were no boats to be found at all. They'd been removed, perhaps for the wedding, or maybe because of what Marie Laure insisted on calling *the incident*.

"Too bad," said Bill, "I was looking forward to a bit of exercise."

"You could try the gym," suggested Lucy, staring at the murky water below the dock where a blue plastic glove was snagged on a submerged branch. "Doesn't it bother you that someone died here?"

"Not especially, if I'm honest," admitted Bill. "It's not like we knew her."

"But what about Elizabeth? She's involved with the family. . . ."

"You can't assume they had anything to do with it. A girl gets herself killed, that doesn't mean the Schoen-Renes are involved. Say you're a killer and find yourself with a body, the moat probably seemed like a pretty good place to dump it. Remember, it was only discovered because Patrick snagged it on his fishing line."

"I wonder," mused Lucy, "what would have happened if Patrick hadn't snagged it. Do you think it was supposed to pop up during the wedding? When all the guests were here?"

"To embarrass the Schoen-Renes?"

"That's one theory. Chris said the girl was in poor health and had been strangled. She was sex trafficked, and whoever was running the brothel wanted to get rid of her."

"Maybe she was causing trouble for them, like demanding blackmail or something. That's the sort of thing that could get a girl killed."

"There you go, blaming the victim. I don't think she was trying to get herself killed, probably the opposite." Lucy's thoughts were flying. "She probably just wanted to get free."

"There's organized crime everywhere," said Bill, adding a warning. "The best thing for us is to look the other way and not get involved."

Lucy knew when she was beat. "I wonder what else is down there in the moat," she mused, changing the subject. "No wonder they took the boats away, they don't want people finding any more bodies."

"Somehow I doubt there are more bodies." Bill started walking off the dock.

"You can't be sure," said Lucy, following him. "And you can't be sure the Schoen-Renes are so innocent. Somebody shot Jean-Luc for a reason. Maybe the reason was something to do with this girl."

"Like what?" asked Bill, leading the way along the moat, around to the front of the château.

"Maybe *he* killed her," suggested Lucy. "It could've been a revenge shooting."

Bill grabbed her arm and looked her in the eye. "Get a grip, Lucy. Jean-Luc did not kill anybody. He does not strike me as a man who goes around strangling young women."

"But why was Jean-Luc shot?"

"I don't know, Lucy, and I don't care," he declared, striding along. "I'm sure it's some sort of misunderstanding. It could've been a mistake. There were lots of important people at the wedding, maybe the shot was meant for somebody else. It's no secret that France has a problem with terrorists, maybe that's all it was. It was probably nothing more than an attempt to disrupt things, a way to remind these rich and powerful people that there's a lot of pain, a lot of anger out there. Unfinished business that needs to be addressed."

Lucy couldn't believe what she was hearing; Bill was quite literally walking away from the truth, refusing to face unpleasant facts. "It wasn't terrorism, Bill, it was a professional hit. The shooter was aiming for Jean-Luc. That's for certain. What we don't know is why."

"Lucky for us, we don't have to know why," said Bill, as they rounded the corner and came to the gravel courtyard in front of the château. "That's what the police are for, and they seem to be on the job," said Bill, indicating a couple of police vans parked by the chapel.

"Let's take a look," suggested Lucy.

"Let's not," said Bill, firmly. "Let's leave them to do their work. Come to think of it, I could certainly use a workout. Do you know where that gym is?"

"Unfortunately, I do," admitted Lucy.

"Well"—he raised an eyebrow and studied her body critically—"if you ask me . . ."

"I didn't," said Lucy, "but I guess I may have gained a pound or two from eating those croissants every morning."

"C'mon," he coaxed, "let's get sweaty."

"Okay," agreed Lucy, "but I can think of a better way than a treadmill."

＊ ＊ ＊

Lucy had to admit she felt in a better mood after putting in some time on the treadmill and stationary bicycle, and it was fun watching Bill huff and puff on the weight machine. Her body felt looser, she'd apparently worked off some of the tension that had cramped and tightened her muscles; her mood was also lighter, freed from the anxiety that had persisted like a small dark cloud, dampening her spirits. Her curiosity, however, was still in full force and she was more driven than ever to find out what was going on. Why had Jean-Luc been shot, and why had a girl's body been dumped in the moat? Those events were not, no matter what Bill insisted, the sort of things you could ignore. But she also realized that as an outsider, and especially as a guest, her ability to investigate was limited. So when she emerged fresh from her shower and dressed, with a long, empty day stretching ahead of her, she was eager to learn if Toby and Molly had any plans for the day when she spotted them on the terrace along with Patrick.

"Hi, guys, what's up?" she asked brightly.

"We're trying to think of something to do," said Molly. "I'd like to do a bit of sightseeing. There's supposed to be some Roman ruins—"

"Boring," announced Patrick, working on his tween voice.

"Think gladiators," said Toby. "They had to fight for their lives. Thumbs-up they lived, thumbs-down they died."

Patrick was doubtful. "Really?"

"Really."

"Will there be bloodstains?"

"After two thousand years probably not," admitted his father. "But we can look and see."

"There's the market," said Lucy. "We could put a picnic together."

"Good healthy fruits and vegetables," teased Molly, getting a groan from Patrick.

"And that chocolate you like," added Toby.

"Okay." Patrick yielded with a long sigh, as if he were being dragged to the orthodontist.

The four were soon off on their adventure, in a borrowed SUV. Bill had declined to go, saying he hadn't finished diagramming those fabulous attic beams that he was thinking of re-creating in the barn he was restoring in Tinker's Cove for a tech wizard. Sara and Zoe also passed, deciding to spend a lazy afternoon by the pool, flirting with the towel boys. Elizabeth was nowhere to be found; it so happened that she had already gone to the hospital to be with Jean-Luc. Lucy didn't mind, she was actually pleased to be able to spend some rare time alone with Toby and his family. She'd never made peace with their decision to move to Alaska and saw this time together as a rare opportunity to renew family ties. Toby was actually more like her than the girls; like her he would work on a problem until it was solved.

"So, Mom," he began, as they departed the château grounds in a borrowed Renault, "do you have any ideas about what's going on here?"

"Yeah," chimed in Molly, "like how long do you think they're going to keep our passports?"

"I wanna go home," moaned Patrick.

"As long as it takes, I guess. Chris Kennedy called the embassy for us, he's got some connections there so it might not be too long."

"So who is this Chris guy?" asked Toby.

"He's actually one of Elizabeth's old boyfriends. He was

with the Secret Service, working here in France on some currency crimes. . . ."

"I thought the Secret Service just guarded the president," said Molly.

"That's only part of what they do. They're involved with the Treasury Department, too. I think. Anyway, he was here in France and they struck up a relationship, but it didn't last. Now he's freelancing, he's got a security firm and Hugo hired him for the wedding."

"Which went all to hell," said Toby, driving rather faster than Lucy would like on the country road.

"Somehow I don't think Hugo was completely honest with Chris. I don't imagine he filled him in on the complete picture."

"What is the picture?" asked Molly. "Organized crime?"

"That's my guess," said Lucy. "I think Hugo, or maybe Marie-Laure, pissed off somebody who wanted to put them in their place. Some crime boss or something." Carried away by her theme, she continued, "We know about the broth—"

"Little pitchers," sang Molly, interrupting.

"Right." Lucy smiled at Patrick, sitting beside her in the back seat. "You know what I mean."

"And here we are," declared Toby, zipping into a handy parking spot. "At the market."

"I don't see a market," said Molly. "Which is weird because it was here the other day."

"That's it," said Lucy. "It's not market day."

"What now?" asked Toby.

Lucy was busy with her phone, checking for a supermarket. One popped right up, a nearby Monoprix. "We will experience yet another facet of French culture: the *supermarché*. You'll love it."

The Monoprix was instantly recognizable as a supermarket, located on the town's outskirts with a large parking area and cart corral, but once inside they discovered *la
différence*. The fruits and vegetables were fresher, the
cheese case a marvel, and the bakery was stocked with
fabulous breads and even more fabulous pastries. Molly
discovered the skin care aisle and was filling her basket
with creams and lotions, Toby was mulling over the endless possibilities in the wine aisle, Lucy was trying to figure
out how many packs of coffee she could fit in her suitcase
as gifts for Sue, and Patrick had discovered a rack of
comic books. Common sense eventually ruled and they
each settled on a limited selection of favorite items, plus
cheese and a baguette, fruit, and bottled water for their
picnic.

As they were leaving, wheeling their purchases to the
car in the parking lot, they noticed the arrival of a police
car. It zoomed into the lot and braked abruptly, lights
flashing, in front of a group of women who were arguing
with a store employee.

"Roma," said Lucy, taking in the women's colorful
clothes. "I bet that employee is accusing them of stealing
and called the cops."

"That's so unfair," declared Molly. "Just because
they're different—"

"No, no," cautioned Toby, laughing. "A chicken just
fell out of her skirt."

They stood watching, fascinated, as the police officers
attempted to pat down the two women, who were protest-
ing mightily. The officers, however, seemed to have the
upper hand until an old wreck of a car arrived, loaded
with several tough-looking men. A loud argument ensued,
with many hand gestures, and ended with the police leav-

ing, much to the store employee's disgust. He shrugged, spat on the ground, and marched back into the store.

The women were not off the hook, however, as their menfolk continued to berate them. Not, Lucy thought, for stealing, but probably for getting caught. The women were quickly bundled into the wrecked car, which sped out of the lot, despite riding low on its worn-out shocks and leaning rakishly to one side.

"We should follow them," said Lucy. "People at the wedding were talking about *les gitans*, as if the Schoen-Renes were involved with them."

"What do you think that will accomplish?" asked Molly. "They're not going to talk to us."

"I don't know, exactly," admitted Lucy. "But it's a lead, the first we've got. And frankly, I don't think we're going to get our passports back until this thing is settled and I'm afraid we're going to have to do the settling. I don't have much faith in the French system."

"Neither do I," said Toby, surprising his mother by agreeing with her. "We'll just take a little ride, see what we will see."

"But I'm hungry," protested Patrick.

"You're always hungry," said his father, starting the car.

The Roma's car was no longer speeding along, it was clearly overburdened and was moving along slowly. Toby didn't press the issue by tailgating, but kept a polite distance, and the car soon turned off into a side road. They continued on past, but then circled back and proceeded down the road. They soon found themselves in a sort of ramshackle neighborhood, not dissimilar to some of the backwoods settlements around Tinker's Cove. There were the same tired old houses, similar collections of aged vehicles parked here and there, some of which worked and some which didn't, chained dogs, and unpaved roads.

"Poverty looks the same everywhere," said Molly. "We could be in Alaska."

"Or even Tinker's Cove," added Lucy, spotting a white limousine which clearly looked out of place. "Hey, I think I saw that limo at the château. It was the night you all went clubbing in town."

"That was the night the girl's body was dumped, wasn't it?" asked Toby, pulling to the side of the road and parking behind the limo. "Want to take a closer look?"

"I sure do," said Lucy, who hadn't seen the connection. When she saw the limo she'd assumed it was for the young people, but perhaps that was wrong. Perhaps it had been used by the girl's killers. She hopped out of the SUV. "If anybody bothers us we can say we're interested in hiring it. We can ask if it's available for rental."

"I'll go with her," volunteered Molly. "You stay in the car with Patrick," she told Toby, "and keep the engine running."

"You got it, babe," growled Toby, in his best gangster imitation.

The two women walked around the limo, consulting with each other as if appraising the vehicle's features. Soon enough a Roma man emerged from one of the dilapidated houses and approached them, doffing his hat to reveal a shaggy head of hair. He sported a five-day beard and was dressed in thrift store finery, baggy slacks and a sleeveless T-shirt, worn espadrilles on his feet.

"*C'est a louer?*" asked Lucy, attempting to resurrect her high school French.

"*Ah, oui,*" agreed the Roma, embarking on a long explanation of the limo's features and rates, very little of which Lucy understood.

They were soon joined by a ragtag group of children, who were curious about them, probably unused to visitors from outside their community. It wasn't the sort of place that would attract tourists, and most locals certainly avoided it. It was only fools like these Americans who occasionally stumbled in, probably lost.

It was time to make their departure, thought Lucy uneasily, noticing the growing number of children, some of whom were pushing and shoving, apparently working out some childish argument. "Sorry," she said, shaking her head regretfully. "I don't really speak French. . . ."

"Okay, okay." The Roma was prepared to attempt English. "Cheap. Very cheap for you."

Lucy and Molly were backing away, heading for their SUV. "Maybe later. Do you have a card?" asked Lucy, indicating with her hand.

"*Ah, oui, oui,*" he said, producing a sharp-looking alligator wallet and extracting a rather grubby business card.

"*Merci, je vous appellerai,*" she said, promising to call as she climbed into the SUV. Soon she and Molly had fastened their seat belts and Toby pulled away as the Roma waved goodbye, smiling broadly and revealing several missing teeth.

Lucy was thinking about that alligator wallet and remembering warnings about Roma pickpockets. She had left her bag in the car but Molly had her African basket tote slung on her shoulder. "Better check your wallet," she suggested.

Molly reached in her bag and sighed. "It's here," she said, relief in her voice.

"With the money?" asked Lucy.

"Ohmigod," she exclaimed, displaying the empty pouch. "How did they do that?"

"Practice, I guess," said Lucy. "Did you lose anything else?"

"No, thank goodness. I only had about fifty euros, I left most of my cash and my charge cards in that little safe in our room." She turned to Toby. "You were watching us. Did you see anything?"

"I was fiddling with the radio, trying to get some music, but I did notice a scuffle. Two kids were fighting behind you. I bet that's when it happened. The whole thing was staged."

"It's my fault," admitted Lucy. "I should've been more careful." She was studying the business card. "But we do have a name. Henri Dumas, and his company, Dumas Frères, CIE."

Chapter Nineteen

When they returned to the château that afternoon, after picnicking and exploring the ruined Roman amphitheater, they were just in time to greet Jean-Luc, home from the hospital. His arm was in a sling and he looked pale, clinging to Elizabeth's arm as he made his unsteady way into the château. His mother, who had been waiting in the foyer for his arrival, rushed to embrace him but he brushed her off, mumbling something, and she stepped away with a hurt expression on her face.

"We're so glad you're home," offered Lucy, who was standing to one side with Toby, Molly, and Patrick.

"Yeah, man," said Toby, "how are you feeling?"

"What's it like, getting shot?" asked Patrick. "Does it hurt?"

Jean-Luc didn't respond, or even acknowledge their concerns, but continued plodding down the hall, supported by Elizabeth, to one of the ground-floor guest rooms.

Seeing Lucy's questioning expression, Marie-Laure offered an explanation. "The doctors said no stairs yet, so he's staying on the entry level until he gets stronger."

"Is he really ready to be out of the hospital?" asked Molly.

Marie-Laure shook her head. "If you ask me, no. But he insisted and the doctors finally gave permission." She sighed. "He's never been sick or injured, you know, and I don't expect he will be a cooperative patient."

"I'm sure he has a lot on his mind," ventured Lucy. "Getting shot must be terribly traumatic, just knowing that somebody wanted to do you harm would be very upsetting. He must feel awfully vulnerable right now."

This was a topic that Marie-Laure did not wish to pursue, merely saying that she wanted to make sure Elizabeth knew where the extra pillows were stored and hurrying off down the hallway to tend to Jean-Luc. Lucy watched her go, thinking that Elizabeth was not only responsible for Jean-Luc's care, but would also have to cope with Marie-Laure's interference.

"If I were Elizabeth," said Molly, "I'd be sure to keep those painkillers coming."

"For Jean-Luc or for herself?" asked Toby.

"Both," replied Molly, chuckling.

"It's still early," said Lucy. "Any plans for the rest of the afternoon?"

"I bet Patrick would like a swim," suggested Toby.

"Good idea," agreed Lucy. "It was hot at the ruins, it will be nice to cool off and relax."

It was wonderfully pleasant at the pool, where just the sight of the cool blue water was refreshing. Sara and Zoe seemed to be making a full-time job of sunbathing, enjoying the attention of the towel boys. Patrick and his father raced each other in various strokes, Molly beat them both with a killer breaststroke, and Lucy simply lolled about in the water, supported by an inflatable raft. She drifted here and there, dabbling her fingers in the water and splashing herself to cool down when the sun got to be too much. While she looked relaxed, like someone without a care in the world, her mind was working overtime. She tried not to think about how long the investigation would take, and when they would be allowed to go home. Little things bothered her, like would Rachel remember to water her plants and how was her aged dog, Libby, faring at the kennel? And then there were the bills, piling up at the post office. The mortgage payment would soon be due, how was she going to pay that? And what about charge cards? She certainly didn't want to incur penalties. She supposed she could make payments by phone, which she'd occasionally done when she discovered a bill she'd overlooked, but she'd never done it while out of the country. This was going to be a big hassle. Life suddenly seemed very complicated.

Worst of all, she couldn't help feeling that in some way this awful situation was her fault. She'd fallen for the dream wedding, imagining the romance and beauty but neglecting to consider the ramifications of taking the whole family far from home. She'd always scoffed at the idea of travel insurance, but now was beginning to understand its appeal. Things could happen, unexpectedly. You could get sick, you could be caught in a tsunami, or you could be involved in a crime! Those weren't the sorts of things you thought about when you were packing, worrying if your clothes were appropriate, or if the walking shoes you'd bought for the trip would be comfortable. You counted your pills, you changed some dollars for euros at the bank, you made sure your passport was current, but you never thought of the disasters that could befall you. Sure, your plane might crash, the odds were against it, but it could happen. So what if it did go down in the middle of the Atlantic Ocean? Your problems would most definitely be over. So why worry?

It occurred to Lucy, as she slid off the raft into the water and rolled onto her back, floating, that it was a very odd situation indeed when you began thinking a plane crash would be preferable to your current problems. So what if their credit rating took a hit? So what if the peace lily died? And face it, Libby probably got more care and attention at the kennel than she did at home on Red Top Road. And as for the drowned girl and the wounded fiancé, well, really, what did it have to do with her? Nothing, she thought, turning over in the water and swimming a few strokes. Nothing and, well actually, everything.

She was suddenly startled by a huge splash, somebody jumping into the pool beside her. When that person surfaced, she realized it was Bill.

"Wow, this feels good. It was sure hot in that attic!" he declared, treading water. "How was your day?"

"Terrific." She swam over and put her hands on his shoulders and fluttered her feet, coming in for a kiss. "Race you to the shallow end?"

He grinned. "You're on!"

Lucy was surprised the next morning when Elizabeth knocked on their door, asking a favor. "I need a break," she began. "Marie-Laure's gone to the church in town to thank God for saving her son, which makes no sense because she has a perfectly good chapel here. I suspect she really just wants to get away for a bit and now I'm all alone with Jean-Luc, who is being absolutely impossible. Nothing I do is right, I'm a bumbling idiot. It's apparently my fault that the French team lost the football match, that the air conditioning is too hot, or too cold, and that the food is terrible. Oh, and the painkillers don't work, which is also my fault."

"I'll go and stay with him," offered Lucy, thinking this was pretty typical male behavior.

"Are you sure?"

Lucy was thinking that this opportunity to question Jean-Luc was almost too good to be true, but she wasn't about to admit that to Elizabeth. "I really don't mind," she said, with a shrug. "I'd like to be useful."

"Well, I really appreciate it. I've got a million things to do, starting with taking a shower."

Lucy popped to her feet and saluted. "Nurse Lucy reporting for duty."

"I won't be long," promised Elizabeth. "I'll be as fast as I can."

"Take as long as you need," urged Lucy. "I'll take good care of Jean-Luc."

Elizabeth gave her mom a quick hug. "You're the best, Mom."

Intent on her mission, and aware that Marie-Laure might return at any moment, Lucy hurried downstairs to Jean-Luc's room. She found him sitting up in bed, shirtless with his bandaged arm propped on a pillow, flipping through the channels with the TV remote. The room, she noticed, was similar to the one she and Bill were occupying, luxurious and spacious with neutral furnishings and subtle floral designs on the curtains and bedding.

"Elizabeth's taking a shower, she asked me to stay with you," she began. "What can I do for you?"

Jean-Luc indicated a bottle of painkillers on the bedside

table. "I can't open it with one hand," he said, giving her a crooked, rueful smile.

She picked up the bottle, which contained an opioid, and raised an eyebrow. "These are pretty strong, is it time for another dose?"

After what Elizabeth had said, she expected him to react angrily, but he simply shrugged instead, which caused him to wince with pain. Speaking with effort, he said, "I think Lizzie gave me some around four in the morning."

"That was six hours ago, I think you're good." Lucy gave him one of the tablets and passed him the glass of water that was already on the nightstand. "Rough night?" she asked.

He nodded. "Especially for Lizzie. I couldn't sleep so I watched TV, which meant she couldn't sleep either." He sighed. "I don't think she's too happy with me."

Lucy smiled, thinking Elizabeth must really be deeply in love with Jean-Luc. That was the only explanation for the fact that she allowed him to call her Lizzie, albeit with that charming French accent.

"She's just tired," said Lucy, seating herself in one of the armchairs. "Do you want the TV? Or something to read?"

"No. Just talk to me," said Jean-Luc. "Tell me what you've been doing. Lizzie said you went to see the Roman ruins."

"Patrick loved them," said Lucy. "He was looking for the gladiators' bloodstains. . . ."

"There were never gladiators there. Much too small. They had plays, speeches, things like that."

"Don't tell Patrick, he'll be awfully disappointed."

Jean-Luc managed a smile, and Lucy decided to venture into more dangerous territory. "We also encountered some

Roma. We got lost on our way to the ruins and found ourselves in their neighborhood. A bunch of kids mobbed us and stole some money from Molly."

"*Gitans.*" He shook his head. "They're trouble."

"But they're not all thieves, right? Some of them operate local businesses, like that guy who has the limo business. I saw that car here at the château. I think it was the night the girl's body was dumped."

"Could be," said Jean-Luc, surprising her with his lack of interest in the timing of the limo's presence at the château. "They come and go, they pretty much run things around here."

Lucy thought of the run-down neighborhood, the obvious poverty. "If that's true, how come they all seem so poor?"

He snorted. "It's like a feudal system. There's the big guy at the top, he's doing just fine. The rest of them do what he says, and are happy for the little bit he gives them."

"But except for the occasional limo rental, and that brothel, what do they have to do with the château?"

"Oh, pretty much everything," exclaimed Jean-Luc, sarcastically. "Who do you think shot me? And dumped that girl in the moat? It was Barban, displaying some muscle."

Lucy's jaw dropped. She'd suspected the château was a front for crime, but hadn't really believed it. But now it seemed that Jean-Luc was admitting her worst fears were true. "Barban?"

"He's the head of the clan, the Gypsy King."

"And he wrecked the wedding just to show he's the boss?"

Jean-Luc sighed. "You might as well know, it's no secret. Papa's in big financial trouble. He got in a bind, a loan came due and the bank wanted their money, which he didn't have. So he was forced to go to Barban, who was oh, so happy to give him the cash he needed. At something like twenty percent interest. But no problem about paying it back, no pressure, as long as Papa made a few changes here at the château. First off, he wanted Papa to provide girls and drugs at the hunts. He resisted at first, but Barban insisted and, surprise, surprise, it was a big success. The hunts were suddenly a lot more popular, and profits went way up—at first. But then costs went up, too, for the girls, for everything, and Papa got in deeper and deeper."

"Does your mother know about this?"

"I'm not sure. I don't think she and Papa discuss money. Not the lack of it, for sure. She thinks she's the lady of the manor and Papa wants to keep it that way. It would kill him to admit that he's broke, that he's a failure."

"But she must have noticed about the girls and drugs, I mean, that farm was practically on the château property."

"Oh, yeah, the girls anyway. I don't think she knows about the drugs. She had this sort of amused tolerance, like boys will be boys, what can you do? So long as Papa was faithful, she didn't mind about the guests. She sees them all as barbarians anyway, anyone who's not French and a landed aristocrat is, how shall I put it? They don't really count, they don't matter to her. Whatever they want, it's okay. 'There's no accounting for tastes, no matter how low,' she'll say. And she means it, it's what makes her such a wonderful hostess. She doesn't judge."

"But she did insist on getting rid of the girls at the farm?"

"Oh, yeah. The wedding, that was different. That was family, and we have an image to preserve. Business is one thing, family is another. The Schoen-Rene family must be above reproach."

"But this is a family business, right? You can't separate the two."

"I think Maman is beginning to learn that," said Jean-Luc, yawning. He shifted around on his pillows and Lucy hopped up to help him and he gave her an apologetic smile. "I don't know why I told you all this. It must be the drugs."

"Don't worry. In one ear and out the other. I can't remember anything these days."

He smiled and closed his eyes. "That's good," he said, drifting off. "Forget, must forget. . . ."

Once she was sure Jean-Luc was out for the count, Lucy got up and tiptoed to the bathroom, grateful for the thick rug. Once inside, she shut the door and retrieved her phone from her back pocket. Hitting contacts, she found Chris Kennedy's number.

He answered on the second ring. "Hi, Lucy. How's it going?"

"Jean-Luc is home from the hospital."

"I heard. How's he doing?"

"I guess he's on pretty strong painkillers, or else he wanted to get a load off his chest. I can't believe what he just told me."

"Yeah . . ." prompted Chris.

"He said his father is in debt to this Roma guy, he called him a gypsy king. His name is Barban. He runs everything around here, according to Jean-Luc. He forced Hugo to bring in the girls and drugs for the guests, he claims this Barban was behind everything: the shooting, the girl in the moat."

"Thanks, Lucy. This is the first I've heard of this." He paused. "I wish Hugo had been more honest with me. It would have helped a lot. I thought this was a straightforward security gig, I didn't realize that they were actually being threatened, targeted."

"You can't blame yourself," whispered Lucy, hearing someone come into the sickroom. "You didn't have the whole story. I gotta go, someone's here."

"Be careful, Lucy, and leave everything to me. These guys are dangerous criminals. You saw what they did to Jean-Luc."

"Will do," said Lucy, ending the call. She replaced the phone in her pocket, flushed the toilet, and washed her hands. Then, towel in hand, she opened the bathroom door and saw Marie-Laure. She was bent over her son with her hand on his forehead, checking for fever.

"Ah, Lucy, what are you doing here? I thought Elizabeth was taking care of Jean-Luc."

Lucy folded the towel. "She needed a break, didn't get much sleep last night, and asked me to help for a bit."

Marie-Laure was not pleased. "She should have told me, and I wouldn't have gone to church. I would have stayed with my son."

"He's been fine," said Lucy, turning back into the bathroom and hanging the towel on its rod. Returning to the sickroom, she continued. "He asked for one of his pills and said he'd had the last one at four in the morning, so I gave him one. He's pretty worn out, he went right to sleep." She smiled indulgently at his sleeping figure. "Rest is what he needs."

"I think I am the best judge of what he needs," said Marie-Laure, somewhat stiffly. Then, remembering her manners, she added, "But I do thank you for taking care of my son."

"No problem," said Lucy, preparing to seat herself.

"Oh, you may go," said Marie-Laure. "I can take over, and I'm sure you'd rather be with your family."

"I'm happy to stay, give you a break . . ."

"No need. I can't think of anything I'd rather do than take care of Jean-Luc."

Right, thought Lucy, leaving the room and aware of Marie-Laure's unspoken message. She could think of nothing more important than caring for Jean-Luc, unlike Elizabeth, who had abandoned him.

Chapter Twenty

The following days had a sort of Groundhog Day quality, in which each day seemed like the day before, primarily revolving around meals. They woke every morning to sunshine, a buffet breakfast was set out in the dining room, mornings were spent in the gym, or the garden, or on little sightseeing excursions. Lunch was served on the terrace, afternoons were spent at the pool, capped by cocktails and a casual dinner on the terrace. Bill checked in with the embassy every morning and got the same response: "Sorry, but we've had no response from the French authorities."

For the most part, Lucy tried to enjoy this extended vacation with her family, but there was also a sense that they were removed from reality and suspended in time. Sooner or later it would all come crashing down when their various responsibilities caught up with them. They were powerless to change their situation, but except for Patrick, were dogged by nagging worries. In France, it seemed, workers had guaranteed job security, but both Sara and Zoe fretted that they might well return home to find themselves unemployed. Lucy knew Ted would welcome her back to her job at the *Courier*, but Bill had several projects in the works and didn't want to let his clients down. His promised delivery dates were fast approaching but nothing was happening at the Weiskopfs' guesthouse or the Jordans' barn renovation. Toby and Molly had both been able to take personal time from their government jobs, but were chafing at the bit, eager to get back home to Alaska. Patrick, however, was picking up French from the château employees as he busied himself helping the gardeners weed the flower beds, hung around the stables, and worked on his butterfly stroke in the pool.

Encountering Marie-Laure on her way to breakfast one morning outside Jean-Luc's room, Lucy was quick to ask how he was doing and offer her services. "He's mending, slowly," said Marie-Laure, with a sigh. "His body is healing but I worry about his mind, his emotions. He is very depressed."

"Perhaps if he got outside, in the fresh air," suggested Lucy.

Marie-Laure shrugged. "I have tried, Elizabeth, too. He refuses to leave his room."

"They say time heals all wounds," offered Lucy.

"Well, time is a harsh master," said Marie-Laure, sounding worried. "It marches on, whether we want it to or not."

Lucy interpreted this to mean that Marie-Laure was growing frustrated not only with Jean-Luc's slow recovery but also with her houseguests' extended stay. "I am so sorry, you have been so kind, but I feel we are imposing on your hospitality."

"No, no, no. You must not worry. I understand that police investigations take time, and Hugo and I are more than happy to have Elizabeth's family stay with us. It is

our wish to make this difficult situation as pleasant as possible. I know it must be stressful for you."

Lucy suddenly felt weepy, and blinked back a few tears.
"It is certainly frustrating, but I am so grateful that you
are putting us up." She paused. "If there is something we
could do to help you, we'd be happy to. I think Hugo
mentioned something about carriage races. . . ."

"Ah, yes, the carriage races. It is a huge event, we are
known for it, and now, well, there is much to do. Elizabeth
is busy with Jean-Luc, he won't let her out of his sight, and
Hugo is too distracted, things are not getting done. . . ."
She straightened her back and gave a brisk nod. "*Bien,* I
must go. I have much to do. Enjoy your breakfast."

Lucy continued on to the small dining room but found
it empty, apart from Zoe and Sara. After wishing them a
good morning, Lucy headed for the sideboard where an
assortment of hot foods were set out in chafing dishes.
Usually she settled for coffee and a croissant, but today
thought she might consider something more substantial.
Moving along the array, she lifted the silver domes to discover what lay beneath, finding omelets, crepes, sausage,
and a mess of something gray. Repelled at whatever it was,
she went straight to the coffee urn and half filled a large
bowl, added an equal amount of hot milk to create café au
lait, grabbed a croissant, and went to join her daughters at
the table.

"Honestly," Sara was complaining, "you're such a slob.
Can't you manage to pick up your dirty undies once in a
while? I got tangled up in your bra last night when I was
trying to go to bed."

"Oh, like you're so neat!" exclaimed Zoe, in a defensive
tone. "You leave your pimple creams and makeup all over
the bathroom sink, and if that's not bad enough, you never

put the top on the toothpaste and leave it running down the side. Yuck!"

Lucy lifted her bowl and took a long swallow of the delicious café au lait and considered her options. She could scold the girls for arguing, which would probably just embroil her in their squabble, or she could remove herself from the situation.

"Oh, right," Zoe was saying, "like you haven't been helping yourself to my expensive prescription cream!"

That was all Lucy needed to hear. Decision made, she picked up her coffee and croissant and stepped out through the French doors onto the terrace. Expecting the usual dazzling sunshine, it took her a moment to realize that the day was overcast, thick black clouds had settled in, and from the high humidity it seemed certain that they were in for a rainstorm. Not just yet, however, so Lucy seated herself at one of the tables and prepared to enjoy her breakfast in solitude.

It was not to be, however. Elizabeth came out, also carrying a bowl of café au lait, and seated herself beside her mother with a huge sigh.

"Couldn't take the heat," suggested Lucy, with a nod toward the dining room.

"Those girls, if they only knew what it's like to have real problems."

Lucy smiled sympathetically. "They're growing restless, we all are." She had a sudden inspiration. "Say, can you suggest some sort of outing? Something that would get us out of here, offer some distraction?"

Elizabeth glared at her mother. "Really? You know what I'm dealing with, right? And you want me to be a tour guide, too?" She glanced at the black clouds gathering overhead. "It's going to rain anyway."

Lucy's jaw dropped. "I'm sorry, I wasn't thinking. I know Jean-Luc is very demanding. . . ."

"Depressed is what he is." Elizabeth's head drooped. "I just don't know how to help him. He's not even trying to get better, wants to be waited on hand and foot. And then Hugo is after me about the carriage races. I'd like to help, I really would, but I just can't. I'm done in."

"Can I help with Jean-Luc?" offered Lucy. "Give you a break?"

"I wish." She pushed the bowl of coffee away. "It has to be me. He won't let anybody else in the room, not even his mother." She stood up, checking her watch. "I've been away too long, he'll be frantic. I've got to get back."

"Well, my offer still stands," said Lucy, watching as Elizabeth dragged herself back inside.

Alone again, Lucy dabbed some strawberry jam on the horn of her croissant and bit, savoring the buttery, berry-filled deliciousness. It wasn't all bad, here, she thought, chewing slowly. But it was odd, she decided, that Jean-Luc was suddenly so opposed to his mother. Did he blame her for the shooting? Did he think she was responsible because she insisted on closing the brothel at the farm?

Those were her thoughts as she ate slowly, attempting to make her breakfast last as long as possible to fill her empty morning. But no matter how small the sips, how tiny the bites, she eventually finished her meal. She sat a few moments, staring at her empty bowl and plate. She ran her finger around the plate catching the last bit of jam, which she licked up, as the first drops of rain began to fall. Maybe Bill had made some progress with the embassy, she thought, hurrying back to the dining room.

There she saw Zoe and Sara had departed, replaced by Patrick, Toby, and Molly. A server, a woman Lucy knew was invariably helpful, was standing by with a puzzled expression on her face and Molly was scolding Patrick.

"You, young man, need to apologize to this nice lady," she was saying, waggling a finger in Patrick's face.

"I won't. You can't make me. It was brains!"

"She was only trying to be nice, to give you a treat," advised Molly.

"Well, it wasn't nice. It was DISGUSTING."

"Just say you're sorry and we'll say no more about it," said Molly.

"I'm never eating again. This place stinks."

"Well, you're not leaving this room until you say you're sorry," said Molly, raising her voice and emphasizing every word. "You need to apologize."

"I won't!"

The server attempted to intervene, saying she was sorry. She only meant to offer the young gentleman a rare delicacy . . .

"C'mon, Molly," said Toby. "Don't make a big deal about this. He's just a kid."

Molly suddenly whirled around, turning on her husband. "Oh, so now I'm the bad guy! I'm always the bad guy! What happened to our united front policy, hunh? You always fold when you should stick up for me." She marched to the door, then turned around. "And civilized behavior!" she snarled, turning on her heel and thumping off down the parquet hallway.

"She'll calm down," said Toby, who had noticed his mother watching the exchange with concern.

"I'm sure," said Lucy, who remembered feeling the same as Molly, when Bill thought she demanded too much of the kids. "But there's no excuse for rudeness," she said, ruffling Patrick's hair. "I do see some chocolate croissants over there, by the coffeepot."

"Please, sit down," urged the server, eager to make amends. "I will bring you an assortment."

"Well," admitted Lucy, "I could use a bit more café au lait, *un demi, s'il vous plaît.*"

"*Avec plaisir,*" said the server, beaming as she bustled around, happy to serve them.

Patrick, biting into his chocolate croissant, gave her a big smile. "Mercy bookoo," he said, getting a pleased chuckle in response.

Lucy nibbled guiltily on a brioche, sipped her coffee, and thought she really should find something to do besides eat. "So, Patrick," she began. "What would you like to do today?"

He drank some orange juice, then sighed. "I wanna go home!"

"Me too," said Lucy, well aware that everyone's patience was wearing thin. She had one last card to play, she'd been carrying it around with her like a lucky charm, waiting for the moment to use it. Now, she thought, pulling the minister of defense's card out of her pocket, the time had come.

"I dunno," she told Toby. "I met this guy at the wedding, a government minister. He said I shouldn't hesitate to call if I needed help." She showed the card to Toby. "But I hate to bother him."

Toby shrugged. "This is kinda crazy. We've been here for more than a week, it can't hurt to try, right?"

"What could he do?"

"A guy like him has lots of contacts, a phone call, and voilà!, we are on our way home."

"Okay, you've convinced me," said Lucy, producing her phone and dialing the number. It rang, and rang, and eventually a recorded voice embarked on a long explanation in French which Lucy deduced meant the minister was *en vacances,* or on vacation. It ended with a beep, indicating she could leave a message, so she did. Just a brief request that he call her at his convenience.

A loud clap of thunder heralded a downpour, which ended any hope of outdoor activity. Sighing, Lucy got up, announcing, "I guess I'll go see if I can find a jigsaw puzzle."

She searched the shelves and cabinets in the various salons, she poked around the billiard room, but found no sign of that Maine rainy-day vacation staple stocked in every cottage, a challenging jigsaw puzzle. Somewhat incredulous at this oversight, she continued on in the direction she believed led to the management offices of the château in search of Marie-Laure. She eventually found a small hallway lined with offices, and in the largest office at the end of the hall, she found Marie-Laure and Hugo. The two were standing with their heads together, as if discussing some grave matter. Before she could catch a word, Marie-Laure sensed her presence and looked up. "Yes? Can we help you?"

"Sorry to bother you. It's just the rain, you see, and I wondered if you had any jigsaw puzzles." She made little motions with her hands, as if assembling a puzzle. "You know, little pieces, you put together to make a picture."

"I know what they are," said Marie-Laure.

"We were going to get some," said Hugo. "It was Elizabeth's idea. She said they are very popular in the US." He scratched his chin. "Then it went out of my head. Pfft." He flapped his hand, indicating the fleeing thought. "I'd forget my head if it wasn't . . ."

"I know, darling. It is very hard without Elizabeth."

"I don't see how I can manage," he said, sadly. "Of course she must take care of Jean-Luc, but who can replace her? It is chaos without Elizabeth."

Lucy noticed that the office, large and luxurious with

corner windows, was in a bit of a mess. Papers and maps were scattered everywhere, along with photos, electrical cords, even bits of harness. Suddenly, although the rain was thundering down outside, the sun rose in her mind. The solution to all their problems: Hugo's need for assistance, and her family's chronic boredom.

"We can help," she said.

"You?" Marie-Laure was doubtful.

"Yes. Not just me, my whole family."

"Your family?" Hugo seemed interested.

"Yes." Lucy was decisive. "We should have a meeting. Hugo, you draw up a list of jobs, things that need to be done. We will divide them up. Many hands make light work, that's what my mother used to say."

"Or a lot of confusion," said Marie-Laure, skeptically.

"Trust me. We can do this."

"American optimism," murmured Marie-Laure.

"They liberated Paris," said Hugo, with a shrug. "Maybe they can do this."

It was agreed that the meeting would take place immediately after lunch, at one thirty, and Lucy departed to advise her family. Her plan was not met with enthusiasm, but they all came around, begrudgingly, in the end. "What else have we got to do?" said Zoe, summing up the general mood.

So, tummies full of ratatouille and baguette, along with a reviving dollop of wine, the meeting commenced exactly on time. Hugo, or rather Marie-Laure, had prepared a whiteboard of tasks, and Lucy tackled them one by one. First up was publicity.

"Zoe, do you have any ideas?" she began, explaining that Zoe worked in the communications department of a sports team.

"Well, sure, I've got a lot of ideas but I don't speak French."

Lucy was not about to admit defeat, not on the first round. "Well, if you wrote up a press release, for example, Elizabeth could translate it, right? While Jean-Luc naps."

Marie-Laure nodded. "It is a good idea," she said. "Zoe, I didn't realize you were skilled in this area."

"I majored in communications in college," she said. "And my ideas for the team have been well received."

"Okay," said Lucy, "let's put Zoe's name up there with publicity." Next, she saw, was *livraison,* a word she was unfamiliar with. "What is this?" she asked. "Keeping the books?"

"No, I don't know the English word," said Marie-Laure, with a little chuckle. "We get all sorts of packages and need to track them, get them to the right places."

"Ah, like a receiving department," said Lucy. "Sara, you are good at cataloguing and tracking, right?"

"It's what I do at the museum, make sure the rocks get back in the right drawers."

"So you could do this, handle receiving?"

"Absolutely," she said, with an affirming nod.

Lucy was on a roll. As she checked off one item after another it seemed there was a family member equipped for every job, except maybe the last, and probably most important. But they'd get to that; first there was a blank next to "*logements.*"

"So what does this involve?" she asked, pointing.

"People, and their teams of horses, come from all over and we help them find a place to stay, we don't have enough room here for everyone. It is not so much the people, but the horses. We have standing arrangements with a number of inns and châteaux in the region, and most of the contestants are returning, so it's a matter of making confirmations, with the guests as well as their hosts."

"Molly, is this something you could do?" asked Lucy.

"It's not unlike finding Section Eight housing, probably a lot easier," said Molly. "My French isn't great. . . ."

"You'll do fine," advised Marie-Laure, surprising Lucy. "Most of the hosts speak English, and we send printed forms, sometimes emails to the guests, with the information. You just fill it in."

"I'll do my best," promised Molly. "And if I don't understand, I will ask for help."

"That leaves event registrations," said Lucy. "I can handle that, I'm used to dealing with a lot of information, dates, times, names. Right up my alley."

"Okay, okay," said Hugo, looking relieved. "I appreciate your help and I think we will manage quite well. The only problem is the job of Jean-Luc, he was the one who every year would lay out the courses for the *routier* and the *maniabilité*. I don't know who can replace him? And of course, there are fences and signs that need to be refreshed and repaired."

"I can do that," offered Bill. "Carpentry is my specialty."

"That would be great," said Hugo. "But still we have to set up the courses. There is the *routier*, which goes for miles through several villages, and then the *maniabilité,* an obstacle course with twists and turns in which the drivers display control of their horses."

"So how did Jean-Luc do it?" asked Toby. "There must be some sort of plan, right? And I suppose you have the fences and barriers stored somewhere?"

"*Ah, oui.*"

"So the plan has to be transferred from the paper to the

ground, right? Marked out in some way, and the obstacles have to be installed. How did he do it? On foot? On a horse?"

"Oh, no, we have ATVs."

Toby brightened up. "ATVs! I'm on it. And Patrick, too! We ride them all the time in Alaska."

"I guess that's your list," said Lucy, smiling proudly as she put in the last names on the whiteboard. "Now we just have to get to work."

"I am amazed," said Marie-Laure, somewhat dazzled. "So much talent. And energy. It is fantastic."

"I just hope we don't goof it up," said Lucy.

"Goof? What is goof?"

Lucy smiled. "Never mind. It's like that old song. We're going to eliminate the negative, accentuate the positive! Onward and upward!"

"So American," mused Marie-Laure, taking Hugo's hand and giving it a squeeze.

Obviously relieved, he nodded with satisfaction. "As Papa would always say, there's nobody like the Yanks. Twice they came to fight for us. He said he would never forget the day they came into Paris."

"Well, yes," said Marie-Laure, suddenly all business. "Come with me. I will get you all settled at your tasks. We begin."

Chapter Twenty-one

It was obvious at breakfast the next day that the various members of the Stone family were enjoying having a sense of purpose. There was a little tingle of excitement in the air as they gathered at the table, eager to tackle the day's challenges. Marie-Laure's instruction session the day before had been clear, concise, and to the point, giving each person a thorough understanding of the required tasks to prepare for the carriage races, which were scheduled to take place in only a few days. Language didn't prove to be the problem that Lucy had feared, as they had paperwork from the previous carriage races to copy, and many of the words were the same in French as in English. Information forms were pretty much the same everywhere and *"nom"* for name and *"addresse actuelle"* were quite obvious. Even Zoe, who was tasked with publicity, had little trouble deciphering the previous year's press releases and was told to use them as the basis for the announcements she was preparing.

Happiest of all, however, were Bill and Toby, who had taken the ATVs out for a test run while the others were taking instruction from Marie-Laure and had a great time zooming along the carriage roads that connected various villages in the area. They'd discovered quite a number of problems that needed to be addressed such as downed tree branches, overgrown bushes, and potholes that needed to be filled, and were busily planning the day's work over hearty omelet breakfasts. Patrick was to be pressed into service as a gofer, driving a lawn tractor equipped with a trailer.

Lucy was pleased as punch with her family's can-do spirit and willingness to help, much preferring these cheerful faces to the bored blank ones she'd found so discouraging. She quickly polished off her omelet and marched off eagerly to the administration offices to tackle whatever challenges the day might bring.

Hugo was already there, talking on the telephone while seated at his huge carved wood desk with its highly polished surface now absolutely clear of any papers, or indeed anything that might indicate work in progress. Seeing her he immediately ended the call. "*Bonjour,* Lucy. I hope you had a good night's sleep because we have a great deal of work to do. Time is running out for these last-minute registrations."

"I did sleep very well," she said. "I think we're all pleased to be able to help out."

"It is much appreciated," he said, "especially in this difficult time."

"So where shall I begin?" she asked.

He got up from the desk and led the way to a connected room, outfitted with a computer station set up on a charming antique lady's writing desk with a fragile-looking chair, as well as an industrial-size printer and a large copy machine. They were all American brands and familiar to her from her job at the newspaper. "Old friends, I know them well," she said, indicating the office machines and getting a relieved smile from Hugo.

"I wasn't sure, I thought they might be different in the States, or maybe you wouldn't know how to use them."

"I'm a pretty good troubleshooter, too, if I say so myself," boasted Lucy, getting a blank look from Hugo. "Problem solver, I mean."

He nodded. "That is good to know." He looked around somewhat vacantly, as if not quite sure what he was looking for.

Lucy noticed a plastic box filled with correspondence sitting on top of a file cabinet and picked it up. "Are these the registration applications?" she asked.

A look of relief flooded his face. "Ah, yes. Exactly. I believe Marie-Laure showed you what to do?"

"Yes," said Lucy, seating herself at the computer station and powering up the PC. "I can take it from here."

He was suddenly concerned. "Where will you take it?"

"Just a phrase," said Lucy, who was scrolling through the list of files, looking for the previous year's roster. "It means I know what to do and will get right to work."

"*Bien, très bien,*" he said, drifting back to his huge, empty desk.

Having found the necessary file she opened a fresh one, intending to toggle between the two, copying and pasting the old information from returnees into the new file, and using the same format for new registrants. There were only about a handful of applications in unopened envelopes waiting for her, so she got right to work. Her system seemed to work quite well, as most of the applications were from returnees and didn't require more than a few clicks of the mouse. When she encountered a name that wasn't on the old roster, she made every effort to get all the information entered correctly, especially those long and confusing French telephone numbers.

After she'd been at it for an hour or so, hunched over the attractive but quite impractical *secretaire*, she noticed she was stiffening up and decided to take a break. She popped her head into Hugo's office intending to ask if she could get him a coffee, but saw that he'd dozed off in his modern, ergonomically designed chair.

She didn't have to go far in search of her coffee as Marie-Laure had installed a table in the hallway and equipped it with a Keurig coffee maker, along with a wide choice of pods, and a covered tray filled with pastries. It was a far cry from the setup at the *Courier,* where the aged Mr. Coffee pot was always half filled with a bitter brew and she might be lucky to find a stale, forgotten donut from Jake's Donut Shack.

Lucy brewed herself a cup of Carte Noire and employed great self-control to resist the pastries, then proceeded along the hallway, where Zoe and Sara were busy in an adjacent office. She told them about the coffee, then continued on outside, onto the terrace. She perched on the stone wall and looked out over the garden, noticing Bill and Toby in the distance, pounding a signpost into the ground. It was warm on the terrace, bees were buzzing about in the nearby lavender bed, and for a moment she regretted opening her big mouth and offering to help out. Wouldn't it be nice to stretch out in one of those inviting chaises and spend the morning in delicious idleness? She took a bracing swallow of the delicious coffee and reminded herself that only yesterday she'd been going out of her mind with boredom. It was simply human nature, she decided, to want the thing you didn't have. Now she had swapped endless leisure for useful employment, but there would no doubt be a time for relaxation in the future and she hoped she would have the sense to appreciate it. Draining the cup, she went back to work on a caffeine high.

Opening the last and rather fine envelope, not the usual office quality but something much more substantial, probably from a high-end stationer, Lucy took a closer look. The return address was engraved, she discovered, and indicated *Château Bienvenu* in the nearby town of *Creneau*. Well, she thought, withdrawing the enclosed application, whoever Django Garcia was he was doing very well for himself. High-quality engraved stationery didn't come cheap as she'd discovered when ordering invitations for a Hat and Mitten Fund gala auction, and M. Garcia hadn't felt the need to economize on his luxurious envelopes. She wondered who M. Garcia was and what he did to be able to afford his no-doubt well-appointed château, and thought Hugo would probably know. She got up to ask him, but found his office was still empty, so she returned to her desk and completed the registration, tucking the confirmation into the comparatively inferior envelope provided for the purpose. Perhaps, she thought, she could make up for the envelope by taking extra care in writing the address and placing the stamp squarely in the corner, so she did, then tossed it into the basket with the other pieces of outgoing mail. Noticing the time, and realizing that the mail carrier was due any minute, she took the basket to the front hall, where she added her envelopes to the others in the basket on the hall table. Then, pleased with herself for remembering that the mail carrier always came around eleven, she went back to her office.

There were no more new applications, so she reviewed the work she'd done, making sure there were no typos. She also took the opportunity to look over the entire roster, curious to see if she recognized any names. Perhaps a member of the English royal family, or a famous celebrity? Finding only French names, albeit some with noble titles, she concluded this was one of those clubby events that only members of a very exclusive community knew or cared about. It would be interesting, she thought, sort of like a sociological experiment, to observe these upper-crust French people in action. But for now, anyway, she'd completed her morning's work, so she put the roster on Hugo's desk and went to join the girls. "Can I help?" she asked, brightly.

"Not really," said Zoe. "I don't know what all the fuss was about, it only took me about ten minutes to write up this press release."

"And as for the *logements*," said Sara, "it's simply a matter of confirming arrangements that the registrants have already made."

"It looks to me like this event really runs itself," said Zoe. "It's been going on for so long, do you know these races began in the early nineteen hundreds?"

"I didn't know, but I'm not surprised," said Lucy. "I've run out of work, myself. There was only one newcomer, everyone else was a returnee. Easy-peasy."

"I don't know what we're going to do for the rest of the day. It'll seem rude if we can polish off in a single morning all the work that was giving Marie-Laure palpitations," said Sara.

Glancing out the window and noticing the mail van proceeding down the drive, Lucy thought help might be on the way. "I bet there'll be some new registrations in the mail. I'll go see."

She was just in time to catch the mail carrier in the foyer as he was collecting the outgoing mail, having already delivered the incoming. *"Bonjour,"* he said, with a smile, before making his departure. Lucy sorted through the correspondence, leaving personal correspondence but gathering a couple whose addresses included a notation for the races. She was bringing them back when she encountered Hugo, red-faced and bellowing, frantically waving the roster in her face.

"C'est une catastrophe!" he declared. *"Une grande meprise!"*

"Did I do something wrong?" she asked, as Marie-Laure came to see what the fuss was all about.

"Regardez!" he screamed, handing her the roster.

"Mon Dieu!" she exclaimed, as soon as she'd seen it.

"What? What is the matter?" asked Lucy, terrified she'd made a huge mistake. Unwittingly, of course, but with the best of intentions she had apparently created a huge problem.

"It is not your fault, you couldn't have known," said Marie-Laure. "But Monsieur Garcia is not welcome here. Not for the race, not for anything."

"He is not, how you say, acceptable," offered Hugo, hanging his head. "A bad, bad man."

"Perhaps all is not lost," suggested Marie-Laure. "Maybe the mail has not gone."

Full of shame, Lucy remembered how she'd been so eager to catch the mail carrier, how proud she'd been of her efficiency. "Alas," said Lucy, handing over the letters in her hand. "These just came."

"So it's too late," said Marie-Laure, sounding as if she'd lost her best friend.

"He was here just a minute ago, maybe I can catch

him," said Lucy, dashing for the door. Stepping outside, she saw Bill in the distance on his ATV. She jumped up and down and waved frantically, eventually catching his attention. He came zooming up and she explained the situation.

"I just saw the van," he announced. "Hop on."

So Lucy climbed on the back of the ATV, wrapped her arms around his waist, and they were off, not exactly like a speeding bullet, but fast enough that they soon saw the little van, chugging down the road. Bill hit the accelerator and they soon caught up, waving at the mail carrier and yelling, "*Arrêtez! Arrêtez!*"

Obligingly, he pulled over to the side of the road and braked.

Lucy climbed off the ATV and approached, smiling and working out the best way to explain her problem in French. He listened politely, but shook his head no, and embarked on a long explanation. It was impossible, he explained kindly, as the security of the mail was a foundation of the Republic of France, and once a letter had been committed to the care of the postal system, it was inviolable. It could not be taken back, oh, no. To do so, he declared, would shatter the very foundation of trust in the postal system, indeed even in the government. It was, he added solemnly in conclusion, included in the Code Napoléon, the very basis of the entire French legal system.

Lucy attempted to convince him that the government would endure the return of a single letter, a letter that shouldn't have been sent, but he remained adamant.

Realizing any further attempt was futile, a crestfallen Lucy thanked him politely for his dedication to his job. She then returned to the ATV, and whispered one word in Bill's ear: "*Merde.*"

When she returned to the château, she went straight to Hugo's office, where Hugo and Marie-Laure were waiting for her, somewhat amused. "It was a lovely gesture, Lucy, but we knew it was pointless," said Marie-Laure, with a sad smile. "The mail carrier would never surrender a piece of correspondence. Never. So, we will have to find another way to discourage Monsieur Garcia's attendance."

"I will talk to him myself," said Hugo. "With apologies. I will explain that a mistake has been made and the roster is already full."

"But that means no more entries," said Marie-Laure. "We will have to exclude some of our dearest friends." She indicated the morning's correspondence, showing him the envelopes. "They come every year, as dependable as Christmas." She shook her head. "And always late."

"I would only *tell* him that the roster is closed," said Hugo, with a sly smile.

"He would find out," said Marie-Laure.

"Why not tell the truth?" suggested Lucy. "Simply explain that a foolish American who was helping out made a mistake. You could all have a good laugh about it."

Hugo and Marie-Laure looked horrified at the thought. "Monsieur Garcia does not have a sense of humor," said Marie-Laure.

Hugo collapsed in his ergonomic chair and buried his head in his hands. "What are we to do?"

Looking at their downcast faces, Lucy suddenly wanted no more to do with this ridiculous mess; she wanted to go home. She'd given it her best shot, she'd only made things worse, and now it was time for a graceful exit. So long, sayonara, it's been nice to know you but now it's time to say goodbye. She hated France, with its ridiculous rules and red tape, and why did they care so much about that stupid Code Napoléon? Didn't these people realize that Napoléon was responsible for the deaths of millions of people, many of them French citizens and soldiers? He should be nothing more than an unfortunate footnote to French history, not revered as a great man, with that gigantic tomb in Paris. No, she'd had it with France. She was an American, by golly, and she wanted to go home.

Chapter Twenty-two

Lucy was back in her room, sulking on the chaise longue and watching a *Friends* rerun dubbed in French, when Bill came in. He was smiling broadly, with a spring in his step and a ruddy glow on his face. "Hey," he said, "are you still worried about that letter?"

"Yeah," she said, clicking off the TV. "It seems I've ruined everything."

"I find that hard to believe," said Bill, heading for the bathroom. When he emerged, face and hands washed in preparation for lunch, he seated himself at the foot of the chaise and rested his hand on her ankle. "Where's your can-do American spirit? We can fix this."

"My can-do American spirit wants to go home to America, where it is understood. Even appreciated." She shrugged. "I just don't get it. Garcia's papers came in this very luxurious envelope, with an engraved address and everything. Much nicer than any of the others. It seemed like they ought to be happy to have him. But for some reason Monsieur Garcia, who has money to burn on stationery and a château to boot, is not good enough for this crowd."

"Maybe it's old money versus new money, something

like that," said Bill. "Or maybe the new money came from something dodgy. Did you ask Elizabeth about him?"

"I did. She didn't know anything about him, but she did say that the Schoen-Renes are actually very snobby. Business is one thing, they make a point of welcoming everyone, but the carriage races are more of a social event for them, and they're only for the in crowd."

"Well, there you go then. This guy's a gate-crasher." Bill was thoughtful. "You can't blame them, really. We all have our social circles, people we're comfortable with. I guess they're entitled to their old-fart friends."

"I suppose so, but you know how I hate being in the wrong," said Lucy.

"So you want to find a way to straighten things out?"

"Well," she began, drawing out the word, "I did a bit of research and, guess what? He lives in the next town."

"And you want to go see this social pariah for yourself?"

Lucy thought of the long hours stretching ahead, hours she would have to fill by pretending to work. If they'd even let her near those new applications, which she doubted. "I've got nothing better to do, and I'd kind of like to see him for myself. See what's so objectionable," she said. "How about you?"

"We're pretty much finished up at the course. They need some new signs put up, that's all, but they won't be ready until tomorrow."

"Road trip?"

"Sure, if it includes lunch somewhere."

"And we'll bring Patrick along, too. Give him a change of scene, get him out of the château."

"Sounds like a plan."

They found Patrick in the library, playing a video game

on his tablet. It was obvious from his languid pose and slow swipes that he wasn't finding the game challenging, or even interesting. Seeing his grandparents, he tossed the little computer aside. "Boring."

"Since we've finished up for the day we're going out for lunch and some sightseeing," said Bill. "Want to come?"

"Sure, anything beats this." He waved his arm at the bookcases. "All these books and none of them are in English! Isn't that crazy?"

"We don't have any French books in our house," said Lucy, then corrected herself. "Well, actually we do have a few Babars I bought years ago by mistake at the airport, thinking they were in English." She looked around at the ranks of burgundy leather bindings, with gold trim. "I bet these books have all been here for forever, like the paintings. Nobody looks at the paintings and nobody reads the books."

"It's tradition!" exclaimed Bill, who'd recently been dragged to the Little Theatre production of *Fiddler on the Roof* directed by Lucy's friend Rachel Goodman.

"Should I tell my folks I'm going with you?" asked Patrick.

"I'll text your mom," said Lucy, producing her phone. "Ready?"

There was no problem about borrowing a car and soon the three were on the road, heading for the local café in town. The waiter there recognized them, greeted them with a big smile, and immediately brought Patrick a plate of *frites* before even taking their orders. Soon they were all happily munching on baguettes filled with *jambon* and *fromage*, along with beers for the adults and a Pellegrino orange soda for Patrick.

Tummies full, they bid adieu to the waiter and hit the

winding road, driving past golden fields and ancient forests to the town of Creneau. Unsure of the exact location of Château Bienvenu, they stopped in a gas station and asked for directions, learning from the attendant's hand gestures that if they continued a bit farther along the road they couldn't miss it.

The gas station attendant was right, the château was right on the road, and unlike the Schoen-Renes' château, it sat out in the open for everyone to see. There were no sheltering trees blocking the eyes of curiosity seekers, no long tree-lined drive designed to impress when the magnificent château was finally revealed. Instead, there were fenced paddocks for horses on either side of a straight drive with a modest painted wood sign announcing CHÂTEAU BIEN-VENU. At the end of the drive a sprawling, low-slung house could be seen, painted dazzling white with bright-blue trim on the doors and windows. A jaunty, red-tiled roof was dotted with doghouse dormers, and there were flower boxes containing red geraniums at every gleaming window. Privately, Lucy thought it should properly be called a manor house, rather than a château, then caught herself. Was she becoming a snob, like Marie-Laure?

"Shall we drive in?" asked Bill.

"Why not?" said Lucy, thinking that while the Schoen-Renes' château was designed to impress, this more modest establishment seemed friendly and welcoming. As if to prove the point, one of the horses trotted over and extended its neck over the fence, then tossed its head and gave a snort before trotting along the fence, as if to show them the way.

"That horse wants to be our friend," said Patrick.

"Yeah," agreed Bill. "Let's see if his owner is friendly, too."

"Fingers crossed," said Lucy, as they proceeded carefully up the drive, following the horse. Reaching the end of the paddock, the horse waited for them to pass, then giving a nod of his handsome head and a flick of his tail, he turned and ran to join his companions.

"Maybe you better wait in the car, in case we're not welcome," said Lucy. "Keep the motor running." She climbed out and squared her shoulders, determined to make her apologies and clear things up with M. Garcia. It was a short distance to the door, which was set right in the middle of the two-story stucco building, and had a carved wood wreath spelling out the word *Bienvenu.*

She was expecting the door to be opened by a maid, or even a butler, but the gentleman who greeted her was dressed in jodhpurs and riding boots, which seemed a fair indication that he was himself M. Garcia. He was about medium height, a bit stocky, but with the sort of well-tended appearance that indicated prosperity. Lucy had come to think of it as a wealthy glow.

"M. Garcia?" she asked, and got a big smile in return. *"Je suis Lucy Stone. Puis-je parlez avec vous pour un moment?"*

He gave her an amused look. "Are you a Mormon?" he asked, in accented English. "Because I am not interested."

"Mormon? No," said Lucy, puzzled. "I am from Campanule. I've come about the carriage races."

"Ah," he said, with a knowing smile. "I presume there is a problem of some sort with my paperwork."

"Well, yes," said Lucy. "You see, I am, well, there's been some confusion and I have been staying there as a guest of the family and I was helping out in the office and I . . ."

He held up his hand. "You signed me up, and Hugo is very upset."

"How did you know?" she asked.

"We Roma are used to such mistakes."

So that was the problem, thought Lucy. M. Garcia was a social outcast because of his Roma heritage. She found this sort of discrimination objectionable, but she was not the host of the carriage races. All she could do was try to smooth things over and correct her mistake. "I really don't know about that," she began. "It was my fault and I am so very sorry, but you see, the problem is simply that there are too many entries. And yours came late. . . ."

"You do not lie well, Madame Stone. The truth is that they do not want me because I am Roma." He was looking past her at Bill and Patrick in the car. "Is that your family? You have brought your son?"

"Actually, my grandson."

"How can that be? You are so young?"

Lucy knew it was simply flattery, but she liked it, nevertheless. "You are too kind. I'm with my husband and our grandson, Patrick. He was very impressed by your friendly horse."

"Perhaps he would like to visit the horses? I often give them some carrots around now, for a treat."

"Patrick would love that," said Lucy.

"And perhaps you and your husband would like a tour? The garden is beautiful this time of year."

"That would be lovely," said Lucy, who was dying to see more of the property. Perhaps she would even get a peek inside?

Lucy hailed Bill and Patrick, who promptly joined them in the sunny courtyard and proceeded to follow M. Garcia to the nearby stable. The stable was decorated in the same colorful style as the château, and was spotlessly clean. A few horses could be seen, their heads poking out of the Dutch doors of their stalls. Each door had a plaque identifying the horse: Sultan, Jazz, Blaze. They followed M. Garcia inside, where they were greeted with the fragrance of fresh hay and polished leather. Lucy's experience of stables was somewhat limited, but she had never seen such a beautiful stable before. The woodwork gleamed, the brass shone, and there was only the mildest, actually quite pleasant, hint of manure.

"Your stable, your horses, are all beautiful," she said, as M. Garcia emerged from a tack room holding a bunch of carrots.

"I am very proud of my horses, they're like children to me," he replied, beaming at Patrick. "And this young man, I bet he would be a fine rider."

"Only on ATVs," said Bill, with a smile.

"Well, we'll have to broaden his experience," said M. Garcia, leading the way back to the paddocks in front of the château. As soon as they appeared, the horses spied the carrots and trotted up to the fence, bobbing their heads. "Do you know how to feed a horse?" he asked Patrick.

"Just hold out a carrot?"

"Almost. Just put the carrot on your flat hand, the horse will take it quite gently."

Patrick did as he was instructed, giggling as the horse's whiskers tickled his hand.

"Can I pet him?"

"Her," said M. Garcia. "This is Philomene. She likes to have her nose scratched."

"It's soft," said Patrick, gently caressing Philomene's velvety nose.

"She's beautiful," said Lucy, admiring the horse's shining coat, muscular shoulders, and delicate legs.

"Ah, but we can't forget Hero and Absinthe," suggested M. Garcia, with a nod at the other two horses in the paddock. "They want carrots, too."

They were crossing the drive, to the second paddock,

when M. Garcia took Lucy aside. "You are a charming lady and you have a lovely family, Madame Stone. I do not want to make any trouble for you. Why not call Hugo and tell him I withdraw my application. No problem at all. Do you have your cell phone with you?"

Somewhat surprised by this unexpected turn of events, Lucy nodded and pulled the phone out of her bag. "Are you sure?"

"Absolutely." M. Garcia was all graciousness. "It is a small matter for me, but perhaps a big problem for you?"

"Well, we are guests at the château and have been unexpectedly detained, but the Schoen-Renes have been very gracious to us and I have felt quite terrible about making a mess of things. And I certainly didn't mean to offend you."

"None taken, and not a mess at all," he said, giving her hand a reassuring pat. "Just give him a call, I can even speak to him, if you wish."

"That would be lovely, so kind of you," said Lucy, dialing the château and asking to speak to Hugo. When he came to the phone, she explained she was with M. Garcia, they'd worked things out, and he wished to speak with him.

Hugo's response was quick. "Put him on."

Lucy handed over the phone and M. Garcia took it, smiling and nodding as he launched into a great deal of rapid French that Lucy took to mean that now that he'd met with her and her lovely family he had no hesitation about withdrawing his application. He understood that people make mistakes and he wished to avoid any awkwardness at all. Especially for this lovely *grand-mère* and her charming *petit fils*. It would be terrible for them to be made uncomfortable in the littlest way on account of him. That he wished to avoid, it was his most fervent wish to avoid any unpleasantness.

Then, most surprisingly, Hugo reversed his objection.

Lucy couldn't believe what she was hearing, coming out of the little phone. "All a dreadful mistake, a misunderstanding," Hugo was saying. "It will be a privilege to include your beautiful equipage, and your handsome horses in our humble event. You may even lead off the parade of carriages, if you wish."

A satisfied smile played on M. Garcia's lips. "You are most kind. How could I refuse such a gracious offer. I willingly accept."

The call ended with expressions of mutual felicitations, and M. Garcia returned the phone to Lucy. "See, no problem. All cleared up." He clapped his hands together. "Would you like to see the garden? I am very proud of my roses."

The tour continued as M. Garcia proudly displayed his rose collection, his fountain, his swimming pool, even a little playhouse mimicking the château for the amusement of his grandchildren. As the day was warm, he invited them inside for a cool glass of lemonade, and Lucy was impressed by the simple, but luxurious air of homeliness. She admired the colorful paintings, mostly featuring horses, and the comfortable, cottagey furniture. Eventually, however, she began to feel that they'd been visiting for quite a while and the Schoen-Renes might be worried about them.

"This has been so lovely," she said, "but we really need to go."

"Must you?"

"I'm afraid so. We've been out all afternoon and I'm sure our hosts are beginning to worry that we're lost, or the car has broken down."

"I wouldn't want to worry them," said M. Garcia, rising and escorting them to the front hall. "It has been a pleasure meeting you, especially Patrick."

"Same here," said Bill. "Can't thank you enough."

Back in the car, making their way down the drive past the paddocks, Lucy had a niggling little worry. "What did you think about that phone call?" she asked Bill. "It seemed friendly enough but I kinda got the feeling there was some sort of shakedown going on."

"What do you mean?" asked Bill, turning onto the road.

"Well, all that polite stuff. I didn't catch it all, but it seemed a little over the top."

"Just Frenchies being French," said Bill, accelerating. He chuckled. "They reminded me of one of those silly skits where one guy is at a doorway and says, 'After you,' and the other says, 'Oh, no, after you,' and they go on like that and nobody gets through the door."

Bill was probably right, thought Lucy, relaxing and enjoying the ride through the beautiful countryside. *Frenchies being French*, she thought, smiling to herself. You had to love Bill.

When they returned to the château, they were surprised to discover Jean-Luc himself sitting out on the terrace, his arm in a sling. A tall, cold drink was on a table beside him and he was looking over some paperwork. "Ah, Elizabeth told me you were out sightseeing. Did you see anything interesting?"

Lucy seated herself on a nearby chair, enjoying the cool shade. Bill and Patrick continued on inside, planning to change into swimsuits. "Actually, we had a very interesting afternoon," said Lucy. "We visited Monsieur Garcia at his château. He was very welcoming and showed us all around the place, he even let Patrick give some carrots to his horses."

"Really?" Jean-Luc furrowed his brow. "Why did you go there?"

"Well," said Lucy, eager to explain her triumph. "I made a mistake in the office this morning and registered Monsieur Garcia for the carriage race. His application came in a very fancy envelope and I went ahead and signed him up, filled out the confirmation, and put it in the mail. The mail carrier came just as your father discovered my mistake and I tried to get the letter back but it was too late, so I thought I would go myself and explain it all to Monsieur Garcia."

Lucy was so wrapped up in her explanation that she did not notice the look of horrified amazement on Jean-Luc's face. His jaw had dropped and he sat, stupefied, and speechless.

"I didn't mention anything about him being Roma, I didn't want to insult him, but he sort of figured it out anyway. Instead, I told him all the places had been filled, and he seemed to accept that. He said he would withdraw his application, no problem, and asked to speak to your father. So I got your father on the phone and Monsieur Garcia did exactly that, said he would withdraw from the race, but your father changed his mind and said he was welcome to participate and could even lead the parade. Isn't that great?"

Instead of getting the praise she expected, Jean-Luc simply shook his head in dismay. "Oh, Lucy, do you realize what you've done?"

"I fixed the problem," said Lucy, beginning to suspect that perhaps the opposite was true. "Didn't I?"

"No. Not at all."

"I don't understand. Monsieur Garcia was so nice. . . ."

Jean-Luc pressed his lips together. "Monsieur Garcia is Barban."

Lucy couldn't believe it. "The crime guy?"

"Himself."

Suddenly, Lucy thought of the *Godfather* movies, and how soft-spoken Marlon Brando had been, making offers that his victims couldn't refuse. Somehow in all that charming chatter M. Garcia, alias Barban, had presented Hugo with just such an offer. All that talk about her lovely family, she remembered, with chagrin. He'd actually been threatening to harm her, or more likely, Patrick. The thought stunned her, horrified her, sent her slumping back onto the chair. "I was an idiot."

Jean-Luc gave her a small, sympathetic smile. "You couldn't have known."

"What do we do now?" she asked, moaning.

"We wait and see what happens. 'Barban' means the wind, and you can't stop the wind. Maybe he will be satisfied to be in the race. Maybe it will be enough. Or maybe . . ."

"What?" demanded Lucy.

"You see what he did to me, or rather, had done after Maman went ahead with the eviction. . . ."

"That was all Barban. And you all knew . . ."

"Of course. You don't deal with a man like him without being aware of the danger, of the possible consequences."

"What about the investigation? The police?"

"I imagine they will go through the motions for a bit longer, then decide the case is unsolvable."

"We will get our passports back and can go home."

"Yes." He smiled, then grew serious. "But until then, you must be very careful. Do not leave the château. Warn the others. Make no mistake, your family is in danger."

Lucy was trying to process this disturbing information, when she was startled by a piercing scream. A woman's scream. Both she and Jean-Luc sprang to their feet and began running inside, following the sobbing sounds that echoed through the halls. Reaching Hugo's office, they found him slumped on his desk with Marie-Laure frantically shaking him, trying to revive him. On the desk, Lucy noticed, there was a handwritten note and an empty pill bottle, evidence of suicide.

Chapter Twenty-three

"He has a pulse," Marie-Laure announced. "Call the *pompiers*!"

Jean-Luc grabbed the phone on his father's desk and punched in the number.

Lucy watched it all, horrified, trying to think of something she could do to help. There was nothing, absolutely nothing, she realized, overwhelmed with guilt. She could hear her late mother's voice in her head, announcing angrily that she'd done quite enough already. And she had. It was her stupidity, her blind blundering that had caused all this trouble. It was all her fault. The best thing she could do, the only thing, was to disappear. So she slipped, unnoticed, out the door and made her lonely way down the long hallway. Reaching the foyer, she climbed the stairs, then continued on past the portraits of ancestors who all now seemed sternly disapproving, to her room.

It was empty. Bill must already have gone to the pool, she realized with a sense of relief. A bit of a reprieve, before she had to tell him what had happened. All because of her. She perched on the edge of the chaise, clinging to the fact that Hugo still had a pulse, and praying with all her heart that he would pull through. The *pompiers* would arrive, she could already hear the siren, and they would whisk him to the hospital. He would be treated, he would recover, everything would be all right somehow and she would be forgiven. Or it would be too late, he would be pronounced dead at the hospital, and she would never be forgiven, not by Marie-Laure and Jean-Luc, not by Elizabeth, not by herself. The carriage races would be cancelled, Barban would demand his money, the château would have to be sold, the family ruined. She would go home in disgrace, carrying this burden of shame until her dying day.

Or not, she decided, rallying. She wasn't responsible for absolutely everything. Hugo had made some very bad decisions which had ultimately led to his involvement with Barban. He was every bit as responsible as she was. In fact, she had only stumbled into a bad situation and tried to help. Ineffectually, yes, she had to admit that. But it was Hugo who had initiated his family's descent down the road to ruin when he'd first gotten involved with Barban.

The siren suddenly went silent, indicating the ambulance had arrived. Lucy went to the window and watched as the EMTs hurried into the château. Help had arrived. Feeling less desperate and marginally optimistic, she decided to call Chris Kennedy. At the very least, he'd be able to offer some advice, and maybe he'd even come up with a plan to keep them safe until they could go home.

"Hi, Lucy, what's up?" he began, in his lovely American voice. It was clear and straight to the point, making her immediately feel she was in good hands.

"It's a big mess here," said Lucy. "Hugo's tried to commit suicide, the rescue squad are here, taking him to the hospital."

Chris was brisk, concerned. "He's still alive?"

"As far as I know."

"What precipitated this?"

"It's a bit of a long story," said Lucy, explaining about her mistake, and Barban's threat. "I don't know what's going to happen, if they'll even go ahead with the carriage races."

"Well, we certainly have to increase security at the château," he said.

"I can't authorize that," she said.

"I will get in touch with the national authorities. They've been watching Barban and building a case against him, but it's taking time. He rules a veritable criminal empire, the tentacles go deep throughout the entire province, including the cops. This might be the opportunity they've been waiting for to finally nab him."

This was not what Lucy wanted to hear and she didn't hesitate to express her frustration. "That's all very well and good, but what does it have to do with me? With my family? How are we going to stay safe?"

"I don't really think you have to worry," said Chris, slowly, considering risk factors. "Barban isn't interested in tangling with a bunch of Americans, his focus is making Hugo pay up, one way or another. He wants his money, and he wants to show off his fancy horses. If that means humiliating Hugo and Marie-Laure, that's all to the good as far as he's concerned."

"He threatened us. My family," said Lucy.

"Just applying pressure on Hugo, and it worked," said Chris. "I'm sure he's enjoying his triumph."

"So you're saying we don't have to worry?" Lucy was skeptical.

"Well, I wouldn't leave the château," said Chris. "I'd

keep the family close, warn them not to talk to strangers, that sort of thing, be aware of their surroundings. But I really think Barban has bigger fish to fry."

"I don't much like being a worm on a hook," said Lucy.

"I think you're off the hook," said Chris, chuckling. "You've played your part and now Barban doesn't need you anymore. But if you'd like," he added, "I could come down and do a security check."

"That would be great," said Lucy. "Bill and I can pay you," she added, remembering the lottery money. "Whatever you charge."

"That won't be necessary," he said, sounding slightly offended. "I'm happy to help. See you soon."

"Thank you, thank you," said Lucy, greatly relieved. Hearing the click of the door, Lucy turned and saw Bill entering, wearing his swim trunks with a towel slung over his shoulder.

"What's going on?" he asked. "I saw an ambulance leaving."

"Hugo tried to kill himself."

"Oh my God! That's terrible." He stood for a moment, absorbing the news. "Will he be all right?"

"I don't know. He had a pulse when he was discovered, that's all I know."

"Why would he do something like that?"

That was the question Lucy was dreading. "It was because of us, because of me," she began. "When we were at Garcia's and he made that call, it was actually a threat. An offer Hugo couldn't refuse."

"What do you mean? He seemed like a really nice guy."

"He's not. He's known as Barban, he's the head of some big crime syndicate. Hugo owes him money, a lot of money, I guess. And he used us to pressure Hugo to admit him to

the carriage races. . . . For some reason it's really important to him to be included in the races."

Bill sat down on the bed in his damp trunks and Lucy
didn't even notice.

"We were like the fly stumbling into the spider's web,"
continued Lucy. "It was too good an opportunity for him
to pass up. All that nicey-nice stuff about our wonderful
family was a warning to Hugo that if he wasn't allowed to
join the race he could do us harm. That's why Hugo reversed himself so quickly."

"I had no idea," said Bill.

"Me either," said Lucy, sitting beside him and taking his
hand. "But I called Chris Kennedy and he's going to come
and beef up security here at the château, he's going to keep
us all safe. He said the authorities have been watching this
Garcia guy and this might be the opportunity to nab him
that they've been looking for."

"What do you mean? Keep us all safe?"

"Well, Chris didn't think we're truly in danger but he
said we should be very careful, just to be on the safe side.
This Barban is a very dangerous man." She squeezed his
hand. "Did you and Patrick have a nice swim?"

"Yeah," said Bill, slowly. "I left Patrick at the pool. He
wanted to work on his butterfly stroke."

"You what?"

"I left him there." Bill got up. "He wasn't alone. The
pool guys were there. And he's a really good swimmer. I
didn't think twice about it."

"Of course." Once again Lucy was flooded with guilt.
Why didn't she warn her family, instead of sitting in her
room, moping. She should have tracked them down, each
and every one, and explained the danger. "This all happened so fast. You couldn't have known. . . ."

"Well, I'll go get Patrick, you gather the family."

"No. I'll go. You stay here and get into dry clothes. Text the kids. Tell them we have important information, they should come straight to our room."

Bill gave her hand a reassuring squeeze. "I'm sure he's fine."

"I hope you're right."

Then Lucy was off, darting through the endless halls and across the enormous expanse of lawn, completely out of breath by the time she pushed through the swing gate in the fence that surrounded the pool area. Her view was blocked at first by the roofed bar where towels and cold drinks were provided, but when she finally got a clear line of sight she saw immediately that the pool was empty. But maybe he was resting, drying off on a chaise. But no, she observed with a growing sense of panic, the chaises were all empty, each with a neatly folded towel on the seat. "Patrick!" she yelled. "Where is he?" Seeing the puzzled expressions on the two pool guys, she attempted French. "*Où est le garçon?*" she asked, panting.

"Patrick?" asked one, the cutest one with long wavy hair, broad shoulders, and mocha skin.

"*Oui!* Patrick!"

"*Parti,*" said the other guy, who had a stubble of beard and a shaved head.

So Patrick had left. "How long ago?" demanded Lucy, aware that she hadn't crossed paths with Patrick on her frantic dash to the pool. Getting blank expressions she went for the French again: "*Depuis quand? Une heure? Quelques minutes?*"

"*Oui, oui,*" they both said, beginning to understand her concern. "*Cinq, peut-etre dix minutes.*"

Five or ten minutes, she thought, she should have encountered him. But maybe he'd decided to visit the stable or wander through the garden, perhaps he didn't go straight back to the château but went to the gym. Her heart pounding, she yelled a curt *"Merci,"* and dashed out the gate, made a quick run through the empty fitness area and on out around the complex of outbuildings to the stable. There she found the horses munching quietly on hay, but no sign of Patrick. Then on through the garden, pausing at the maze to yell his name, and encountering a gardener.

"Ah, Patrick," he said, nodding. "Very nice boy."

"Is he here? *Ici?*"

A sad shake of the head.

There was nowhere else to look, except at the château, so she began running back, her mind considering a million possibilities. The game room? Knocking some billiard balls around? The kitchen, begging a snack? Maybe he was back with his parents, showering, or playing a video game on his tablet. Hope against hope, it all dissolved the moment she entered the lobby and saw Molly's face. She looked absolutely terrified, you could practically see her heart thumping beneath her T-shirt.

"Lucy, any sign of him?" Molly asked. She was standing next to Toby, hanging on to his arm, and surrounded by Sara, Zoe, and Elizabeth, all with anxious expressions on their faces.

Lucy shook her head. "Not at the pool, or the stable. I spoke to one of the gardeners but he hadn't seen him. Have you checked inside? The kitchen . . ."

"Everywhere," said Toby.

"I think we should call the police," said Bill.

It was then that Elizabeth's phone chimed its happy little tune and she grabbed it. "It's him. Garcia."

She listened, nodding as he spoke, responding in French.

Then they heard Patrick's voice, saying he was eating ice cream and was going to ride a horse. "What fun," said Elizabeth, using every bit of strength she had to keep her voice cheery and neutral, to maintain the fiction that Patrick was not a kidnap victim but simply visiting a friendly neighbor. She finally ended the surreal conversation, saying, "Be a good boy." Then Garcia was back on the line, his threatening growl not friendly at all. When the call ended, she gave her desperate family a recap. "He's got Patrick, Patrick is fine. But he wants Hugo to give him every penny he owes, by the start of the race tomorrow, and he'll return him. And"—her voice broke as she struggled to continue—"he said if we call the police, we'll never see Patrick again."

"What can we do? We don't even know if Hugo is alive," exclaimed Bill.

"And if he is, it isn't likely that he can come up with this money," said Sara. "I mean, I'm pretty sure he would have if he could have."

"Where's Marie-Laure? And Jean-Luc?" asked Lucy. "We need to tell them."

"They're both at the hospital with Hugo," said Elizabeth. "We have to call Chris. He'll know what to do."

"I already have," said Lucy. "He's on his way."

"Well, that's it, then," said Toby, pulling Molly into a hug. "We just have to wait."

"And pray," said Lucy.

Chapter Twenty-four

Too frazzled to even consider eating, the family clung together in Bill's and Lucy's room, waiting for developments. Lucy could hardly bear to look at Molly, feeling that she'd been responsible for the kidnapping. If anything happened to Patrick, and that was as far as she could allow her thoughts to go, if he were harmed in any way, she vowed she would make Barban pay. She had no idea how she would do that, or what punishment she could possibly deliver, but deep in her heart she knew that she would find a way. If he hurt Patrick, it would be her mission to destroy him.

"It's not your fault, Mom," said Elizabeth, breaking into her thoughts. "You couldn't have known that Garcia is Barban. I've been here for almost a year and I had no idea. Marie-Laure and Hugo, even Jean-Luc, they purposely kept me in the dark." She nodded. "I think it was a big mistake. If only they'd faced it squarely and in the open, Barban wouldn't have had this power over them."

"That's how these guys operate," said Toby, who was sitting on the edge of the bed, beside Molly, who was lying down, clutching a handful of tissues that she used to dab at her eyes. "They sense weakness and use it. It was pretty obvious that the Schoen-Renes were snobs, very concerned about keeping their status as members of the upper crust."

"Yeah. They never said a word about that girl in the moat, or even when Jean-Luc was shot. They pretended it was all a big mystery," said Zoe. "But they knew all along what was going on."

"They would have lost face if they told the truth," said Sara, "and that's the last thing they would have wanted."

"But now, of course, they must realize they made a bad bargain," said Bill. "So you lose face, a few friends drop you, and pretty soon everyone forgets. Now they're in danger of losing everything, even Hugo's life."

"I feel like it's all my fault and I'm so sorry," confessed Lucy. "I'm the one who pushed this trip, nagged you all until you agreed to come. We should have stayed home and sent presents."

"But I'm really glad you all came," said Elizabeth. "I didn't foresee any of this, and neither could you. But as awful as it is, it's better to be facing it together."

Molly sat up, her face red with anger. "Easy for you to say. It's not your child who was kidnapped."

Elizabeth apologized immediately. "Of course, you're right, Molly. But we'll get through this and Patrick will come home safe and sound."

Molly fell back against the pillows and reached for more tissues. "I want Patrick," she wailed. "Why aren't any of you doing anything?"

"We're doing exactly the right thing. We don't want to blunder about and make things worse," said Bill, in a reassuring voice. "Chris will be here soon and he'll know what to do. Until then, we just have to wait."

"That's right," added Toby. "Face it, we're not calling the shots here. Barban has to make the first move."

"That's just an excuse," sobbed Molly, turning away so her back faced the others. Toby stayed beside her, rubbing her back.

Finally, after what seemed an eternity, there was a knock on the door and Chris came in. They all turned to face him, waiting breathlessly to hear what he had to say.

"Okay," he began. "The police have been contacted—"

"Oh, no!" screamed Molly. "That's exactly what Barban said not to do!"

"It's okay," said Chris, in his sensible, reassuring way. "There's no other way, we have to bring the police in. But it's a crack team, their entire focus is kidnappings, and we can rely on them to bring Patrick home safe and sound."

"What about the money?" asked Toby.

"The transfer, it's all marked bills provided by the police, will take place tomorrow, during the carriage race, which Barban insists must go on as planned."

"Does he know the police are involved?" asked Elizabeth. "Who's been talking to him."

"Me. Only me. I said I was representing the family," said Chris. "He doesn't know about the police, though he probably suspects as much. As long as everyone sticks to the plan, that's the important thing. Don't talk to anyone outside of the family, don't try to meddle, let the pros handle this."

Lucy thought Chris was talking to her, and she felt the color rising in her cheeks. "No meddling, I promise," she said.

"So, let's call it a night," suggested Chris. "You guys should try to get some sleep, tomorrow's going to be a busy day. As for me, I've got some work to do."

They began to leave the room, hugging one another and offering reassurances that it would all be okay. Toby helped Molly get to her feet and she clung to him, a portrait of tragedy. Elizabeth was last, whispering a few words to Chris. Then they were all gone and Lucy and Bill were left alone. "I could use a drink," said Lucy, indicating the minibar. "A whiskey, please."

"Good idea," said Bill, extracting a couple of mini bottles. They each ended up downing two apiece but the alcohol didn't provide the sleep they craved. They spent the night tossing and turning, praying that Patrick was being well cared for, but imagining him afraid and confined as a prisoner in some filthy, dark hole. In the back of their minds, of course, lurked the dreadful possibility that he was already dead, although neither dared to voice such a terrible thought.

Next morning Lucy discovered her appetite had returned; having skipped dinner she was eager for breakfast. She wasn't alone, the whole family had gathered in the small dining room and were digging into the omelets, pastries, and coffee that were on offer. Molly was there, too, picking at a bit of fruit salad. She was careful to avoid Lucy, which was fine with her. She really couldn't face her daughter-in-law until Patrick was recovered, safe and sound. They performed a wary dance, keeping well clear of any contact with each other. They were just about finished eating when Chris popped in, with good news.

"My operatives have found Patrick," he began.

Molly interrupted. "Is he . . . ?"

"He's fine. He's being kept in a converted *pigeonnier* on Barban's estate. It's really a guesthouse, quite luxurious, and they've probably fed him a story so he has no idea that he's actually been kidnapped. From what they observed, he's actually having a great time, playing video games and eating ice cream. We're keeping an eye on the place, ready to move in if needed, but we're planning on letting the transfer go ahead. Once Barban has arrived at the race, my men will grab Patrick and bring him to safety. Jean-Luc will be waiting at the appointed location with the money."

"When is all this taking place?" asked Toby.

"Sometime during the race," said Chris. "Barban insisted that it has to go on exactly as planned."

"Any word about Hugo?" asked Lucy.

"He's doing okay. He himself spoke to Barban, explained he's in the hospital, and that Jean-Luc will deliver the money." He paused. "Barban was okay with that, he even wished Hugo a swift recovery."

"I'm not surprised," said Lucy. "For a master criminal he seems to have very good manners."

"Well," observed Toby, "they said the same about Hitler."

"Let's not be fooled by his charming manners," advised Chris. "Barban's a cunning criminal under that thin veneer of civility. Everything could change in a second, so we all have to stay on our toes. The race is about to get underway, so I think we should all head out to the racecourse, acting like nothing is the matter. Got it?"

"Got it," said Bill, leading the way.

The walk through the château seemed endless and Lucy had to force herself to take each step, as if she were going to face a firing squad. Her heart was pounding and she was terrified and consumed with worry about Patrick. But stepping outside, she was met with a dazzling sight. The courtyard in front of the château was entirely filled with handsome horses, harnessed to lovingly restored carriages of all sorts. Others unable to fit in the courtyard were lined up in the driveway. It was like a trip back in time, she thought, when horses provided transportation instead of automobiles. Back then, little more than a hundred years ago, this would have been a frequent scene as aristocratic visitors arrived at the château for a country house weekend. Elizabeth was busy greeting all the contestants and distributing the numbers that they would pin onto their sporty, canvas jackets. The horses were eager to go, snorting and tossing their heads, but they had to wait while glasses of port were distributed to the drivers, and the rules explained.

Surveying the scene, Lucy realized that one contestant, the most important, was missing. There was no sign of Barban and his team. Terrified that something had gone wrong, she tugged on Bill's sleeve. "He's not here," she said when the starting gun was fired and the teams were off, racing down the course that Toby and Bill had marked out.

Bill had his phone plastered to his ear, taking a call, and she strained to hear the news. What she finally learned was devastating, worse than she'd imagined: the raid on the *pigeonnier* had been a bust, there was no sign of Patrick. She felt her heart tighten in her chest and began to feel faint. Bill saw her start to sway and grabbed her, holding her tight. "Look!" he cried, "he's here."

Together they watched as a colorful Gypsy wagon pulled by a pair of magnificent black horses, their manes and tails trimmed with a rainbow of ribbons, suddenly joined the race, thundering after the pack. A smiling Barban was holding the reins, and beside him, hanging on for dear life, was Patrick, grinning from ear to ear.

No sooner had Barban been spotted than Bill called for Toby and the two men jumped on the ATVs that had been thoughtfully readied, in case of an accident. They zoomed

off, bouncing alongside the track, passing the racing carriages and gaining on Barban. Lucy strained to watch, as
the first carriages began to disappear into the woods,
closely followed by Barban's wagon and the two ATVs.
She was fearing she would lose sight of them when, suddenly, she saw the Gypsy wagon take a turn in the opposite direction, veering off the course and heading for the
drive and the main road.

Noticing a little Mini parked in the courtyard, with a
young woman sitting on the hood and watching the race
through binoculars, Lucy asked for a lift. "Can you follow
that wagon? And the ATVs?" she asked.

"Sure," said the girl. "I'm Bridget Beresford, by the way."

"Nice to meet you," said Lucy, introducing herself as
she fastened the seat belt.

"So what's going on?" asked Bridget, hitting the accelerator and causing the little car to leap forward. "What's
with that Gypsy rig? I never saw it before."

"That's what I want to find out," said Lucy, hanging on
to a grab bar as they bounced along. Some distance ahead,
she knew there was a stone bridge, and it was there that
she saw the wagon had stopped. French officers had
blocked the bridge, armed with automatic rifles, and Barban had no choice but to give himself up.

He hopped down nonchalantly from the wagon, then
lifted Patrick down, chucking him under the chin. Then he
raised his hands, and was quickly handcuffed. "No matter," he said, as he was led away to a patrol car. "I have a
very good lawyer."

"What's happening?" demanded an enraged Patrick.
"Why did they stop the race? We would have won."

Lucy enfolded him in a big hug, squeezing hard and getting a protest. "Let me go," Patrick demanded, wiggling out
of her grasp. "Why are they arresting Monsieur Garcia?"

"It's a long story, Patrick," said Lucy. "But first we have to go see your mom. She's been very worried about you."

"She always worries," said Patrick, with a shrug as Lucy led him back to the Mini. "Hey," he exclaimed, noticing the car. "Cool ride."

Bridget flipped the front seat forward so he could climb in the back, then got in herself. When Lucy joined them, she said, "Do you think you could tell me what's going on?"

"Sure," said Lucy. "Patrick doesn't realize it but he was kidnapped by the guy in the wagon. He's a local crime boss named Barban."

"That's crazy," said Patrick. "I wasn't kidnapped, I was invited to visit, and I had a great time. It was a lot more fun than hanging out at that boring old château. I got to ride a horse, and feed the rabbits, and play with the goats. And I could have anything I wanted to eat. It was pretty cool."

"Oh, Patrick," said Lucy, rolling her eyes. "If you only knew . . ."

"Well," he answered, sounding downhearted, "I have a feeling I'm going to find out. Am I in trouble?"

Lucy was thoughtful, then finally spoke. "I think your mother may have a few words for you about going off with a stranger."

"He wasn't a stranger, Grandma. You took me to his farm and introduced me to him."

Once again, as they reached the courtyard, Lucy felt guilt settling on her like her grandmother's old gray sweater, the one she kept on the back of a kitchen chair to wear when she popped outside to pick a tomato or hang up the laundry. It was a familiar feeling.

Chapter Twenty-five

A few days later they all went to the official *reconstitution* at the local courthouse in which the *juge d'instruction* presented the case. This was not a trial, Chris explained, but a preliminary procedure. The trial would take place later. The purpose of the *reconstitution* was to set out the facts of the case and to bring the accused to a realization of his crime. It was also designed to provide the victims with an understanding of the motives precipitating the crime, and perhaps some sense of closure.

Lucy found the procedure reminded her of the inquests that she'd seen in old British movies, in which a coroner sought to determine a cause of death. They were all gathered in a rather dusty, court-like room, seated on uncomfortable chairs. The entire Stone family, including Patrick, were present, as were Hugo, Marie-Laure, and Jean-Luc. The *juge d'instruction* was seated at a large desk, and Barban himself was seated to one side, accompanied by several police officers. There was also an interpreter, a serious, scholarly appearing young woman, provided for the benefit of the English speakers.

When everyone was settled, the *juge d'instruction*

opened a folder and began. He was a tall, lean man with owlish eyeglasses, and turned the pages of his report with long fingers. The case, as he explained, included many crimes, beginning with Hugo Schoen-Rene's agreement with Barban involving the establishment of the brothel on château property and the presence of the prostitutes at château events. The *juge d'instruction* cast a baleful glance at Hugo, as he described alleged violations of the laws concerning human trafficking and Hugo was seen to shift uncomfortably in his seat, no doubt aware that he would be facing charges in the matter himself.

The *juge d'instruction* continued, recounting how Hugo had been unable to meet Barban's increasing demands for payment regarding the illegal services provided. When one of the girls, now identified as Stefania Poritzkaya, escaped from the brothel, she was caught and killed, and her body was dumped in the moat as a threat. Barban was furthermore angered when Marie-Laure cleared out the brothel in anticipation of the wedding festivities, and he had Jean-Luc shot in retaliation.

"It became a game of cat and mouse," the *juge* continued. "Monsieur Garcia's pride was damaged, so he came up with a plan to enter the carriage race, which he rightfully assumed would embarrass his enemy, Hugo Schoen-Rene. The presence of the Americans at the château gave him an opportunity to further pressure Monsieur Schoen-Rene and he hatched a plan to kidnap the young American boy, Patrick Stone. Thankfully, the boy was recovered unharmed, and that will be considered favorably at the trial."

Barban smiled at this, and gave Patrick a friendly little wink.

Observing this, the *juge d'instruction* allowed himself a

disapproving sniff. "However, Monsieur Garcia has so far refused to cooperate with investigators, refusing to identify any participants in this criminal enterprise, and that will most certainly be a negative factor." He then enumerated the charges against M. Garcia: sex trafficking, extortion, murder, attempted murder, and finally, kidnapping. A trial date would be announced soon.

He stood up, everyone stood up, and Barban was led out of the courtroom and back to his cell. Once he was gone, the *juge* made his departure, leaving the room. There was a scraping of chairs as the Stones and Schoen-Renes got to their feet. Jean-Luc patted his father's shoulder, telling him not to worry. Marie-Laure shrugged, disdainfully dismissing the whole procedure. "A big show about nothing. Hugo will pay a fine, Barban will get off."

"How can that happen?" asked Lucy.

"Maybe a pay-off, maybe mitigating factors like his mean mama, or maybe he'll manage to escape. Trust me, people like him don't go to jail."

"Is that right?" she asked Jean-Luc.

"Maman is never wrong," he replied, with a smile.

They were making their way out of the building when they were hailed by the lead investigator in the case, who presented them with their passports. "You are now free to leave France," he said, sounding as if he couldn't quite understand why anyone would want to leave.

"It will be great to go home," said Lucy, pressing her passport to her heart. "Thank you."

"Bon voyage," he said, then took Hugo aside.

"Oh, dear," murmured Zoe, as they started down the stairs. "Do you think they'll really charge poor Hugo?"

"I hope not," said Lucy. "He has certainly suffered a great deal."

"If you ask me, he deserved it," said Elizabeth, rather sharply. "If he'd been stronger none of this would have happened."

There was something in Elizabeth's expression, in her rigid posture and the hardness of her eyes, that didn't bode well for her future at Campanule, thought Lucy. And probably not for her relationship with Jean-Luc. That was confirmed at the farewell dinner that evening.

It was quite like old times, thought Lucy, as they gathered for a final celebratory meal around the table in the beautiful large dining room. The table was covered with antique damask linen, the family china gleamed, the crystal sparkled, and a great deal of silverware was lined up beside the plates.

"Tonight we say goodbye to our guests," said Marie-Laure, "and we will be very sad to see you go. This has been a difficult time, full of unexpected events, and I am forever grateful for the grace with which you all adapted. So this dinner is our way of saying thank you and wishing you bon voyage."

Lucy felt some response was required, so she gave Bill a little kick under the table. Taking the hint, he got up. "I would like to thank you for your wonderful hospitality, your patience with us Americans, and to wish you all happiness in the future."

Champagne was poured, toasts were drunk, and everyone settled down to what they expected would be a delicious dinner. But before the soup was served, Jean-Luc stood up. "There is something I need to say, for Elizabeth and me. We have talked and considering everything that has happened, we have agreed to end our engagement."

While not entirely unexpected, Lucy found this news quite saddening. And for Marie-Laure and Hugo, it seemed cataclysmic. "Oh, no," she moaned. "Is there nothing to make you change your minds?"

Jean-Luc smiled and shook his head. Elizabeth sat silent, stoically. "This is for the best," he said, "but no reason for sadness. We are best friends, forever. And now, we must celebrate. As the English poet once said, 'All's well that ends well.' Is that not true?"

Lucy raised her glass, and touched it to Bill's. "All's well that ends well."

Next morning, as they were driving to the airport in the rented van, Sara and Zoe wanted to hear all about the broken engagement. "It was you, wasn't it? You decided to back out, right?" asked Sara.

"It was mutual," insisted Elizabeth.

"But he would have gone ahead with the wedding just because his mother wanted it so much," suggested Zoe.

"Maybe," admitted Elizabeth.

"Nothing against you, but I never thought he was really all that keen," said Sara. "He didn't seem like he was really in love."

"For what it's worth, I thought he was gay," offered Molly.

Listening to the girls, Lucy felt a surge of sympathy for Elizabeth. "Lay off, girls, Elizabeth's been through a difficult time. It's never easy to break up."

"Actually," began Elizabeth, eager as ever to contradict her mother, "it's no big deal. I shouldn't admit it, but when that shot rang out and Jean-Luc fell, I had this huge sense of relief. The wedding was off. But they said he was going to recover, and he came out of the hospital and I was taking care of him and I pushed those thoughts away. I tried, I really tried to be his good little future wife, but the more I thought about it the more I realized that I wanted to marry the château more than the man.

"And, all that time, I kept thinking about that room with the awful wallpaper. The château suddenly didn't seem so great, it seemed to be smothering me."

"So one of you had to go," offered Lucy. "It was a question of you or the wallpaper."

"And Marie-Laure made it very clear that the wallpaper was staying."

They all laughed. "I think you made the only sensible choice," said Lucy.

"And how exactly are you going to support yourself?" asked Bill, always the concerned father.

"Oh, I called Monsieur Loiseau, the manager at the Cavendish. When I left he told me I always had a job there and, well, they're taking me back and I'm even getting a raise."

"I think there's more to this than the wallpaper," said Zoe. "Like maybe there's someone else? You looked quite cozy with Chris."

"Maybe," admitted Elizabeth, with a shrug. "We have a date this weekend . . . who knows where it will lead?"

That news was received with hoots and laughter all around, and when they arrived at the airport there were hugs, and a few tears. "I'm going to miss you," Lucy told Elizabeth, hugging her close.

"Me too," said Elizabeth. "But there's Zoom and Face-Time and we'll all be able to stay in touch. Especially you, Patrick. I want to keep my eyes on you and make sure you stay out of trouble."

"Oh, believe me, we'll be keeping a close eye on him from now on," said Toby.

"Great," grumbled Patrick, shuffling along behind his parents, dragging his roller suitcase.

It was when they were all in line at security that Lucy

whispered into Bill's ear, "Do you think that Chris actually might be the guy for Elizabeth?"

Bill shrugged. "If this trip has taught me anything, it's that you never know what will happen."

"So true," agreed Lucy, as a frightening thought occurred to her. "Oh, no," she moaned.

"What's the matter?" asked Bill.

"How am I going to face Janice Oberman? She'll want to know all about the wedding and I'll have to admit that it didn't happen after all."

"Who's Janice Oberman?" asked Bill.

"Supermom. She's got four daughters and she's marrying them off one by one. So far two are married, one is engaged, and one is swamped with proposals."

"And none of yours are," said Bill. "You must be a terrible mother. . . ."

He paused to hand over his passport to the agent, then continued, "But you're a terrific wife."

Lucy's day of reckoning came sooner than she expected, on the very first day she went back to work at the *Courier.* She'd just settled herself at her desk and powered up her PC when the little bell on the door jangled and Janice Oberman came bustling in. "Well, tell me all about it," demanded Janice, who was dressed for action in Capri-length leggings and a bright pink workout top that revealed every bulge. "I'm just coming from Jazzercise, so much fun! But I heard you were back and had to come right over to hear about the wedding." Slightly out of breath, she paused, waiting expectantly.

"Well," admitted Lucy, with a sigh, "things didn't work out. The groom had a, well, a sort of accident, and, Elizabeth changed her mind."

"My goodness!" exulted Janice. "What a comeuppance! What sort of accident was it? Couldn't they reschedule?"

"It turned out that he wasn't quite the man Elizabeth thought he was," said Lucy, lamely.

"Rather late to discover that!" declared Janice, her chins jiggling. "After the wedding was planned and the whole family traveled to France!"

Lucy shrugged. "True, but sometimes it happens that you realize you never knew someone until, well, something unexpected happens."

"Is she brokenhearted?" asked Janice, in a hopeful tone.

"No. She has other fish to fry."

"Don't tell me someone else came along? Maybe an old flame?"

Just then, Phyllis cleared her throat. "Janice? I've been wondering, has Taylor had her baby yet?"

"Oh, I guess I'd forget my head if it wasn't attached," said Janice, searching in the small trunk of a purse she always carried. "Here it is!" she proclaimed, producing a birth announcement with a photo of a very red-faced, scowling newborn. "A beautiful big boy," gloated Janice, waving the photo in the air for Lucy and Phyllis to see. "Twenty-two inches and ten pounds ten ounces."

"My goodness, that is a big baby," said Phyllis, whose expression seemed to indicate she was rather happy she'd never had to deal with birthing any baby, much less a large one.

"It all went well?" inquired Lucy, also concerned.

"Oh, Taylor's a champion. She was only in labor for four hours!"

Lucy's and Phyllis's eyes met. "How wonderful," said Lucy, a veteran of much longer labors.

"And have you met the little fellow yet?" asked Phyllis. "He's what, two weeks old now?"

"Um, well, not yet," admitted Janice.

"I suppose they want time as a family," suggested Lucy. "A couple of weeks to get to know little . . . what did they name him?"

"Oh!" Janice was happy to get on firmer ground. "Jetson! Because Taylor is a flight attendant, you know."

"How cute," said Lucy, remembering a cartoon series on TV and thinking poor little Jetson was stuck with an unfortunate name.

"So when will you be flying in to see Jetson?" asked Phyllis, not willing to let Janice off the hook.

"Um, they'll let me know when they're ready," said Janice, looking so sad that Lucy was beginning to feel sorry for her, an emotion that didn't last long.

"Ah, Lucy," said Janice, adroitly changing topics. "Didn't I hear that Zoe is living with a man? Does that mean that wedding bells are in her future?"

"No chance," admitted Lucy. "They're just friends."

"Oh, too bad," sighed Janice, clearly tickled. "Such a shame." And with that she marched triumphantly out the door, which jangled behind her.

Phyllis started to say something, but Lucy shook her head and held up a cautionary hand. "Don't, don't say a word," she said, overcome with a laughing fit and clutching her tummy.